THE
EDWIN DROOD
MURDERS

BEING THE SECOND DICKENS JUNCTION MYSTERY

PRAISE FOR

If Frank Hardy had come out, opened a bookstore, and moved to a Dickens-obsessed Oregon small town, he might have grown up to be something like Simon, the protagonist of Christopher Lord's charming new mystery, *The Christmas Carol Murders*. Full of homespun characters and curious goings-on, Lord's mystery is a love letter to both Dickens and to the small town amateur detectives who've kept the peace in hamlets from River Heights to Cabot Cove.

—Chelsea Cain, *New York Times* best-selling thriller writer

Christopher Lord has all but immortalized Charles Dickens—his characters, his enthralling sense of story, his entire fictional universe. From the opening pages, *The Christmas Carol Murders* is an enjoyable contemporary spin on the lush psychological environs of Dickens's own territory. With this story of a small town bookseller turned gumshoe, Lord emerges as a bright new voice in mystery.

—Evan P. Schneider, author of
A Simple Machine, Like the Lever

THE CHRISTMAS CAROL MURDERS

A delicious romp through the world of Dickens wonderfully imagined in the twenty-first century by Christopher Lord. *The Christmas Carol Murders* has it all: mystery, eccentric characters galore and a touch of frivolity. You don't have to be a Dickens fan to fall in love with this novel.

—Margaret Coel, author of *Buffalo Bill's Dead Now*

The Christmas Carol Murders is a smart, satisfying and contemporary twist on the literary landscape of Charles Dickens. It features a likeably urbane amateur detective, an unforgettable cast of supporting characters, and a juicy mystery that puts the trappings of Christmas Past, Present, and Future to new and grisly uses. Whether you've read Charles Dickens or not, *The Christmas Carol Murders* will delight and surprise you.

—Pamela Smith Hill, award-winning author of *Laura Ingalls Wilder: A Writer's Life*

The Edwin Drood Murders

Harrison Thurman Books, Portland 97210

© 2013
All rights reserved. Published 2013.

Illustrations by Tina Granzo.
Book design by Alan Dubinsky.
Editing and production by Indigo Editing & Publications.

Printed in the United States of America.
21 20 19 18 17 16 15 14 13 12   1 2 3 4 5

ISBN: 978-0-9853236-3-9

Library of Congress Control Number: 2013934259

THE DICKENS JUNCTION MYSTERIES

THE CHRISTMAS CAROL MURDERS
THE EDWIN DROOD MURDERS

THE
EDWIN DROOD MURDERS

BEING THE SECOND DICKENS JUNCTION MYSTERY

by

CHRISTOPHER LORD

MAPS & ILLUSTRATIONS by TINA GRANZO

HARRISON THURMAN BOOKS

For Evan, at last

A brilliant morning shines on the old city. Its antiquities and ruins are surpassingly beautiful, with the lusty ivy gleaming in the sun, and the rich trees waving in the balmy air. Changes of glorious light from moving boughs, songs of birds, scents from gardens, woods, and fields—or rather, from the one great garden of the whole cultivated island in its yielding time—penetrate into the Cathedral, subdue its earthy odour, and preach the Resurrection and the Life. The cold stone tombs of centuries ago grow warm, and flecks of brightness dart into the sternest marble corners of the building, fluttering there like wings...

The service comes to an end, and the servitors disperse to breakfast. Mr. Datchery accosts his last new acquaintance outside, when the Choir (as much in a hurry to get their bedgowns off, as they were but now to get them on) have scuffled away...

Mrs. Tope's care has spread a very neat, clean breakfast ready for her lodger. Before sitting down to it, he opens his corner-cupboard door; takes his bit of chalk from its shelf; adds one thick line to the score, extending from the top of the cupboard-door to the bottom; and then falls to with an appetite.

The Mystery of Edwin Drood
Charles Dickens
June 8, 1870

Except for a few personal letters, these were the last words Charles Dickens wrote. Later on June 8, 1870, Dickens suffered a stroke during dinner. He died the next day without regaining consciousness, leaving his novel half-finished.

During his lifetime Dickens revealed only the vaguest clues about his intentions for the conclusion of *The Mystery of Edwin Drood* and left behind no written evidence of substance.

Or did he?

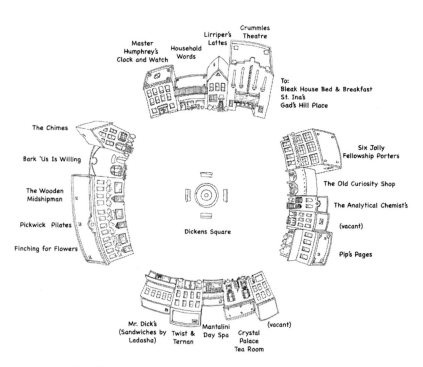

Master
Humphrey's
Clock and Watch

Household
Words

Lirriper's
Lattes

Crummles
Theatre

To:
Bleak House Bed & Breakfast
St. Ina's
Gad's Hill Place

The Chimes

Bark 'Us Is Willing

The Wooden
Midshipman

Pickwick Pilates

Finching for Flowers

Dickens Square

Six Jolly
Fellowship Porters

The Old Curiosity Shop

The Analytical Chemist's

(vacant)

Pip's Pages

Mr. Dick's
(Sandwiches by
Ladasha)

Twist &
Ternan

Mantalini
Day Spa

Crystal
Palace
Tea Room

(vacant)

Zach's Map of Dickens Junction, Business District

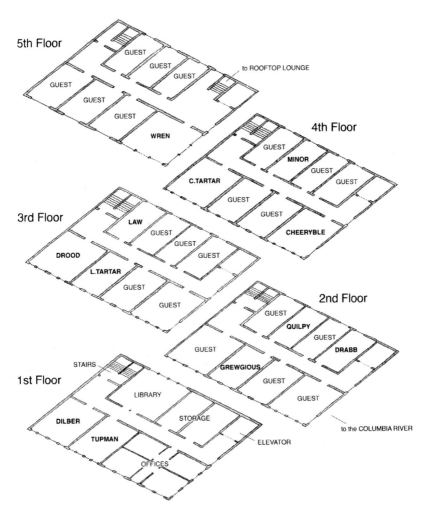

Floorplan of the Hotel Elliott

Detective Boggs's List of Suspects

Simon Alastair, owner, Pip's Pages bookstore

Silas Cheeryble, autodidact conferee*

Osma Dilber, Dickensiana curatrix emerita

Buckminster Drabb, PhD, leading scholar of the Twinn tradition*

Edwin Drood, conferee

Morgan "the Great" Grewgious, stage hypnotist

Bettina Law, PhD, conference chair, United States Chapter (Western Sector) of the International Society of Droodists

Dean Minor, PhD, leading scholar of the Jasper tradition*

Daniel "Quilpy" Quill, Dickensian blogger

Cecily Tartar, conferee

Lionel Tartar, MFA, conferee

Neva Tupman, conferee

Jennifer Wren, actress, scholar

* "The Weird Sisters"

Other Junxonians/Visitors

George Bascomb, artist, Simon's close friend

Zach Benjamin, reporter, *Household Words*, Dickens Junction's weekly newspaper

Josephine Boggs, detective, Clatsop County Sheriff's Office

Myrtle Crump, Portland visitor

Bartholomew Cuff, security chief, Hotel Elliott

Solomon Dick, mayor, Dickens Junction; Simon's distant cousin

Abel Gjovik, deputy, Clatsop County Sheriff's Office

Jude Hexam, chef and housekeeper, Gad's Hill Place

Apassionata Midge, assistant, Bark: Us Is Willin' Pet Supply and Day Care; Head Custodian, Dickens Square statue

Viola Mintun, owner, Crystal Palace Tearoom

Brock Spurlock, part-time employee at Pip's Pages

Bradley Sturgess, editor-in-chief, *Household Words*

The 17th Triennial Conference of the United States Chapter (Western Sector) of the International Society of Droodists

Agenda

April 15

Noon–5:00 p.m.	Registration/Check-in	Hotel lobby
6:00–7:00 p.m.	Cocktail Hour (includes heavy hors d'oeuvres)	Hotel library, first floor
	Dinner on your own (see list of local restaurants in conference packet)	

April 16

7:30–9:00 a.m.	Continental Breakfast & Welcome	Bettina Law, conference chair Hotel bar, basement
9:15 a.m.–noon	Plenary Session: "Dickens in the Next 100 Years: Why *Drood* Matters"*	Silas Cheeryble, Buckminster Drabb, Dean Minor, panelists; Bettina Law, moderator Columbia River Room, basement
12:15–1:45 p.m.	Lunch	Hotel banquet room, basement
2:00–5:00 p.m.	Bus Trip to Fort Clatsop, Astoria Column	Meet in hotel lobby
5:00–6:30 p.m.	No-host Bar	Conference Center
6:30–9:00 p.m.	Ethelinda Award for Lifetime Achievement in Droodism or Dickensiana (dinner included)	Osma Dilber, special guest Hotel banquet room The Great Grewgious, hypnotist
	Entertainment	Hotel banquet room

* Discussion questions will be accepted in advance. Please see Bettina Law.

April 17

The Hotel Elliott and Conference Center
Astoria (and Dickens Junction), Oregon

7:30–9:00 a.m.	Continental Breakfast	Hotel bar
9:15 a.m.–noon	Breakout Sessions:	
	"What was in Mrs. Crisparkle's Cupboard: Food in *Drood*" (seating limited to ten!)	Cassandra Orth Liberty Room, basement
	"New Divots in the Datchery Dilemma"	Dean Minor Columbia River Room
	"Charles Dickens and Wilkie Collins: Friends or Rivals?"	Silas Cheeryble Vernonia Room, basement
12:15–1:45 p.m.	Lunch	Hotel banquet room
2:00–5:00 p.m.	Breakout Sessions:	
	"When 'Heaven's Hard Drunk' Wasn't Enough," or "When Princess Puffer came to Astoria: The Opium Trade in Dickens's London and Nineteenth-Century Astoria"	Osma Dilber; Winifred Duddle, laureate emerita, Clatsop County Historical Society Columbia River Room
	"Miss Twinkleton's Globe: The Geography of *Edwin Drood*"	Louella Pardiggle Vernonia Room
5:30–6:30 p.m.	No-host Bar	Hotel banquet room
7:00–9:00 p.m.	Buffet Dinner: All-you-can-eat No program	Hotel banquet room

April 18

7:30–9:00 a.m.	Continental Breakfast	Hotel bar
9:00 a.m.–4:00 p.m.	Bus Trip to Dickens Junction: dedication of the Sapsea Head, Dickens Junction; shopping; Dickens Family mausoleum	Meet in hotel lobby
6:00–7:00 p.m.	No-host Bar	Hotel rooftop lounge (staircase near room 501)
7:00–9:00 p.m.	Dinner on your own	
9:00p.m.–late	Entertainment (optional)	The Dueling Duoos Brothers, accordionists extraordinaire Suomi Hall (transportation available, see staff)

April 19

7:30–9:00 a.m.	Continental Breakfast	Hotel bar
9:15 a.m.–noon	Plenary Session: "At Last! The Truth of Number Plan Six"	Buckminster Drabb, Columbia River Room
Noon—12:15 p.m.	Closing Remarks/Droodist cheer	Bettina Law; Simon Alastair, conference coordinator Columbia River Room
12:15–2:00 p.m.	Conference ends/Check out	Hotel lobby

This will be the best conference ever!

Bettina Law, conference chair
Simon Alastair, conference coordinator

Quilpy's Quill

April 2

I've been blogging for-EVAH about the upcoming Droodist conference. I got my press pass and registration today!! Quilpy can't afford a Columbia River-view room at the fabulous Hotel Elliott in Astoria, but I'll be there with Dingley Dell bells on! Click below to learn how you can $upport Quilpy's Quest for a Queen (-size bed, that is).

HAWT news! International star of stage, screen, and tube, two-time Ternan Award-winning actress Jennifer Wren will be there, too! Jen-girl (I'd go straight for her, wouldn't you?) must be pitching a new project—maybe the long-awaited movie musical of DROOD, or that Broadway-bound revival of THE FROZEN DEEP, with JenWren re-originating the part once played by Dickens's sweet tart Nelly Ternan? Look for ALL the goss here.

Local Junxonian Osma Dilber will be honored for her most excellent lifetime commitment to the preservation of Dickensiana. Ms. Dilber is even luckier to be the owner of the Heart of Helsinki, one of the most famous—and fabulous—gems in the world (besides yours truly!!!)

Long-time Droodist rivals Dean Minor
and Buckminster Drabb will be trading
papers and, no doubt, fisticuffs to boot—I
want a ringside seat for that!!!

But the most major and heinous goss is that
Bucky Drabb promises a ginormous reveal.
Could he be talking about the DaVinci
Code of DROOD—Number Plan Six, the "lost"
last page of Dickens's notes where he
identifies the fate of the missing Edwin
Drood? You better refresh me every five
minutes or you'll miss breaking news!

Local bookstore owner and G-g-g-gay gumshoe
Simon Alastair will be helping with the
festivities. Hope I see the boyfriend
and my soon-to-be BFF, überhottie Zach
Benjamin, just named one of the fifty
sexiest journalists in the USA! (Didn't
that magazine get MY glamour shots?)

BTW, I'm still taking applications for
Quilpy's Cabin Boy Contest, to pick a
cabin mate for my triumphant return to the
Caribbean in July. If you want to be my top
(I'm on the bottom bunk, if you get my warp
and woof), send your story to quilltop@
quilpy.com no later than May 1st.

Some lucky fella will be licking
salt off my margarita rim!

Be Back Soon...

Click HERE to upgrade Quilpy
to the bed he deserves!

xoxo

April 15

Noon–5:00 p.m.	Registration/Check-in	Hotel lobby
6:00–7:00 p.m.	Cocktail Hour (includes heavy hors d'oeuvres)	Hotel library, first floor
	Dinner on your own (see list of local restaurants in conference packet)	

DAY ONE

Simon Alastair pushed away the barely touched break-fast that houseboy/chef Jude Hexam had laid before him. This morning he had several things on his mind. Food wasn't one of them.

"Sorry you didn't like it, dude," Jude said.

"We have a no-dude rule here," Simon told him mat-ter-of-factly. "I'm old-fashioned that way."

"No worries," Jude said, a goofy grin spreading across his handsome face. In his three days on the job, Jude had used that expression frequently, Simon noticed; maybe he really was worry-free. As Simon reasoned, at twenty-two, with his looks and talent, Jude must assume that no worries would ever line that gorgeous face and brow. "What should I call you, then?" Jude asked.

"Simon will do," he answered.

"Okay, boss," Jude said. He removed the leek and Camembert frittata, whole-grain toast with artisan butter, and fruit cup. Jude could cook, Simon had to give him that. Jude put the plate on the kitchen island and began cleaning up the gas cooktop.

Simon shook himself out of his reverie. "I'm sorry," he said. "Breakfast was fine. I'm preoccupied." He looked at the open laptop in front of him, and then closed the lid.

"Reading more about your sexy man?" Jude asked.

"That pesky Mr. Quill," said Simon, trying to smile and clear his head. "He's been blogging about the conference for weeks. Good for publicity, bad for my nerves. I'm glad it's finally starting, so Mr. Quill will stop guessing and can report whatever passes for reality—as he sees it."

Simon looked at his watch; at the same time, he heard Zach's car outside. He should go, but he wanted to talk to Zach. And he wanted to be alone with him when he did it.

"Jude, would you please start the laundry?"

Jude washed his hands and dried them on his kitchen towel. "Sure," he said. He left the kitchen.

Simon could hear Jude emptying the hamper and carrying the clothes to the upstairs utility room when Zach came through the back door of Gad's Hill Place and into the kitchen.

Simon saw Zach's beauty as if for the first time. Newly forty, Zach Benjamin was five feet eleven, 175 pounds, with jet hair beginning to gray at the temples, piercing blue eyes, and high, clean-shaven, olive cheekbones. To-day, in addition to his black leather bomber jacket, Zach was wearing a maroon pullover sweater and brown narrow wale corduroy slacks.

Zach kissed Simon, then poured himself some coffee and stood at the island. He casually began eating the remainder of Simon's breakfast.

"You look like a college professor," said Simon.

Zach finished a mouthful of frittata before answering. "I wanted to look academic for the Droodists."

"Your press credentials aren't enough?" said Simon. "You and Quilpy."

Zach nodded his head in the direction of Simon's computer. "I'm looking forward to meeting the little shit."

"As Brock might say, he's crushing on you," said Simon.

Zach's killer eyes sparked in Simon's direction. "Jealous?"

Simon could tell that Zach was in a teasing mood, but Simon was not. "Maybe a little."

Simon knew he had nothing to worry about. He and Zach had fallen into a satisfying and comfortable relationship for one so new. Zach had found an apartment in Astoria, but it was more or less an expensive place to stash the stuff he had accumulated throughout his itinerant career. He was on the road frequently for the monthly travel feature he wrote for *Household Words*, the Junction's weekly paper, but most nights he was at Simon's. Simon liked it that way.

"Well, you needn't be jealous of a cocky young blogger," Zach said, echoing Simon's thoughts. He stepped away from the island, reached over, and traced a delicate fingertip along Simon's brow, as if trying to erase the wrinkles there. "You look troubled."

"Maybe I should Botox," said Simon.

"Not for you," Zach said. "Besides, I want your face to show excitement when I enter the room."

Miss Tox, Simon's tortie Devon Rex, crossed the kitchen floor and rested on the heat register nearest Simon's legs. As a diversion, Simon picked her up and put her on his lap. She kneaded his khaki slacks in a desultory fashion, then curled up and tucked her head underneath her paws.

He took a breath. He wasn't quite ready for what he wanted to say.

"I've been thinking about Brock and Bethany," he said instead. "What if I paid for the entire wedding?"

Brock Spurlock, Simon's assistant at the bookstore, was getting married in July to Simon's former housekeeper, Bethany Cruse. Brock had agreed to stay on at the bookstore until June, but Bethany had quit earlier, to start putting their new life together. Her departure had led to Jude Hexam's hiring.

Zach moved back to the island. He now lowered his coffee mug. His eyes were distracting Simon from his purpose at one level, and driving him toward it at another. "Think about it, Simon. How would you describe them?"

"They're young, in love, and they'll have beautiful children."

Zach finished the frittata and put the plate in the dishwasher. "And independent, strong-headed, and fiercely proud. They want to do this for themselves, on their terms. You can't come in and take that away from them by paying."

"It would be so easy for me," said Simon.

"But not easy for them." Zach sat at the nook table and took Simon's hand. "They don't want things to come easily, Simon. They want the world on their terms and through their own efforts—and sacrifices. And if good things don't come, then they don't. That's how most young people feel these days."

"And I am no longer young, which is why I'm not getting your point?"

"Not young in *their* eyes," Zach said. "Money is too easy for you. You don't ever have to worry about it." Although Simon didn't live lavishly and worked as the owner of Pip's Pages, he had never had to earn any money, only manage responsibly the estate he inherited from his grandparents.

"Then what?" Simon asked. This topic, which he had brought up to avoid the other one, suddenly wasn't making him feel good, either.

"Here's a thought," Zach said. "Offer to match their savings when they get ready to buy a house, subject to some maximum amount. That way you can give them a boost, but allow them to reach their own goals, which will make them value them all the more."

Simon wrote a number on a piece of scratch paper and pushed it to Zach.

"Whoa," Zach said. "That's quite a match."

"It will give them something to work toward. Isn't that what you suggested?"

"It is." Zach laughed. "I think it will be a proper motivator for them both to take second—maybe third—jobs to earn their half."

Simon took a breath. "While we're on the subject of living accommodations"—he continued gazing into Zach's eyes—"move in with me. It's time."

"Whoa again." Zach gently pushed himself away from Simon and sat back in his chair.

"It's what I want," said Simon, "for both of us. After all, it doesn't cost me any less or any more for you to be here."

"Food," Zach said.

"We can split that. Everything else I already pay for whether you're here or not, so why not be here? That way you can save some money for whatever you want."

"Is this about money?" Zach asked.

"Not at all. But I've been worried you would think it was."

Zach leaned forward. "Well, maybe, it's about money—and the fact that I don't have much—but it's really about commitment, isn't it?"

Simon could feel his body tense. He willed it away. "I want commitment. I'm tired of being by myself. I want to be in a relationship and all of the messiness that goes with it."

"Including kids?"

Now Simon pushed himself back. "You want children?"

"I don't know," Zach said. His face was relaxed, alert, and still gorgeous. "I've never gotten far enough in a relationship to have that discussion." He scratched his chin. "But…Yes. I want children around the house, like my sisters. Shrieking and crying and laughing. Laughing."

Simon had never imagined the patter of any feet on the floor of Gad's Hill Place, except those of Miss Tox.

Simon started calculating. If they had a child, Simon would be more than sixty-five when he, or she, graduated from high school. Would Simon's tired old bones make it up the gymnasium bleachers to cheer her, or him, or them—*them?*—on? Diapers, and driving, and dating—oh, my.

"I'll have to think about that." Simon didn't want to appear negative, but he needed time to process this more complex vision of a life with Zach than he had previously drawn in his mind. "I'll have to think."

"You know I love you," Zach said. They had first used that word with one another about a month ago during a long weekend in Ashland while Zach was collecting material for a *Household Words* article about the Oregon Shakespeare Festival. "But I've never lived with another man—I mean, not like this. I've shacked up a lot—" He paused. "Let me rephrase that—I've shacked up, but never the full boat that you're offering. So I've got to think about things like money…freedom…partnership. I've been on my own my whole life; at least you've been in other long-term relationships."

"That doesn't mean I'm any better at them than you are," said Simon. "My two long-term relationships both left me. So I'm not perfect."

Zach cuffed Simon's ear, gently. "Not even close, mister." He tried to give Simon a gentle kiss, but Simon pulled back.

"So you're saying no?" That wasn't quite the answer Simon had expected, not the payoff he had hoped for from the risk.

"I'm saying…not yet." Zach stood and moved toward the door. He picked up his laptop case and slung the strap over his shoulder. "I'll give you my answer when the conference is over. In the meantime, we've both got work to do." He turned and put his hand on the doorknob.

Simon remained in place, his knees rigid. He was trying to control his words, his temper, the pain surging toward his throat. "This isn't going the way I wanted."

Still holding the door, Zach turned back to face him, his eyes like lasers. "Not everything does, Simon."

Jude took this inopportune moment to return to the kitchen, whistling a tune.

"How is number fourteen today?" he asked, referring to Zach's ranking in a very popular magazine's list of the fifty sexiest journalists. Zach's new-found notoriety was one of the more interesting byproducts of Zach's article about the murders Simon had solved during the Junction's *Christmas Carol* festivities. *The Huffington Post* had picked up the article, it had gone viral, and Zach was now a poster boy for the *Cougar Beat* crowd.

Simon felt gentle anger give way to defeat, with maybe a hint of sadness.

"See you at the hotel," Zach said to Simon, without even a smile for Jude, and then was gone.

Simon tightened the belt of his Burberry trench coat as he strode down Gad's Hill toward Dickens Square and Pip's Pages. Rain fell lightly; mist filaments draped from the tops of the evergreens and the tender spring leaves of the oaks and other deciduous trees. A tarpaulin of fog stretched across Youngs Bay, visible beyond the square.

On cold, comforting mornings (although this one was no longer comforting), Simon never wanted to leave Dickens Junction. At age three, Simon had been taken in by his grandparents after the death of his parents in an automobile accident. Grandfather Ebbie Dickens had founded the town of Dickens Junction in 1950, and Simon, his only grandchild and heir, felt a strong obligation to continue using family money to support and nurture his grandfather's dream.

Since the unpleasantness last Christmas, Dickens Square actually had bounced back and looked more vital than it had in years. Several new businesses, including The Analytical Chemist's, an old-style pharmacy including a small soda fountain, and Master Humphrey's Clock and Watch, had opened to brisk post-holiday business. Cricket's Hearth Cards and Gifts and the two adjacent stores were no longer in operation, but Simon had persuaded the new owners to offer appropriate rents in exchange for potentially stable clients. Indeed, three other new ventures had started up: The Wooden Midshipman, offering nautical-themed gifts and high-quality antiques; Bark: Us Is Willin' Pet Supply and Day Care; and The Chimes, a cellular phone store, a necessary concession to modern times. And Mr. Dick's (with Sandwiches by Ladasha) had transformed from a video-gaming parlor into an upscale family-friendly restaurant. Ladasha Creevy's cutting-edge menu had received a recent shout-out in *Bon Appétit* and several rave reviews by fierce foodie bloggers.

And the most important revitalization: Dickens Junction was once again free of tabloid journalists looking for dirt on grisly murders and newly refocused on its intended purpose: celebrating the life and art of Charles Dickens.

Simon stood in front of Pip's Pages. The storefront next door, formerly Micawber Investments, was still empty, but Simon was mulling expansion opportunities. His shop's current window display, in honor of the conference, featured the "sensation" novels of the nineteenth century. Among the prominent titles, besides *Edwin Drood* itself, were the Wilkie Collins warhorses *The Moonstone* and *The Woman in White*. Other titles included *Lady Audley's Secret*; *Dr. Jekyll and Mr. Hyde*; *Trilby*, the George du Maurier novel that introduced Svengali to the world; and *The House of the Seven Gables*. Although the conference appealed to a narrow band of individuals, the display had stimulated sales and generated good discussions.

Brock Spurlock, looking pumped up from his early-morning workout in a gray muscle tee and pressed casual slacks, was working in the Mystery section when Simon entered the store.

"Hey, boss," he said. "What kind of a name is Ngaio, anyway?"

"It's Maori," said Simon. When Brock failed to respond to that, he added, "Dame Ngaio Marsh was from New Zealand."

"A Kiwi," Brock said. "Got it."

Simon walked over to the counter and tidied the stack

of copies of *The Scarlet Letter: A Pop-up Book* that he intend-ed for the relatively skimpy Children's section. He felt a bout of fussiness coming on, and Brock's naiveté nudged him over the edge. But what was really bothering him was the question of his status with Zach.

Zach had been adamant about getting his own apart-ment instead of staying on at Simon's from the beginning, had said he was too independent to live off Simon's lar-gesse. But was what Zach called his independence just male stubbornness? Why couldn't he move in with Simon, now four months into their relationship, when it was so obvious (at least to Simon) that the two men had some-thing solid that was going to work?

Simon's role in solving the recent murders had been horrible and painful but also had given him greater con-fidence and a more secure notion of himself. So he had expected Zach's response to his suggestion that morning would be an unqualified yes. Zach's mild rebuke, and his own resulting petulance, struck the wrong notes.

Simon tried to refocus. "Are you sure you'll be all right here by yourself while I'm at the conference?" he called to Brock.

"I'll be fine. Anyway, Bethany wants me as busy as pos-sible so I'm not around. She's says I'm not helping." He scratched his head. "She had me tasting Jordan almonds yesterday. What's that about? Nuts are nuts."

"Listen to her," Simon advised, "but don't try to pre-tend—really be interested. And you'll find that you are, if you listen to the information she's sharing. Remember that she has excellent taste—she chose you."

"For a gay guy, you know women pretty well."

"I'm sure you have charms that I lack." Simon checked his watch. He was due at Osma Dilber's in a few minutes. Brock didn't need him. This should be comforting. It wasn't. Simon was fussing just to fuss. "If you need me, I'll have my cell, of course, and you've got Zach's too, right?"

Brock pointed at the door. "Go," he said. "Get your Drood on."

When it was built in the 1930s, Osma Dilber's bungalow had been considered country living for those who knew the hustle and bustle of Astoria's rowdy waterfront a few miles away. Now the whole area was country living for Portland's booming activity a mere two-hour drive away. Simon climbed the wide concrete steps to the spacious front veranda with its original planked porch. Even as he turned the crank of the bell in the center of the solid oak door he could see slow movement through the leaded prismed sidelights. The door opened and Osma peered out.

"I knew it would be you," she said, her distinctive voice like water on gravel. She led him into her front parlor.

Osma Dilber was four feet ten inches in low heels, with a figure that had once been trim but now was indistinct under the color-crazy muumuus that she wore everywhere. Today's version, pink and purple orchids on lime-green crimped satin, shimmered as she moved into the Edwardian parlor next to the entry hall.

"Please," she said, gesturing with an arthritis-knobbed hand, "please sit. I'm almost ready to go." Simon noticed a suitcase near the stairs. Osma wanted to be close to all of the conference action; she had elected, unlike Simon, to stay at the hotel instead of returning to Dickens Junction.

A Cavalier King Charles spaniel came running into the room, all ears and eyes, yipping and jumping at Simon's shins.

"Mrs. Pipchin," Osma said sharply. The dog stopped jumping and went over to Osma, who had sat in a flowered chintz easy chair.

Simon sat opposite Osma on the matching overstuffed couch. Little had changed in the forty years he had been visiting here. This room was a true parlor: flower-print wallpaper, flowered upholstery with crocheted antimacassars, glass-fronted curio cabinets filled with porcelain teacups and collectible spoons. One étagère housed Lladró cat figurines in pale blues and lilacs; a lace-doilied parfait table displayed a selection of Osma's prized Victorian Majolica beehives. Dark draperies, held back with tasseled swags, framed the leaded windows. The room was thick with attar of roses.

Seated with Mrs. Pipchin in her lap, Osma seemed like another ornament in the room, one that time had used and burnished, but still glowed with the life-force of its artisan. She was eighty-one years old, her face wrinkled and jowly but with lively gray eyes (one had a slight cast in it), tiny etched lips, and gently receding chin. Mrs. Pipchin licked Osma's hands. Prominent among the burls and knots of the advanced arthritis that had ended her days as a champion tatter was an immense ring, a brilliant red ruby surrounded by diamonds.

"You're looking at my horrible hands," Osma said. She held them up as if to flutter her fingers, but her joints were so bad that the gesture, except for the glittering gem, looked like twisted twigs caught in a storm.

"No," said Simon. "I'm admiring the Heart of Helsinki."

Osma smiled. "I'm not rich," she said in her whiskey voice, "but I have rich memories."

Although she had never been famous outside the bubble in which she, Simon, and the other rabid Dickensians dwelled, her ring, and its story, had been. Osma had inherited the ring from her grandmother. The first Osma, the Finnish Nightingale, a celebrated beauty at the turn of the century, immigrated in 1910 to Astoria with her husband, lutefisk baron Jarno Erkkila, who had given the first Osma the jewel-encrusted ring as a birthday present. When the Nightingale's daughter presented her with her first grandchild twenty-some years later in Astoria, grandmother Osma (whose family fortune would be lost in the Great Lutefisk Plunge of 1932) gave baby Osma the ring as a christening present. In the forty years that Simon had known her, he had never seen her without it on her wedding-ring finger. Osma never married, but Simon's grandfather Ebbie hinted over the years that she enjoyed a colorful and occasionally mysterious past.

"Would you like some tea?" Osma asked.

"I don't think so," Simon answered, "but thank you for the offer." In this room, Simon felt himself relax.

It was impossible to be overwrought among so much stillness, and the contretemps with Zach seemed so far away from this tatted and porcelain world. Still, they were on a schedule. He checked his watch. "We should leave for the hotel."

"Of course," Osma said. She clamped the arms of the easy chair and started to push herself up. Simon crossed the room and offered to help, but she shooed him away. "I will let you help me with my bag," she said. From a narrow hallway closet, she removed and then slowly wrapped herself in a heavy patterned shawl. The combination of shawl and muumuu produced a cacophony of colors.

Simon lifted the suitcase while Osma turned out the lights in the parlor and hall, and then picked up her purse on a coat stand in the hallway.

"Who's taking care of Mrs. Pipchin while you're at the hotel?" Simon asked.

At the mention of her name, Mrs. Pipchin trotted over and stood near Simon, her tail and hips twitching.

"Bark: Us Is Willin' has started a new home-visit program," Osma said. "Apassionata Midge will stop by twice a day to walk Mrs. Pipchin while I'm away, check her food and water, and make sure she's comfortable."

Simon gave his arm to Osma at the top of this stairs; this time she accepted. The two slowly descended to the street level and Simon's car. Simon inhaled the fresh air absent of Osma's scents and memories.

He helped Osma with the car door; after shutting her side he put the suitcase in the trunk, got in the car, and began driving.

"It's been forty years since the Droodists met in the Junction," Osma said. Simon drove up Gad's Hill Road toward the waterworks and over the other side toward Astoria. "Your grandfather and your father would be so proud that you brought them back." Osma was one of the dwindling number of Junxonians who retained a personal connection to Grandpa Ebbie, who had died almost twenty years earlier. It was a significant part of what made Simon's feelings for her so warm and protective. She patted Simon's leg. "I am, too," she added. "Otherwise I would not have been able to attend. I don't travel well anymore."

Simon smiled. "You're the guest of honor," he said. Until her seventy-fifth birthday, Osma had served as the curatrix of Grandpa Ebbie's celebrated collection of Dickensiana, now housed in the Osma Dilber Wing of the Astoria/Dickens Junction Regional Library. The Droodist Society had decided to honor her for her years of service. "It's going to be a great conference," he added. He thought about some of the difficult personalities he would face. He took a breath. "I'm hoping there won't be many fireworks. Some of those academics are fierce."

"I'm hoping for a firestorm," Osma said, a twinkle in her good eye. "What's better than a room full of prima donna Droodists?"

Simon and Droodist Conference Chair Bettina Law had chosen the historic and refurbished boutique Hotel

Elliott in downtown Astoria to be the host site, with meeting and dining facilities in its cozy below-ground conference center.

Simon helped Osma check into her room early. The hotel staff was kind enough to locate her on the first floor, near the hotel library and business center. She decided to rest a while, so Simon left her and went back to the lobby.

The Hotel Elliott's tasteful lobby had been fully restored in the last decade to a degree of elegance beyond its 1924 opening-day functional practicality, which was still visible in the framed black-and-white photograph over the polished mahogany lobby desk. A few Droodists milled about the conference registration table on the other side of the lobby.

Bettina Law came around the table to give Simon a hug. "At last," she said, "the Droodists are back."

Bettina was a petite Asian American, fifty-one but looking much younger, with alert dark eyes and an inky pixie cut. She wore a custom-tailored navy herringbone suit with three-quarter-length sleeves, a deep portrait collar that framed her round face, and a slim skirt. Even with the blue python peep-toe heels, the top of her head was barely even with Simon's chin. Bettina had a PhD from Columbia University in comparative literature, was considered the world's leading expert on "the Datchery problem" in *Edwin Drood*, and knew everyone in the Dickens universe. She had been chair of the Droodists for several years. Since Bettina had relatives in the area, Simon got to see her several times a year, and thought of her as a friend as well as a colleague.

"Any excitement yet?" he asked.

Bettina reclaimed her seat at the registration table. Simon remained standing. "Of course," she answered. She turned her head and watched as a giant of a man in a too-tight suit approached. "I shall let Mr. Cuff tell you himself."

The man held out a massive paw for Simon to shake. "Bartholomew Cuff," he said. Simon imagined the floor vibrating with the bass notes in Cuff's voice. He was in his early thirties and several inches taller than Simon—clearly over six feet—with at least 220 pounds of solid muscle. A whisper of blue ink on his skin peeked out from his white shirtsleeve cuff. Simon imagined that the tattoo traveled all the way to the shoulder. "Chief of hotel security."

Bettina introduced Simon and then said, "Mr. Cuff can't convince Bucky Drabb to let the hotel handle the security of Number Plan Six."

Cuff shook his head, which was attached directly to his overmuscled shoulders. "I showed Mr. Drabb the hotel safe in its double-locked room, but he says he will manage everything himself."

"The stubborn little shit," Bettina said. "That document, *if* it is genuine and *if* it contains anything like what the rumor mill says, will turn Drood scholarship on its head."

"I'd offer to try to convince him myself," said Simon to Cuff, "but Bucky and I aren't exactly collegial."

Bettina smiled. "Yes, Simon once suggested that Helena Landless was too strong-willed to have been subject to

Jasper's mesmeric influences, and Bucky wouldn't speak to him for months."

Cuff's dumbfounded reaction to this explanation told Simon that Cuff was anything but a Droodist.

Simon noticed a clutch of people pressing against the lobby's plate-glass windows. Muted sounds pushed through, with shouts and cameras flashing. The lobby door opened and two people entered.

"Jennifer Wren," Bettina whispered. A young man holding an iPad and toting a battered leather cargo bag almost danced around the movie star as she stepped toward the registration table. Every few seconds he dropped the bag in order to take her picture with his phone.

That Ms. Wren arrived without an entourage was a relief. Simon thought she looked younger in person than on television (he knew from his occasional dip into the Internet that she was twenty-seven). Her long brown hair flowed freely, and her clear blue eyes scanned the foyer with intelligence and caution. She wore a ruched black jersey dress that accentuated her figure and gleaming perfect legs, and black flats. The only real color was around her neck, a loosely knotted Hermès scarf, a variegated basket-weave design of vermilion, pink, and cream.

The young man beside her, almost her height, was several years younger, and had a boyish quirky face with a short stubby asymmetrical nose. His short brown hair lay close to his head, and green eyes flashed out from the goofy-cute features. He was wearing a gray hooded sweatshirt and baggy jeans. The elastic of his briefs showed whenever he moved his arms. He spoke in a breathless way, his voice cracking occasionally like a teenager's.

Jennifer Wren turned to him, a pleasant but disconnected look on her face. "Mr. Quill, Quilpy," she corrected herself, "I will be happy to give you an interview for your blog later, once the conference is underway, and if you stop taking my picture. But right now I would like to register and then visit my suite. I have had a difficult time getting here. Please excuse me."

Her voice was calm, respectful, not at all what Simon might have expected from someone so young and famous. On the other hand, she wasn't merely a celebrity, but a Dickens scholar as well. Her master's thesis, *Behind the Proscenium Arch: Dickens and the Theatre*, had been published, sold well to the general public, and was often cited in the academic literature.

She surprised Quill also; he stood back and pocketed his phone. "Thank you, Ms. Wren."

"Please," she said to Quill, "call me Jennifer. There's no red carpet here." Then she flashed a real smile for Bettina.

"Jennifer," Bettina said, "I'd like to introduce you to Simon Alastair. Simon, Jennifer Wren." Bettina handed Jennifer her registration packet.

"I'm pleased to meet you," Jennifer said, before Simon had a chance to say anything. "I've read and heard so much about Dickens Junction. I've wanted to meet you for years, ever since you sent that charming letter."

His day brightened with this revelation. Simon turned to Bettina. "I had the honor of seeing Ms.

Wren—Jennifer—in her breakthrough role on Broadway as Little Nell—her first Ternan Award at fifteen."

"I was lucky," Jennifer said. "So many girls auditioned."

Her voice was soft and genuine, not studied, as Simon had imagined it would be. If it weren't for her exceptional beauty, she might be just a regular person. He was starstruck, a humbling thought.

"What are you working on now?" Simon asked.

"My production company is developing two projects," Jennifer answered. "The first is a Broadway-bound production of *The Frozen Deep*. Of course, if you read Quilpy's blog, you already know that I'll be playing Clara—the part that Ellen Ternan was hired to play. Second—and this is in the very early stages of discussion—a new big-screen adaptation of *Edwin Drood*. With me as Helena Landless."

"How exciting," Bettina said.

"I'm obviously too old to play Rosa Bud," Jennifer added, "and if we don't get started soon, I'll be more suitable for Princess Puffer."

Simon laughed. He noticed Quilpy in the periphery keyboarding on his iPad, no doubt already blogging about his newest "bestie," Jennifer Wren.

"I'm hoping we'll be able to visit during my stay," Jennifer said. "Maybe I'll even be able to meet the sexy journalist boyfriend I've read about." She smiled.

Simon blushed. Even Jennifer Wren read the tabloids. Or had someone read them for her.

"Zach would love to meet you." At this he felt a twinge of regret for his own last meeting with Zach; had he been out of line at breakfast?

47

Jennifer peered toward the glass doors. "I need to get my luggage," she said. She had booked the presidential suite on the fifth floor. "Excuse me." She strode back across the lobby and returned to the black town car that Simon glimpsed through the closing door. As Bettina turned away to help register another conferee, Quill strutted toward Simon.

"Daniel Quill," he said, giving Simon's hand a hard squeeze and shake. Up close he displayed even more of that boyish handsomeness that was, no doubt, his stock-in-trade. The crooked nose added vulnerability and impishness. "But call me Quilpy," he added, flashing tiny perfect teeth. "Everybody does, unless they call me something worse."

"I feel that I already know you," said Simon. "From your blog."

"Everybody reads it, don't they? I get almost as many hits as Perez Hilton. Now that the Ayn Rand frenzy is over, people are back caring about what really matters—Dickens." He shifted his weight from one foot to the other. At no time did he stand still. Simon was tempted to take him by the shoulders to stop him from moving, even temporarily.

Simon couldn't help himself, though—the kid was a cutie and a charmer. Go with that. "Well, Quilpy," he said, "welcome to Astoria and Dickens Junction. I hope you won't find us too boring."

"Dude," Quilpy said, the word like nails on a blackboard to Simon, "this is *a total eclipse, bro*. Do you think Bucky Drabb will drop a *Drood* deuce this week?"

Simon moved away, as if excessive use of slang might be contagious. "If *Professor* Drabb," said Simon diplomatically, "really has found the missing half of Dickens's Number Plan Six, and *if* it really contains the first—the only—clue to how Dickens would have ended *Edwin Drood*, his discovery would be momentous. But I have not seen his documentation."

"Has anybody?"

"I don't know. I'm not an intimate of Buck—of Professor Drabb's."

"You don't like him."

Simon felt his lips tighten. "I didn't say that."

"You didn't have to, dude. Your face did." Quilpy smiled. "Don't worry. Your secret's safe with me. I don't blog everything I hear. If I did, I'd be dead." He tapped his iPad. "That reminds me—and I'll give you a photo spread if you give a big reveal—the *real* goss about how you solved those murders?"

Simon checked his watch. "I must go," he said. "I have some administrative responsibilities."

"Drag you later," Quilpy said, his neck already stretching and checking the crowd for the next interesting tidbit. "Tell that boyfriend I think he's hawt."

So that's how it's pronounced, Simon thought. "You can tell him yourself." Another little pang. "He'll like it."

Near the lobby desk stood a man Dickens himself would have described as portly—more than six feet tall, probably more than three hundred pounds, with a shock of overlong white hair, a trim white goatee, and a protuberant belly that stretched his white dress shirt. He was wearing a charcoal suit and canary paisley tie. He turned around as Simon greeted a colleague next to him.

"Mr. Alastair," the large man said, his voice commanding and mellifluous at the same time. "I am Morgan—'the Great'—Grewgious."

The talent. "Mr. Grewgious." Simon's hand was lost inside the big man's ham-sized but still strangely elegant hand. "I've heard wonderful things about you."

"From Ms. Law," Grewgious intoned, as if delivering the name from Mt. Sinai. He placed a hand at Simon's back, moving him away from the lobby desk and toward the plate-glass windows. Despite his size, Grewgious moved with a dancer's grace. "I had the pleasure of making her acquaintance during one of my performances at sea." He paused and stroked his goatee.

Simon nodded politely. "She called me as soon as she returned from her cruise to say that you would be perfect for this conference."

Grewgious had long lashes above his piercing blue eyes; they fluttered now. "I have done a little research since I received this most unusual invitation," he said. "I do not know much about Mr. Dickens, but I have learned that he had a lifelong fascination with hypnosis, which he would have known as mesmerism."

"Yes," said Simon. "Dickens was a competent practitioner, claiming to have used it to benefit many people, including his beleaguered wife, Catherine."

"So I have read," said the Great Grewgious. Simon wondered what his friends called him. "But I, of course, use my training for entertainment purposes only. I am not a scholar." He said it as if he had studied at Plato's knee.

A young woman Simon didn't recognize entered the hotel lobby. Simon touched Grewgious's arm. "Excuse me," he said. "She looks lost. I'll go help her."

Grewgious looked over. "Of course, of course. Perhaps I will see you at the cocktail hour."

Grewgious moved toward the front desk, and Simon crossed the lobby to where the young woman stood, a battered flight bag beside her. She was around twenty-five, average height, overweight, and dressed in a close-fitting flowered print dress that would have been unfashionable in any era. She wore scuffed white flats. Her legs were bare. Her thin, brown, shoulder-length hair would have been a nice frame for her face had she taken better care of it. Rhinestone-winged eyeglasses completed her ensemble.

"May I help you?" Simon asked.

"I need to register for the conference," she said. She had a high-pitched voice with a singsong delivery that made her sound like a child.

"Over here," said Simon, gesturing to Bettina at the registration table. "Miss—"

"Neva Tupman," she said. "Ms." She brushed a limp lock of hair off her face.

Simon introduced himself. "I don't believe I've seen you before."

Ms. Tupman looked at her shoes, then at Simon. "I'm new," she said.

"Are you a Jasperite?" Simon asked, trying to lighten the tone. "Or one of the Landless Leaguers?"

"What?" She bit her upper lip.

"Your theory about the murder," Simon continued, "or whether there was one."

"I don't know. I'm here to learn," she said, looking around the room. Simon followed her gaze—Grewgious was consulting with the desk clerk, poring over a brochure of local sights and pointing at various pictures with his room key. Quilpy keyboarded away in a corner, pausing to look up only when Jennifer Wren returned to the lobby and waited a discreet distance behind Grewgious to check into her suite.

"Of course," said Simon. "Well, I suggest you register and then rest or tour the town. I hope we'll see you at the cocktail hour later today."

"Yes," she said. "I want to meet everyone as soon as possible."

Neva picked up her flight bag. As she crossed the lobby, three men entered the hotel, all talking over one another.

Buckminster Drabb, the first man in the door, was the most striking—a dandy in his early forties, with a round shaved head, deep doe-brown eyes, and a better-than-average build for someone who spent more time in musty research library stacks than in a lap pool. Today he was wearing a Savile Row navy suit and pinstriped blue shirt with white spread collar and hand-stitched pink repp tie. Drabb considered himself the premier American *Drood* scholar, a status many of his colleagues disputed behind his back, especially after a few cocktails.

His dapper look was interrupted by a jarring detail: He wore a handcuff on his left wrist. The other cuff in the pair was locked around the handle of the aluminum briefcase he gripped tightly.

The real drama had begun.

"You're insane," Drabb said to the elder of the two men with him. "We've been over this a hundred times. Mrs. Tope would *not* have recognized her."

Drabb was insulting Dean Minor, whom Simon considered the preeminent American *Drood* scholar still actively teaching, a man in his early sixties, small and slender. He had on a tired fawn corduroy jacket and dark chinos that Simon thought could use a fresh pressing. He wore large trifocals and today, for some reason, a second set of glasses rested on his thinning gray hair. Simon imagined that he would have been handsome enough in his youth, but life in the stacks had dried him out. He was known for his prickly personality, particularly when challenged by glib upstarts (as he had once called Drabb in front of Simon).

"Just because you keep repeating yourself, Bucky, doesn't mean you're any closer to being right," Minor snapped. Drabb hated being called Bucky, but everyone did it.

"Boys, please," said the third in the group, a cherubic man about forty, short and wide with soft features, such as a doughy mouth now formed into a too-tight smile. Silas Cheeryble's warm brown eyes were almost hidden by his plump cheeks. He rubbed stubby fingers through his overlong mousy brown hair as he shuffled, almost ran, to keep up with the other two as they approached the front desk. "You both have valid points."

Drabb wheeled around on the soles of his black ostrich cap-toe brogues. "No, we don't, Silas. This is not one of your 'oil on troubled waters' moments. Either Mrs. Tope would or would not have recognized Helena in the Datchery disguise. Let's talk about shoulder pads."

"Like yours?" Minor asked. "Would she have needed some as dramatic as these? You might land a small aircraft here"—he touched Drabb's suit—"or here."

Cheeryble giggled. Like Simon, he was not a scholar, but an enthusiast for whom Dickens was a passion. A draftsman in his work life, he devoted a significant portion of his free time to the study of *Edwin Drood* and its possible endings. Simon thought Cheeryble too often kowtowed to the academics, even though his self-taught knowledge was formidable and respected.

Bettina called these three the Weird Sisters, the witches from Macbeth, a play that Dickens referred to extensively in *Edwin Drood*. They were almost always together, always arguing.

"Welcome to Astoria and to the Junction," said Simon, moving across the lobby and greeting them. "Dean, Silas, Buckminster. Welcome."

Drabb acted as if Simon weren't there.

"The Jasperites have had the upper hand since 1870," Drabb said to Minor. "And you've all claimed that the 'mystery' of Edwin Drood died with Dickens. Well, it didn't. You'll have to wait a few days, when this will all be moot. You'll sing a different tune, then. After you see. Number. Plan. Six." He jiggled the attaché case in front of him.

"I'm excited," Cheeryble said.

Drabb looked down at the top of Cheeryble's head. "I'll bet you are," he said. "Bettina!" he said sharply, almost shouting across the lobby. "I need to see you right away."

"What a prick," Minor said, but Cheeryble wasn't listening. He was gaping open-mouthed at a young man now standing inside the hotel lobby door. Simon stared also.

The young man brushed raindrops from his trench coat and then lifted his head so Simon could see his face. He was in his late twenties, with tawny skin, brooding sharp eyebrows, thick lashes above menacing eyes, a rich lower lip, and starry white teeth. His hands moved with leopard-like grace—his fingers flicked at imaginary raindrops as if he were striking piano keys, a mesmerizing gesture. Simon thought him one of the most handsome men he'd ever seen. He caught Simon's eye and approached.

"You are Simon Alastair," he said in a lightly, strangely accented baritone.

"You have me at a disadvantage," said Simon, taking the beautiful hand in his own, sensing the strength behind the grip.

"Let me remedy that right away. I am Lionel Tartar. From the Seychelles. I returned to the United States several years ago to finish my studies and complete my dissertation—*Umbra and Penumbra: Death and Dissociation in* Our Mutual Friend *and* Edwin Drood. I thought this conference would provide at least a footnote or two." The teeth gleamed.

"That's a challenging topic," Cheeryble said with admiration.

"Not so challenging as time-consuming," Tartar answered, turning the fullness of his gaze to Cheeryble, whose knees seemed to quiver. Tartar's razor-sharp eyebrows were arched and poised to strike. "There's more material than I can use, that's for sure."

"Where are you studying?" Simon asked.

Tartar named an Ivy League university. "But I am most proud of my undergraduate work," Tartar continued. "I was one of the last pupils of the late Obadiah Twinn."

Cheeryble whistled through his teeth at the name of the most controversial Droodist scholar ever.

"You look too young to have studied with Professor Twinn," said Simon. "He retired twenty years ago from Meriwether University."

"Thank you," said Lionel. "I had the privilege of being tutored by Professor Twinn in a special independent study project just before he died."

"You're lucky," Cheeryble said. Simon introduced the two men, who then shook hands. "I met Professor Twinn once," Cheeryble continued, "at a one-day workshop on the iconography of the *Drood* monthly number cover. Fascinating."

Tartar nodded. "One of his specialties," he said. "You were lucky to have been there." He cast his glance around the lobby. "I'm looking forward to what I can learn here from such distinguished colleagues as yourselves." Tartar excused himself and walked over to the hotel lobby desk to check in.

"Well," Cheeryble said, all smiles, his tiny eyes winking. "Obadiah Twinn indeed." He rubbed his hands together. "This puts a crank in the cauldron."

Simon spent the rest of the afternoon working on background administrative details—checking with the catering staff about the meals and verifying the availability of the laptops, screens, wireless mikes, and other electronics needed for the next few days. This conference, unlike the last one, had drawn a record number of new attendees both interesting and mysterious, most likely because of Drabb's grandstanding. All of this busyness had helped Simon push away the details of his breakfast confrontation with Zach, which was already starting to melt into another tempest in a teabag.

Simon decided to check to make sure that everything was in order for the upcoming cocktail reception. The library/business center was located on the first floor above the lobby. It was a cozy room, and the Droodists would fill it up.

The room looked lovely. A portable bar had been set up near the wall of windows that overlooked the narrow back alley, and Finching for Flowers in the Junction had supplied several vases of stargazers and hothouse gladioli. Two of the walls were mahogany, artisan-crafted, floor-to-ceiling bookcases filled with books ranging from leather-bound sets of classic authors to more contemporary trade and mass-market titles. On the same wall as the door and opposite the windows, a computer, printer, and fax sat on a table next to two laptop carrels. Additional leather-bound volumes lined shelves above the computers.

Simon examined some of the titles. Many were contemporary romances and thrillers—beach books that Simon seldom read, and therefore did not stock at Pip's Pages. Most hotel guests were visiting Astoria and the Junction as part of a vacation, so probably weren't looking for Proust, Kant, or Kafka. There were a handful of classic mysteries, book-club selections, and prizewinners.

Simon was most interested in the leather-bound volumes. The complete works of Twain, Fenimore Cooper, Hawthorne, Melville (but not the poetry), Washington Irving, and Louisa May Alcott took up one entire bookcase. Then on to the British authors: Austen, Eliot, Hardy, Dickens (a gift from the Dickens Foundation upon the reopening of the hotel in 2006), a smattering of Thackeray (you could have *too* much Thackeray). A selection of other greats: Tolstoy, Trollope, Dostoyevsky, Dumas, and Balzac. Above the topmost shelf of the bookcase closest to the door, and barely within Simon's reach, rested a collection of plaster or resin busts of authors. Dickens had pride of place in the center, flanked by Shakespeare and Dickens's great friend Wilkie Collins.

Simon touched the Dickens volumes, arranged in chronological order of publication. Except that someone had placed *Great Expectations* before *A Tale of Two*

Cities. Simon carefully pulled the two books from the shelf, reversed their order, and returned them. *Our Mutual Friend* and then the final and unfinished novel, *The Mystery of Edwin Drood,* completed the collection. Simon straightened the row until it looked perfect.

An attractive young blond wearing a black tuxedo entered the library. Her nametag said, *Suzanda since 2009.* (*What,* Simon wondered, *had she been called before that?*) She greeted Simon, went behind the bar, and began doing an inventory.

Bettina Law followed shortly. "Ah, Simon," she said. "Prepare for the deluge!"

Over the next few minutes, the Droodists arrived, queued for drinks, and then broke into small but increasingly noisy clutches. Except for the stunning Lionel Tartar and the winsome Neva Tupman, Simon knew the rest of the Droodists as they arrived. He didn't count Grewgious as someone he could know or not know. Neither did he count young Quilpy, who was now engaging Zach in animated conversation. Zach's presence made Simon feel a pang, although he was almost beginning to forget what the contretemps had been about. Simon moved through the crowd toward them.

"I can't believe you haven't read *Pickwick Papers* yet," Quilpy was saying to Zach, taking a glass of white wine from a server (Blenda since 2011) circulating through the library with a tray of wine and well drinks.

"I've known Simon only four months," Zach said, giving Simon a quick kiss. The warmth of his lips on Simon's was a tiny sting of pleasure, and possibly a signal that

Zach also had put aside their earlier discussion. "He has given me a reading list, and *Pickwick Papers* is on it."

"It wasn't so much a list as a group of suggestions," Simon gently blustered. "He's reading *Our Mutual Friend* right now."

"So," Zach said to Quilpy, looking down into the shorter man's eyes, "how did you decide to become a Dickens blogger?"

Quilpy smiled as he watched Lionel Tartar cross the room to introduce himself to Jennifer Wren, who stood near the window in an aqua slant-hemmed cocktail dress and red leopard-print buckle pumps that highlighted her perfect calves. The Hermès scarf was artfully arranged at her neck, intensifying the beauty of her face.

For a moment, Quilpy returned his attention to Zach. "I filled a niche that needed filling." Quilpy stood taller. "I get a million hits some months. So there was obviously a need, wasn't there?" He craned his neck to look over Zach's shoulder again. "Who's the hotness?"

Zach's and Simon's backs were to the library door; they turned around in response to Quilpy's question. In the doorway chatting with Neva Tupman stood a curious young man, twenty-five or so and more lanky than lithe with his six-foot-plus frame. His most arresting feature was his hair: short, uneven platinum spikes held in place with a thick coat of shimmering gel. He had light-brown eyes behind a pair of old-fashioned black-framed eyeglasses. The glasses sat on a large pointed nose with a distinguishing bump just below the bridge.

He wore a plaid, long-sleeved shirt and olive chinos. Simon thought him unconventionally handsome.

"Well," Zach said in answer to Quilpy's question, "we're going to find out soon, because here he comes."

"Ms. Law asked me to find you," the young man said, addressing Simon. "My name is Edwin Drood."

Simon felt Zach's eyes on him; he kept his eyes on the young man.

"Is it now," Quilpy said. He was practically bouncing out of his shoes.

"Yes," Edwin Drood said. His voice was soft and kind. "My grandparents were the Quinsy Droods from Nether Puddledown, Dorset," he explained. "Everyone in the family, of course, has been devoted to Dickens, so it's only natural that I end up here, don't you think?"

Quilpy watched Drood with great interest. The two men were the same age but about as different in temperament as two men could be, Simon guessed. Like himself and Zach.

"Well," said Simon, "welcome to Astoria. You must have been a very late registrant. I would have remembered your name, and been on the lookout for you."

"Just yesterday," he said. He took a gin and tonic as Blenda passed by with her tray.

Zach and Quilpy introduced themselves.

"The blogger?" Drood asked.

"A fan," Quilpy said to Zach.

"Yes," Drood continued, now looking at Zach, "I recognize you from that article. You're more handsome in person than in print."

"Let's mingle," Quilpy said, taking Drood's arm. "What larks! See you later, boys." And off they went. As they passed by Jennifer and Lionel, Drood bent his head down slightly and away, as if he had stepped on something as he passed.

"I'm sorry about this morning," Zach said.

"Don't worry about it," said Simon. "It's nothing."

Zach chuckled. "It's not nothing. That's just it. It's everything."

Simon checked Zach's face for a sense of irony; there was none. Moving in together *was* everything at this point. But to say more now would be petulant, needy. Simon resisted the effort.

As if Zach sensed Simon's struggle, he filled the silence. "I think I'll wander, try to arrange interviews with some of the less famous Droodists. Local color to balance out the celebrities."

As Zach went in one direction, Simon moved to the periphery to absorb the scene. He occasionally saw Drood's platinum spikes, taller than anything in the room except the massive Grewgious, and assumed that wherever Drood was, the feisty Quilpy would be nearby. Simon eventually found himself near the Weird Sisters, each clutching a drink and arguing again.

"The greatest piece of Droodist scholarship in the last century was Obadiah Twinn's *Anyone but Jasper*," Bucky Drabb declaimed. His left hand was empty, Simon noticed. The handcuff and briefcase were gone. "No essay has been so plangent, so wry, so..."

"Obtuse," Dean Minor spat.

"If I might offer some thoughts," Silas Cheeryble started, but Drabb interrupted him.

"What mystery is there," Drabb asked, "if it's Jasper?"

"It's the *how*," Cheeryble offered, "not the *what* that Dickens was interested in."

"You believe in the Forster Fraud," Drabb said.

Minor and Cheeryble gave him a quizzical look. "What the f---?" Minor asked. "Is this some half-baked new theory?"

"I assure you that it is fully baked," Drabb said. "Just wait until my presentation." He downed the rest of his Sazerac in one swallow.

Simon extended his arms. "No need to argue in the social hour. Save it for the plenary sessions when everyone can benefit from your exegesis." Simon couldn't resist an occasional ironic use of academic jargon.

"Or your next vicious screed," Minor added, his eyes intent on Drabb. He took another drink as Blenda and her tray passed once more through the room. Another server (Tor since 2009) stopped and offered canapés: lutefisk bruschetta, cockle ceviche in paper cups, and slick, warm rumaki skewers. Cheeryble helped himself to five rumaki, licking his fingers afterward.

Simon turned to face Drabb directly. Drabb had changed his tie for the cocktail hour; this one was even more beautiful than the one before, a stair-step weave in aubergine and silver. Simon had a sudden case of cravat envy.

"I see you've done something with your security issues," he said, gesturing to Drabb's naked left wrist. "I hope that

Bartholomew Cuff has persuaded you to leave Number Plan Six in the hotel safe."

"I have made suitable arrangements," Drabb said. As he did so, he accidentally bumped the elbow of the Great Grewgious, almost causing Grewgious to spill his gimlet. Drabb turned and apologized. Grewgious gave him a bland smile and nod. He looked like Burl Ives as the Ghost of Christmas Present, minus the fur-trimmed robe.

"I have taken care of it myself," Drabb continued to Simon. "It's in my room, or it's on my person right now, or it's wherever it needs to be so that I know it's safe. I don't trust anyone. Not the hotel, not even you."

"I understand," said Simon. "But I hope you understand Bettina and me, also. We only want what's best for your safety."

"There's a world of crooks and thieves out there, but I'm smarter than they are. They don't have PhDs in Victorian fiction."

Simon tried to suppress a smile, but couldn't. "I'm sure you're right about that," he said. "So that would rule out most of the people here, wouldn't it?"

Drabb didn't get Simon's jest. "These people are jealous. I'm about to blow up the smug little Droodist world by showing incontrovertibly what Dickens intended to do with the second half of the novel. I've got the proof." He tapped Simon's chest.

In the interests of peace, Simon overlooked this intrusion into his personal space. "We'll all be on tenterhooks until your presentation. I hope you have a pleasant evening, Buckminster."

Sometime while Simon was talking with Drabb, Osma had entered the library and was now in animated conversation with Jennifer and Lionel. Osma's good eye glittered almost as much as the Heart of Helsinki did when she made a gesture. At one point, Neva Tupman passed between Simon and Osma, moving languidly through the crowd, making eye contact with various conferees, sometimes going up to a small group and engaging in brief conversation. From first impressions, Simon had assumed she would be out of her element, and, while she still seemed that way, she was also making a pleasant impression on others. Before Simon looked away, Neva Tupman stood next to Drood and engaged him in banter fascinating to both of them. Quilpy stood nearby, wanting, Simon imagined, to tear Drood away to someplace more private.

"I've had the best offer from this amazing man." Bettina's voice caught Simon's attention. Zach was with her. "He has offered to buy me dinner if I regale him with the tawdry history of your Droodism." Zach grinned. "How could I refuse?"

"There's little to tell," Simon suggested.

"I'm not so sure about that," Zach said. "I've already heard about the night you and Bucky Drabb had one too many Drambuies and ended up in the Central Park fountain, fighting over whether Fagin was a pederast or just misunderstood."

"I also received a dinner invitation from Silas Cheeryble," Bettina added.

"Bring him along," said Simon.

"Should we ask Osma to join us?" Bettina asked.

Simon looked over in time to see Jennifer put her arm on Osma's shoulder and laugh warmly. "She seems to be in good hands," he said. "We can check in with her after dinner for a drink. May I suggest Maison D'Être for dinner?"

"Such Dickensian characters at this conference," Silas Cheeryble said, taking his last bite of wild boar ragu with pappardelle and frizzled leeks.

Maison D'Être was around the corner from the Hotel Elliott, a narrow but deep space with high ceilings and textured wallpaper. Amber- and black-speckled blown glass sconces dripped pools of warm buttery light on the walls. The food was eclectic and delicious.

Simon had forgotten how funny Cheeryble could be when he wasn't in the penumbra of Bucky Drabb and Dean Minor. In Simon's view, Cheeryble's admiration for the trappings of academia made him lose perspective on the quality of his own keen insights into Dickens. He also possessed the insinuating habits of a genial gossip—Simon felt himself drawn toward a type of small-group conversation he seldom had. He usually had such discussions as this only with Zach or his longtime friend George, or when deep in Droodist business with Bettina. Not in groups over dinner and drinks in a public space.

"I can't recall when we've had so many Droodists under thirty," Bettina said, spearing a roasted Brussels sprout half and dipping it black-truffle butter sauce. "There's that strange Ms. Tupman, and Quilpy, and Lionel Tartar—"

"And someone actually named Edwin Drood," said Simon.

"The most peculiar one of all," Cheeryble said.

Bettina nodded agreement. "I will mention our newbies at tomorrow's plenary session," she said. "There's too much talk these days about the old authors not being relevant. These young people suggest otherwise."

"I'm not so sure," Simon warned. "Ms. Tupman's Dickens education is thin, and Quilpy's here because he's riding the cultural wave associated with the two-hundredth anniversary of Dickens's birth. He'll move on to Hardy, or James, or someone else when it suits him."

"Or to whichever writers *hawt* dudes are reading," Zach suggested.

Simon's morning pout now seemed foolish and juvenile compared with the twitch of desire he felt as he looked into the dark sapphires of Zach's eyes, pupils dilated in the lambent light above their alcove table.

"Young Tartar impressed me," Cheeryble said. "Such an interesting background—exotic heritage, that unusual accent...Where exactly are the Seychelles, anyway?"

"Northeast of Madagascar, off Africa's eastern coast," Zach said. "Tartar's Dickens vitae may be solid, but I don't trust him. He wasn't happy when I told him I had been to the Seychelles." Zach speared a glazed baby carrot and chewed slowly. "For example," he said when he had finished his bite, "Tartar told me he doesn't speak Creole. He says it's because he left the Seychelles as a child, but I'm not sure."

"Tartar seems too smart to be in Drabb's camp," said Simon.

"He is?" Bettina asked.

"He studied with Obadiah Twinn," Silas told her.

"How unfortunate," Bettina said.

"Not to Drabb," said Simon. The wine was affecting him—Simon felt himself moving toward full-on gossip mode. But this discussion could be important: Drabb had already disrupted the conference with his spy briefcase and prima donna behavior. As conference coordinator, Simon felt an obligation to protect the Droodists and the Hotel Elliott. Who other than Cheeryble might know the full range of what Drabb was up to? Nothing ventured, nothing gained.

"He bragged all night about his secret document," said Simon. "What does he mean by the Forster Fraud, anyway?"

Zach leaned forward. "If you're going to talk shop, re-member that I had never heard of *Edwin Drood* until I met Simon."

"Drabb sent an e-mail about a month ago," Cheeryble answered, "and used that phrase in passing. It piqued my interest, so I did some sleuthing."

The others at the table drew closer.

"When Dickens died," Cheeryble continued, "*The Mystery of Edwin Drood* was half-finished. Dickens's notes, or number plans, as he called them, consisted of sheets of paper folded in half lengthwise, one sheet for each of the monthly installments."

Simon knew that all of Dickens's novels had been published in installments, some in weekly but most in

monthly parts, or numbers, as Dickens called them—
but all of this would be new to Zach. Cheeryble must
have sensed this; his explanation was neither tedious nor
condescending.

"On one half of the fold," Cheeryble went on, "Dickens
listed the installment's chapter titles and key plot points
for those chapters, on the other half more general comments, sometimes foreshadowing for future installments.
With me so far?" Cheeryble asked Zach.

Zach nodded.

"So, when Dickens's biographer and literary executor
John Forster turned over his collection of Dickens man-
uscripts, letters, and papers to the Victoria and Albert
Museum in London, the page for Number Plan Six—the
installment that Dickens was working on when he died—
was not included. Forster's widow, Eliza, didn't turn it over
until years later. What is most significant is that Number
Plan Six was half the size of the other plans; it was only
the right-side list of chapter titles, and no detail about
the contents of the chapters. So the question is—what
happened to the other half of Number Plan Six?"

"This sounds so cloak-and-dagger," Zach said.

"I suspect," Cheeryble went on, "that Drabb believes
he has discovered the missing half of Number Plan Six,
and that it contains notes in Dickens's handwriting that
might identify what happened to Edwin Drood—whether
he was dead or alive, and, if dead, who murdered him."

"Who separated the two halves of the number plan?"
Bettina asked Cheeryble. "Was it Forster or his widow?"

"Or Dickens himself?" Zach suggested.

Simon smiled softly to himself. That was yet another thing he loved about Zach: He was working his way—slowly—through the Dickens canon, but he was always interested in learning more, and in helping Simon learn more. Simon doubted he could have solved last winter's murders without Zach by his side.

"There's very little critical ink on what may have happened to the plan," Cheeryble said by way of an answer to Zach's question, "or why Number Plan Six is a unique size. Noted Droodist Arthur Cox argues persuasively that Forster, Mrs. Forster, or some random museum employee, removed the half sheet for pragmatic reasons: It was blank. And it was blank because, anticipating his own death, Dickens chose not to reveal the novel's secrets even in his working notes until after he had written each installment. But some fringe Droodists, seeing a conspiracy everywhere they look, have begun to speculate that John Forster may have suppressed—even destroyed—the half of the number plan with its clues to the mystery's final solution."

"Why?" Zach asked.

Cheeryble rubbed his hands together. "So that Forster could then claim that *The Mystery of Edwin Drood*, Dickens's last gasp, was the perfect mystery novel—because it could not be solved."

"In spite of a thousand Droodists writing a million words," Bettina said.

"No wonder Drabb carries his secret in a handcuffed briefcase," Zach said. "It must be worth a fortune."

"As with fine art, the black market in Dickensiana is horrid," Bettina said. "Unscrupulous collectors take the most amazing things and hide them from the world for their own pleasure. If this document is real, I can think of a handful of people who would pay any price just to possess what no other person could—the secret that Dickens took to his grave."

"When you put it that way—" Zach said.

"—people might kill for it," Cheeryble finished.

After dinner, Simon and Zach went to the bar in the hotel basement. Cheeryble declined to join them in order to prepare for the next day's panel discussion with Drabb and Minor. Bettina also retired to answer e-mails and work on Droodist Society administrative tasks.

The hotel basement bar was spilling over with Droodists. Drabb and Minor were elbow to elbow at a cocktail table scattered with gin and tonics and a half-ravaged bowl of peanuts, furiously debating some point or other. Over in the opposite corner, Grewgious was chatting earnestly with Drood and Quilpy. Drood had his back toward the darkest part of the bar, where Jennifer Wren and Lionel Tartar talked at a two-top, their heads nearly touching. While Zach offered to wait at the bar for service, Simon took a booth as far away from the rest as possible, a corner seat that gave him a clear view of everything and everyone.

"Lionel, darling!" A tall, dark woman strode across the floor of the bar. She wore a skin-tight silver lamé dress that highlighted her toned legs. Her sleek black hair was long and close to the face, and she had penetrating dark eyes and high, sharp cheekbones that caught the muted light of the bar. By the time she had made it to Lionel's and Jennifer's table, Lionel was standing, almost shielding Jennifer from the new arrival. Simon decided to help Zach at the bar with the drinks so that he could discreetly eavesdrop.

"You haven't answered my calls," she said, kissing him on both cheeks. Lionel's hands were on her upper arms as if to push her away, but he returned her kisses mechanically. He turned both himself and the stranger around so that Jennifer could see them. She stood.

"Ms. Jennifer Wren, my sister, Cecily Tartar," he said. Jennifer held out her hand, but Cecily embraced Jennifer and hugged her close.

The brother and sister were twins—their faces were eerily similar, with Lionel's features showing the masculine reflection and Cecily's the feminine.

"I'd know you anywhere," Cecily said. "How divine to see you."

"I didn't expect you here," Lionel said to his sister.

"I can see that," Cecily said. "If you had listened to my voice mails, you would have known that I was coming."

"You are also a Dickens scholar?" Jennifer asked.

Simon watched as Cecily flashed the real movie star her version of a Hollywood smile. It was a good likeness. "Not like my brother, but I dabble. I don't usually care for the later Dickens, like *Drood*—so overly ripe, so tired."

Zach paid for the drinks and returned to their table. Simon followed reluctantly, watching the brother, sister, and movie star continue talking until Cecily moved away and introduced herself to the two present Weird Sisters. The men stood as she approached. Simon couldn't hear any of their voices this far away.

"He wasn't happy to see his sister," Zach said.

Simon nodded agreement. "Another last-minute registrant. Her name wasn't on the list that Bettina and I went over earlier."

"Before I knew you," Zach said, taking Simon's hand, "I thought that Dickens was just another author. Now, of course, I realize that he's an institution, but a furtive one, like a secret society. You'll have to teach me the secret handshake."

"When we get home…" said Simon, weaving his fingers through Zach's.

The last of Simon's earlier mood melted away, in part displaced by the increasing interpersonal conflicts and tensions of the conference itself. He could pout another time.

Osma Dilber came into the bar. She had changed into a muted caftan and flats. She smiled when she saw Simon and Zach.

"I was too excited to go to bed yet," she said when she arrived at their table. "After meeting Jennifer Wren and all." She looked at Zach, then at Simon. "She invited me to her suite for a cocktail, and then ordered in dinner, just the two of us. Isn't that grand?"

"Certainly is," Zach said.

"She's the nicest thing," Osma continued. "Not at all what you'd expect from someone so famous. She fussed over the Heart." Osma held out her hand, letting the gems' facets catch all of the soft light and send it back out as bright needles. "She showed me some of her own pieces that she travels with. Very nice things."

"You've made a new friend," said Simon.

"So has she."

Lionel and Jennifer crossed the room together, heading for the elevator. Jennifer gave Osma a wave and a wink.

Zach left the table to order Osma a white wine at the bar. As Simon watched, Cecily passed Zach, giving him an intense look. Grewgious, Minor, and Drabb all watched her from their tables as she stepped up to Simon and Osma. Grewgious was the first to look away.

"I'm Cecily Tartar," she said, holding out her hand first to Osma. "You must be Osma Dilber."

Osma looked surprised. "I'm pleased to meet you," she said, "but how do you know me?"

"Two ways," Cecily said. She smoothed her skirt and sat next to Osma. "I read up on your accomplishments after I first heard of this conference from my brother, but what really intrigued me is this." She reached for Osma's left hand and held it in the light, carefully adjusting her grasp so that the ruby-and-diamond ring winked.

Simon was surprised by such a gesture of familiarity, but Osma, he gathered, was used to it after a lifetime of owning a famous ring. He was also suspicious of this stranger's keen interest in the ring.

"I can't believe I have the honor of viewing the Heart of Helsinki. I'm a gemstone grader by profession," Cecily added, "and a gem historian."

"An unusual occupation for a woman," said Simon.

"For anyone," Cecily said. Her eyes flashed a keen intelligence, as if she were sizing Simon himself up for grading. "The boys in Antwerp weren't always happy to have me apprenticing beside them, until I proved that my eye was as good as theirs."

"You know the history of this ring?" Osma's clear eye gleamed with delight.

"I'm more familiar with its companion, the Star of Stockholm," Cecily said. Held in Cecily's tawny manicured fingers, Osma's aged hands looked like driftwood burls. As if to prove her credentials, Cecily recited a brief history of the gemstones.

"Amazing," Osma said, her face glowing.

Zach rejoined them, and Cecily introduced herself.

"So, having seen the Star of Stockholm years ago in Malmö, part of my interest in coming here was to see the Heart for myself," she said. "Gem cutters around the world comment on its perfect facets and the artistry of the diamond settings."

"My goodness," Osma said to Simon. "I feel as if I'm on *Antiques Roadshow*."

"It is a gemstone without price," Cecily said. "It is perhaps too famous to sell, although I'm sure many collectors would pay handsomely for it with no questions asked."

"We have two priceless objects in our midst," Zach said. When Cecily gave him a quizzical look, he summarized the dinner discussion about Drabb's possible bombshell.

"Yes," Cecily answered, "Lionel told me something about that." She turned to Simon. "Mr. Alastair—Simon—I certainly haven't meant to neglect you."

He smiled. "Not at all. We think Osma is a treasure, too, not for her jewelry alone."

Cecily's gaze was as intense and exotic as her brother's, but her eyes lacked warmth. Simon thought that the Tartar twins were constantly evaluating their environment and calculating how the world could be turned to their advantage. They were alike—but were they close?

"What about the conference," he said to her, "do you find most fascinating? The unsolved mystery of the book itself?"

Cecily shook her head.

"The occult tropes like opium and mesmerism?"

"Hypnosis does not interest me," she said.

"So you won't be attending tomorrow night's presentation?" Simon nodded his head in the direction of the Great Grewgious, still in conversation with Drood and Quilpy. Minor and Drabb had joined them, an unlikely grouping for sure. Simon wished he could eavesdrop on their conversation.

"Parlor tricks. I don't mean to be disrespectful," she said, patting Osma's ringed hand. "Of course I'll be there for the dinner in Ms. Dilber's honor." She placed Osma's hand in the woman's lap and stood. "But I don't consider the exploitation of hypnosis for stage tricks to be entertainment. You must please excuse me," she continued. "I've been traveling all day. I'd like to rest and be refreshed for tomorrow. I hope to see all of you in the morning. Now, good night."

As she crossed the room, Simon watched half of the strange table—Drabb, Grewgious, and Minor—follow

Cecily's departure, three sets of eyes moving left to right as she passed toward the elevator. Drood was looking at Simon, and Quilpy seemed lost in contemplation of Drood's peculiar handsomeness. In this light, Drood's shocks of platinum hair flickered like candle flame.

"I should go, too," Osma said, picking up her wine glass. "Do you think they'll let me take this to my room?"

"I'll vouch for its safe return," said Simon, "if anyone asks."

"All right, boys, see you in the morning."

"May I escort you back to your room?" Zach asked.

"I'm fine," she said. "Thank you. You're both such dear boys. I'm lucky to know you." Zach and Simon stood; Osma hugged each in turn and then, her caftan stirring around her, left the bar.

"I'm exhausted," said Simon. "Let's go home."

"All right," Zach said. "But I hope you're not too tired to teach me that special Dickensian handshake."

April 16

7:30–9:00 a.m.	Continental Breakfast & Welcome	Bettina Law, conference chair Hotel bar, basement
9:15 a.m.–noon	Plenary Session: "Dickens in the Next 100 Years: Why *Drood* Matters"*	Silas Cheeryble, Buckminster Drabb, Dean Minor, panelists; Bettina Law, moderator Columbia River Room, basement
12:15–1:45 p.m.	Lunch	Hotel banquet room, basement
2:00–5:00 p.m.	Bus Trip to Fort Clatsop, Astoria Column	Meet in hotel lobby
5:00–6:30 p.m.	No-host Bar	Conference Center
6:30–9:00 p.m.	Ethelinda Award for Lifetime Achievement in Droodism or Dickensiana (dinner included)	Osma Dilber, special guest Hotel banquet room
		The Great Grewgious Hotel, hypnotist Hotel banquet room
	Entertainment	

* Discussion questions will be accepted in advance. Please see Bettina Law.

DAY TWO

"Welcome, Droodists," Bettina said from the dais. The 17th Triennial Conference of the United States Chapter (Western Sector) of the International Society of Droodists came to order.

As Bettina continued her opening remarks, Simon, standing at the back of the room, counted forty-six attendees, a conference record (Grewgious apparently decided to sleep in).

There was Osma, in the front row by the center aisle, taking in every word. Simon had faced no opposition when he approached the executive committee with the idea of making Osma the recipient of a Droodist lifetime achievement award.

Cecily and Lionel Tartar sat apart; Lionel was next to Jennifer Wren, who was next to Osma, and Cecily was seated next to Silas Cheeryble's chair, which he had vacated to wait in the wings for his upcoming panel discussion.

There was Neva Tupman, surfing on her iPhone, and there was Edwin Drood, white flames above his head—his chair almost touching Quilpy's, and turned away from Jennifer and Lionel. Quilpy was reading his iPad. The young men's shoulders touched whenever either shifted in his seat.

Simon was gently envious of what lay ahead for them, both risks and rewards, and maybe also envious of their youth. On the other hand, he had much to be thankful for. Zach, after all, had not immediately and categorically rejected his request that they move in together, merely postponed his response. After last night's "secret-handshake" training, Simon was feeling less fussy and anxious. He was, at heart, a pragmatist. If Zach said yes, what changes would his full-time residency at Gad's Hill Place create? Dirty socks on the floor, or someone to share the household chores? No matter—Simon had Jude for those. Better sex, or a slow decline to bed death? Or did the latter only lurk on the other side of parenthood? Parenthood. Could Simon see a swing set in the backyard, linty binkies under every sofa cushion, a car seat in the BMW? And the diaper bag—best not to think of that right now.

While Simon's thoughts wandered, he kept partial attention on Bettina, who was finishing her first question to the panel: What would Dickens think of the status of *Edwin Drood* among his works, this many years later? Would he be surprised? Flattered? Frustrated?

Drabb and Minor began arguing at once.

"Dickens would be horrified," Drabb said, "at the machinations of his old friend and executor John Forster, for the liberties that Forster took with the text of the unfinished installment number six, and the tampering he did to the number plans."

"What tampering?" Minor demanded.

"He's referring to what he calls the Forster Fraud," Cheeryble said.

"Which is what you'll all be calling it after I present my paper," Drabb said between his teeth.

"Let's save that discussion for then," Bettina said, looking out as conferees shifted uneasily in their chairs.

Certainly the last thing Bettina wanted was a room full of brooding Droodists. Simon considered intervening, but that would display a lack of confidence in her, and Bettina Law was a highly competent scholar. If she couldn't keep Drabb in his place, no one could.

Drabb shifted in his chair. "In spite of what I said about Dickens being horrified, he would also be pleased that every single one of his works, even the unfinished one, has never been out of print since the day of publication. About how many authors, besides Shakespeare, can that be said? Even some of the Bard's works have been lost."

"Well said." Cheeryble smiled. "Since I'm not a scholar, I'll take the common reader's approach and say that Dickens still matters, and *Drood* matters, because Dickens tells great stories with memorable characters, and re-creates times and places that might otherwise be lost to us forever. And because his writing changed peoples' lives for the better."

"Scholar or not, Silas," Minor said, "you've echoed my sentiments. Yes, we can study Dickens for his use of doubles, river imagery, unreliable narrators, and even, if you must, this post-deconstructionist babble about excreta and gender fragmentation, whatever that might be. But at the end of the day you will have Scrooge, Fagin, Mr. Pickwick and Sam Weller, Sarah Gamp, Sidney Carton, Wilkins Micawber, Miss Havisham, and Wackford Squeers, among the rest. And you will have laughed—and cried. Not much else matters."

"How unacademic a thought," Cheeryble said. "Congratulations."

The room laughed and applauded, everyone feeling this rare display of collegiality and bonhomie.

Simon stepped out of the meeting room and made his check-in calls to the bus driver and guide for the tour of Fort Clatsop and the Astoria Column. As he finished his call, Neva Tupman exited the meeting room and crossed the bar toward the elevator.

"Ms. Tupman," Simon called. "Is anything the matter?"

"I'm tired," she said. She pushed her limp brown hair away from her face. Today she was wearing low-waisted jeans and a peasant blouse that did not quite cover her midriff. She could wear something more suitable, Simon thought. "I traveled a long time to get here. I need to rest."

"Does that mean you won't be taking the tour this afternoon?"

"Probably not. I want to be fresh for dinner tonight."

"And the show, I suppose."

"Absolutely. I love magic."

"The Great Grewgious is a hypnotist."

"Whatever," Ms. Tupman said as she walked toward the elevator. "It's all good."

Simon stood at the edge of the bus parking area at the Astoria Column atop Coxcomb Hill, looking north across the Columbia toward the Washington state side of the river. The day was cool; it was misting but not raining, though deeply overcast. Today you could not see Saddle Mountain to the south, or much of the detail of Astoria below, fog-bound even this late in the afternoon.

Simon turned around to view the column. Most of the Droodists who had accompanied Simon to Fort Clatsop, and now here, had ascended the top of the sgraffito-decorated monument. He could see Silas Cheeryble on the narrow observation deck at the top; Simon was surprised that he had climbed the 164 steps. Dean Minor was on deck also, holding a pair of binoculars. Cecily Tartar and Osma Dilber were examining the commemorative paving stones at the base of the column. Osma, no doubt, was pointing out the names of people she knew or had known who had donated money for the restoration and preservation of the column in the previous decade. Cecily, bent over in order to hear Osma, nodded appreciatively now and then.

On the way back to town, Simon asked the bus driver to take the long way: down the backside of the hill on Gad's Hill Road, past Dickens Junction, and along Youngs Bay, approaching Astoria from the southwest.

As the bus descended the hill and arrived on the ridge, only a few blocks from Zach's duplex, Simon pointed out the heavily wooded one-square-block cemetery where his grandfather's mausoleum brooded under a brace of newly leafing maples.

"My grandfather," he said into the bus intercom system, "the founder of Dickens Junction, is buried there, in the family mausoleum that was modeled on several Victorian structures. We'll stop by on the day we visit Dickens Junction. It's a pretty cemetery."

Zach's text message said that he would be waiting for Simon in the hotel bar. After escorting Osma to her room so that she could rest before the dinner honoring her, Simon descended to the bar. He found Zach in a corner booth, hard at work on his laptop. Two martinis sat beside him.

"You're just in time." He gave Simon a quick kiss.

"Cheers," said Simon. He and Zach clinked glasses. Simon took a sip of the martini—perfect, no vermouth to muddy up the Aviation gin. If he were going to have only one cocktail, then it had better be a good and pure one. "Just in time for what?"

"My much-needed break," Zach said. "Today's productivity has been measured more by dead ends and missing information than by rich veins of journalistic ore."

"Say more."

"Well, let's start with Drood."

At that moment, Drood himself and Quilpy drifted into the bar, shortly followed by Jennifer and Lionel. Drood and Quilpy were in Simon's full sight; Jennifer and Lionel took a table blocked from view by a large potted palm. He could see that Drood, while listening to Quilpy's ever-present chatter, was stealing glances at the impossibly beautiful young couple. Drood held his cocktail in front of his face as his eyes moved in the direction of where Lionel and Jennifer sat.

"Are you listening to me?" Zach touched Simon's arm. "You appear distracted."

"People-watching," said Simon. He lowered his voice. "Tell me about Drood."

"That's just it." Zach sipped at his martini. "There's nothing to tell. At. All. No social networking. Anywhere. Can't search for him without coming up with the Dickens character."

"*I* don't social network," said Simon.

"You're not twenty-five," Zach said. "It actually is strange that Drood doesn't have a presence on any of those sites. Quilpy, for example, has over one million fans and five thousand friends on itsmyface.org. Your lovely assistant, Brock, has more than four hundred friends."

"How can a person even know four hundred people, let alone call that many friends?" Simon asked.

"Think of them as contacts—or hookups—not actual friends," Zach said. "But in any case, Edwin Drood doesn't have a page on any of the social networks, so I couldn't find out a single thing about him, except that he's not related to anyone named Quinsy Drood of Nether Puddledown, Dorset, as he told us yesterday."

"How do you know that?" Simon asked.

"There's no such place," Zach said, "and no such people."

Simon sipped his martini.

"Now, Drabb's another story," Zach continued, a glint in his eye from the little bombshell he had dropped. "He's a pretty interesting character."

"I'd expect you would find a lot about him on the Internet," said Simon. "He's well-known in academic circles, has published articles, books, bibliographies. He's prolific."

Zach agreed. "Yep, I found all of those. And lots of references to his mentor, Obadiah Twinn, the 'controversial polymath' with the peculiar theories about Dickens's true designs for *The Mystery of Edwin Drood*."

"Many people consider Twinn an egghead and a crackpot," said Simon. "I met him years ago but, since I wasn't an academic, he didn't have time for me."

"Unlike Twinn's last mentee, a very young Lionel Tartar," said Zach.

Across the room, Drood and Quilpy were talking and laughing. At one point, Quilpy reached out, apparently to touch the bump on the bridge of Drood's nose, but Drood drew away and took Quilpy's hand instead, making both of them laugh.

The Great Grewgious strode into the bar with Bettina Law. He was in a tuxedo, which gave his substantial frame additional gravity and dignity, and he had trimmed his goatee. Bettina was in a black party dress, more feminine, flouncy, and shimmery than her usual tailored taste, but it flattered her figure and softened her look.

They approached Simon and Zach's table. "Good evening, gentlemen," Grewgious said, his voice honey-rich. "I hope you will be attending the performance tonight."

"I wouldn't miss it," said Simon.

"We shall both be there," Zach said.

"As you know, I ask for volunteers from the audience to participate on stage." He turned to Zach. "I'm hoping you'll agree to be one. I think you might have just the stage quality I'm looking for."

Zach smiled at Simon. "Why not?" he said to Grewgious. "I've got nothing to lose."

"Nothing but your dignity," said Simon.

"I'm not worried about that," Zach said.

"Ms. Law has also agreed to volunteer," Grewgious noted.

Bettina beamed. "It's for a good cause. If we can't laugh at ourselves in this profession once in a while, it would cease being fun."

"I sense," said Grewgious to Simon, "that you are not the adventurous type."

"I can be spontaneous," said Simon, "if I'm warned in advance."

"You are not, perhaps, the best candidate for hypnosis. A willing participant is needed, someone who is suggestible and can relax. I think you would fight a hypnotic state."

"I probably would."

"On the other hand," Zach said, "I'll try anything twice."

Grewgious looked around the room and stopped on Drood and Quilpy. "Excuse me," he said. "I need to make sure of my other volunteers. I shall see you all after dinner."

Grewgious's large body practically glided toward the table with Quilpy and Drood. He began talking to Drood. Bettina sat beside Simon.

"What an interesting pair of young men," she said. "Mr. Quill is rather a surprise. He's bright, articulate, funny, and obviously loves Dickens, or at least loves to gossip about people who love Dickens. And he could hardly keep his hands off Drood all afternoon."

"Young love," Zach said.

"I can handle that all right," Bettina said, raising her glass in a toast. "And I'm intrigued by Drood, though it's so hard to call him that, isn't it? If anything, he looks more like a young Datchery to me—with that white spiky hair and all, almost a costume."

Simon checked his watch and stood. "I need to dash home and change for dinner." He kissed Zach. "I'll see you both at the banquet."

When Simon returned to the hotel lobby, dressed in an Armani double-breasted tuxedo with black-diamond studs, Grewgious was standing at the front desk talking with the night manager (Sven since 2006). Sven held a brochure and was pointing at something in it; Grewgious leaned in to hear him better. Then Grewgious put his hand on Sven's shoulder and spoke, nodding his head as if in thanks. Simon was too far away to hear what was said. Grewgious pocketed the brochure. The desk phone rang.

"Mr. Alastair," said Sven from across the lobby, "that was Ms. Dilber. She will be down directly."

The elevator door opened and Osma emerged, a vision in glimmering winter white and diamonds. The floor-length beaded evening gown, through the magic of darts and tucks, gave her a youthful silhouette as she moved across the floor. The Heart of Helsinki stood out against the gown like a drop of blood on snow.

"The guest of honor," Grewgious announced. His voice was so deep the floor almost shook, Simon thought. Like James Earl Jones's, very, very smooth, compelling.

"You look radiant," said Simon.

"This gown," Osma explained, "like the Heart, belonged to my grandmother. The Finnish Nightingale, in her later years, was more like a turkey than a songbird. Thank goodness for Catriona Boggle, the dressmaker at Frills and Furbelows in the Junction. She altered it so that I could wear it tonight."

"You are a treasure for the eyes," said the Great Grewgious in his stagiest voice. He took Osma by one elbow, and Simon took her by the other.

"How lucky I am," Osma said.

Grewgious held the elevator door so that they could all descend to the large basement conference room, now turned into the banquet room. The room was already noisy with the Droodists, in evening gowns, dark suits, and tuxedos, finding their places at the banquet rounds. Simon helped Osma up the platform to the head table. She sat to the left of the lectern next to Bettina Law; Buckminster Drabb sat on Bettina's other side. Simon, Dean Minor, and Louella Pardiggle, the other members of the Droodist executive committee, sat on the other side of the lectern at the head table.

Simon waved down at Zach seated with Quilpy, Drood, and Bradford Sturgess, Zach's boss and the editor-in-chief of *Household Words*. After finishing his Dungeness crab cocktail, Simon went over to Zach's table. Sturgess, a tall, slender man in his early sixties, usually looked rumpled, but tonight was starched and pressed in a tuxedo. Except for Drood, who was wearing a gray seersucker jacket and black acid-washed jeans, all of the men at the table were in formal wear. Quilpy looked out of his element in his rented white dinner jacket but, as Simon's friend George often said about some young man or other, he still cleaned up nicely.

"We members of the fourth estate must put on a good front for the public," Sturgess said, ironically pompous. "You're looking at the past, present, and future of this profession," he said, first pointing to himself, then to Zach, and finally to Quilpy. He patted Quilpy on the back. "I've offered him a job, but he prefers to work solo."

"More nimble that way," Quilpy said, munching on a crouton.

"Are you having a good time?" Simon asked Edwin Drood. "I haven't had much of a chance to speak with you since our introduction."

Drood nodded his head; the short platinum spikes were so stiff with product that they didn't quiver. "Fabulous so far, even if much of it is over my head."

"Like 'transubstantiation,' or whatever Bucky Drabb was blathering on about this morning," Quilpy said.

Simon chuckled. "'Jasper's optitive counterfactuals and transgressive valences,' I believe Drabb said. But blather all the same." The men laughed. Simon continued, looking at Drood's lovely eyes behind the weird retro glasses perched awkwardly on the bump on his nose, "I take it that you are more fan than scholar."

"Exactly," Drood said. "A fan. And I'm pretty new to Dickens, compared with most people here."

"He hasn't even heard of *Mugby Junction*," Quilpy said. "Think of that." Quilpy put his arm around Drood. "But stick around and I'll teach you everything you need to know. About Dickens, too." He giggled at his feeble double entendre.

Simon was pleased that Quilpy was too taken with Drood to be putting his callow moves on Zach, unsuccessful though those would have been. "I'll talk with you all later." Simon returned to the head table. Minor, when not provoked by Drabb, was a delightful conversationalist, and he, Simon, and Louella Pardiggle entered into a lengthy discussion of the Princess Puffer Paradox.

In the excitement of the intellectual engagement, Simon forgot the feuding Tartars, the mysterious Edwin

Drood, the beautiful Jennifer Wren, the pompous Grewgious, the stubborn Drabb and his scholarly bombshell, even his own anxiety over his and Zach's living arrangements. He lost track of time. This was the reason he loved the Droodists, the most extreme faction of the Dickensian community. When he realized where he was again, the floating-island desserts were being removed from the table and Bettina was standing at the lectern.

"Our purpose tonight," Bettina said, "is to honor one of the finest Dickensians I've ever known: Osma Dilber. Osma is receiving the highest honor the International Droodist Society bestows—the coveted Ethelinda Award for Lifetime Achievement in Droodism or Dickensiana— for her preservation of the Dickensiana collection housed in the newly named Osma Dilber Wing of the Astoria/ Dickens Junction Regional Library and for her assistance to scholars wanting access to that collection. Ladies and gentlemen, Ms. Osma Dilber."

With Simon's help, Osma made her way to the podium as the audience gave her a standing ovation. "Thank you all, so very, very much," Osma said. She removed a small pair of reading glasses from her clutch and unfolded a piece of paper. "Thank you, Bettina, and thank you, Simon, for nominating me for this prestigious honor. But the real honor, these last fifty years, was to belong to this community, bound by a common love for Dickens and his work."

As Osma spoke, Simon remembered her through the years of their friendship, her kindness to him as a child, as comforter to him at the death of his parents and, later, his grandparents. She patted his back when his two long-term relationships ended over Simon's love for Dickens Junction. She was the person he had known longest in his life, and he had watched her change from a vibrant woman to one whose glow had diminished but remained, if only in ember form. He wiped his eyes.

Osma took a small bow as she finished her speech. "You all have made my life so rich with your kindness, your interest, and your requests for help. Thank you so much."

Bettina handed Osma the Ethelinda plaque. "Thank you all for coming to dinner," Bettina said. "We will have a brief intermission while we reconfigure the room for the show. The Great Grewgious will begin his performance in thirty minutes."

When the meeting-room doors reopened and Simon, Zach, and the Droodists filed in, the Great Grewgious stood erect and still on one side of the slightly raised stage. In his tuxedo and with his considerable abdomen, he cut an imposing figure and cast an even larger shadow. Five chairs were lined up in a neat row beside him.

"Please, everyone," Grewgious said, as conferees began filling the semicircles of seats in front of the stage. "Sit close. You'll want to see and hear everything."

Osma sat beside Simon, with Quilpy next to Zach on Simon's other side, and Drood on Quilpy's right. "I don't think you should do this," Quilpy said. "It's dangerous, and it's lame."

"It's not lame," Drood said, his voice sounding tired. "It'll be fun. Watch."

At the far end of the front semicircle, Jennifer Wren was playing with the ends of her Hermès scarf and chuckling at something Lionel was murmuring. Bettina had taken the empty seat next to Osma; Neva Tupman sat behind Osma. As Simon looked around, the only person he did not see that he was especially looking for (although he didn't quite know why) was Cecily Tartar, apparently holding true to her insistence that hypnosis was not her cup of tea.

"Welcome, Droodists," the Great Grewgious began. "As you all know, probably much better than I, Charles Dickens was a serious devotee of hypnosis, or mesmerism, or animal magnetism, as he would have called it. From what I've read, I believe that Dickens would have been able to accomplish the feats you'll see me do tonight. Who knows, the Inimitable might have been better than the Great!"

Grewgious waited; polite applause followed. He bowed.

"Will the volunteers please come to the stage?"

At that, Drood, Ms. Tupman, Bettina, Drabb, and Zach stood.

"Here goes nothing." Zach gave Simon's shoulder a squeeze as he passed on his way to the stage.

Grewgious led Ms. Tupman, looking even mousier in the harsh light, to a chair at one end of the stage and then placed Drood, Drabb, Law, and Zach, who was farthest from Simon's side of the stage.

"Now," Grewgious began, "make yourselves comfortable. Hypnosis is nothing more than relaxation." His voice was like melted chocolate, creamy, with a sheen, and dripping with dark comfort. "Listen to my voice. Do not listen to other sounds, do not think distracting thoughts. Push them away as if they were the gentlest of breezes, nothing more. But if you do notice other sounds, they will take you deeper, deeper into a relaxed state. Nothing will harm you; nothing will alarm you. It feels good to have your eyes closed, feel your lids heavy and dark. You are calm and relaxed, and you will simply become more like yourself."

Years earlier, Simon had tried hypnotherapy to overcome a fear of small planes because of a then-boyfriend's love of flying. His therapist had instructed Simon to imagine himself as a bluebird passing through bands of color on a floating chair, moving through his levels of fear and then letting the fear fall away. The sessions had taken away some of his fear of flying, but now that the boyfriend was gone, Simon did not rush to enter any flying object that lacked jet engines.

Grewgious continued talking and strolling across the stage. He leaned in to Zach, and spoke quietly, then moved to Drabb and did the same thing, followed by stops beside Bettina, Ms. Tupman, and Drood, each time touching the participant on the shoulder and speaking directly and softly into one ear. Sometimes what was spoken must have been a question, since, their eyes remaining closed, Drabb, Zach, and Drood all responded to Grewgious in low voices that did not travel beyond the edge of the stage.

After speaking to Drood, Grewgious stepped to the edge of the stage.

"I have reminded each of the participants," Grewgious said, "that they are among friends, and that friends often chuckle at us as a form of approval or support. You may find yourself laughing at something you see—at least I hope you do. The subjects believe, in their hypnotized state, that laughter is a form of approval, and may result in further behaviors that will provoke the same response. So, feel free to express your enjoyment of what you see, but please do not shout out any of their names or otherwise try to distract the subjects. They are deeply relaxed." He looked down at Jennifer Wren. "May I borrow your beautiful scarf? I think it may become useful later on."

Jennifer removed the scarf and handed it to Grewgious, who ran it through his fingers as a magician might, then draped it loosely around his own neck. The pink basketweave design popped against the black of his tuxedo.

"When I was searching for volunteers today," Grewgious continued, "I tried to find people who had unfulfilled wishes, something in their lives that they might want to do, but were afraid of. That's one of the things hypnosis can unlock, something I'm sure Dickens was quite interested in—the release of inhibitions. Much like alcohol, hypnosis can unlock the mind from patterns and practices that inhibit you from being who you want to be. Now, you can't be compelled under hypnosis to behave in a way truly contrary to your character, but you can release unfulfilled desires or suppressed behaviors. Let's see if we can loosen up our volunteers tonight."

Grewgious stepped over to Neva Tupman, who sat demurely with her hands in her lap, her face forward, eyes shut. Her glasses were askew, the rhinestones crooked chips of light above her eyes.

"When I spoke to Ms. Tupman earlier," he said, "she told me she loved visiting her grandparents at their farm in rural Oregon when she was young. May I call you Neva?" he asked.

"Yes," she said, her voice soft but audible.

"Please open your eyes," Grewgious said. Neva did so, blinking a few times and looking out over the audience, but not, Simon thought, anywhere in particular. "And is it true," Grewgious continued, "that you said you loved all of the animals at the farm?"

"Yes," Neva said.

Grewgious put his hand on her shoulder. "Please stand. Let's remember some of those animals," Grewgious continued, his voice firm, smooth, lilting. Simon felt sleepy. "Like the farm cat. Do you remember the cat?"

"Mouser," Neva said.

"Mouser," Grewgious repeated. "How did he move? Why don't you show us?"

At that request, Neva began swaying slightly and then started walking, pressing close to Grewgious as she passed him, dragging one hand behind her and letting it linger on Grewgious's arm.

"And sound?" Grewgious said. "How did Mouser sound?"

Neva began mewing in a high voice, and repeated her action of brushing against Grewgious. Dean Minor and a few others started laughing. Simon noticed Quilpy's quizzical expression, his eyes focused on the stage.

"What about the other animals?" Grewgious asked. "You mentioned cows."

"Yes."

"Show us the cows, and let us hear them."

Neva lowered her arms and began lumbering across the stage, and mooing. More members in the audience were laughing. Grewgious's other four volunteers remained quiet in their chairs.

"Hear the laughter," Grewgious said to her. "You're doing a great job."

He continued with Neva, having her replicate additional barnyard animals—a rooster, a chicken, a sheep—and then he led her back to her chair.

"Thank you, Neva," he said. "You can rest now. All of the animals are sleeping in the barn. You may close your eyes."

She sat as before, arms folded in her lap, eyes closed.

On the other side of the empty chair next to Simon, Quilpy was searching for something on his iPad.

Grewgious moved on to Bettina.

"May I call you Bettina?" Grewgious asked.

"Yes," she answered in a quiet voice.

"Please open your eyes." She did so. "Bettina, you told me today that your mother had taken you to see a performance of Joan Sutherland in *Il Trovatore* in San Francisco in the 1970s, and that for a brief time afterward your passion in life was to become an opera singer. Is that correct?"

"Yes."

"And I believe you told me that you sang coloratura, like Joan Sutherland."

"Yes."

Grewgious looked at the audience while he helped Bettina to her feet. "Perhaps, then, Bettina, you would sing something that you sang when you hoped to be famous like Joan Sutherland." Grewgious's voice was soothing, his repetition of the diva's name slow and stately, like a low gong.

"All right," Bettina said. She stood straight and tall, pulling herself to her full five feet, and began singing, softly at first, then with greater volume, the "Queen of the Night" aria from Mozart's *The Magic Flute*.

Simon recognized immediately, as did the rest of the audience, why Bettina became a Dickens scholar instead of a singer. But what she lacked in technique, she more than made up for in enthusiasm and volume, and as she strove to achieve the infamous ha-has, as Simon called them, the money notes that an audience has paid to hear, she sounded like glass breaking, or metal striking concrete. Several audience members covered their ears; all roared with laughter.

Grewgious stopped her in the middle of the third ha-ha. "Thank you, Bettina. It is often said that practice makes perfect. But not everything said is necessarily true. You may sit down."

Grewgious moved across the stage toward Buckminster Drabb. As he did so, he pulled softly at the Hermès scarf and let it drift across his shoulders until it dangled from his hand.

"Mr. Drabb," Grewgious said, "may I call you Bucky, which I believe is the nickname used by your friends?"

Bucky said something Simon didn't catch.

"Buckminster, then," Grewgious said in his deep voice. "You and I had a pleasant chat today. You knew from a very young age that you wanted to spend your life studying the life and works of Charles Dickens. Is that correct?"

"Yes." Grewgious helped Drabb stand away from his chair.

"Please open your eyes." Drabb did so. "I also recall," Grewgious added, "that, among other things, you were first attracted to Dickens because of his theatricality—when reading him, you could see his characters on a stage in your mind. I'd like you to show us some of that theatricality yourself by bringing one of those characters to life for us right here, right now."

Grewgious took the Hermès scarf and draped it over Drabb's shoulders. "Use this shawl, if you wish, to bring yourself into the character of Nancy from *Oliver Twist*. Show us the woman whose attempt to help Oliver find a better life resulted in her murder."

Grewgious stepped away from Drabb, whose posture almost immediately softened. Simon watched Drabb's demeanor shift from masculine to feminine as Drabb bent his elbows and knees, drew the scarf around his shoulders, and clutched the two ends as if he were cold.

With a gentle sway, he began walking across the stage, one end of the scarf now dangling as if it were caught in a breeze. He raised his chin and began to sing. In a clear

tenor, Drabb began "As Long as He Needs Me," from
Oliver! and did a pretty good job at a Shani Wallis imper-
sonation, right down to the working-class British accent.

The audience, at first laughing at Drabb's performance,
eventually stopped to pay him more serious attention. It
was a plaintive performance, beyond gender, that had
its own magnetism. It demonstrated the power of released inhibitions under hypnosis. No one who knew
Drabb's feisty and sometimes snarky scholarship would
have ascribed to him this tenderness or talent. Simon
was impressed.

Grewgious let Drabb sing his final notes, with a lovely
vibrato any professional singer would envy, and the audience clapped with genuine appreciation. Drabb seemed
unaware of the applause, because he slowly removed the
scarf and handed it back to Grewgious, who folded it and
placed it inside his breast pocket.

Jennifer Wren stood and began walking toward the
door. As she passed by Simon she leaned toward him.
"Bathroom break," she whispered. "So sorry."

Grewgious led Drabb back to his seat. He bent over
and spoke into Drabb's ear. Drabb's face was impassive,
no trace of the recent emotions that had passed over it.
Grewgious spoke to him softly, and Drabb closed his eyes.

"Well, that was unexpected, wasn't it?" Grewgious said to
the audience. "What you don't know about your colleagues
might fill volumes, yes?"

He reached Edwin Drood's chair. The young man sat
like the others, still, head facing forward, eyes shut behind his boxy black glasses, hands in his lap. Grewgious

whispered something to him, helped him to his feet, and then said, "May I call you Edwin?"

"If you wish."

"Please open your eyes."

Drood did so, his eyes dewy behind the ungainly spectacles.

"When I asked you to volunteer earlier today," Grewgious said, "you hesitated, but then said that you might as well, because you had been working too hard lately to keep your 'bad side' suppressed. Isn't that true?"

"Yes."

Simon was watching Quilpy, who was again paying close attention to the stage. Quilpy had bitten one of his fingernails until it bled.

"So why don't you let your 'bad' side come out to visit, and tell your 'good' side how it feels to be kept in check."

Drood had been standing in a relaxed stance, one leg bent, one hip out. The instant that Grewgious stopped talking, Drood drew himself up to full height and crossed his arms, and his face became pinched, his forehead furrowed.

"You're going to fuck everything up," Drood said, his voice deeper than Simon had heard it in casual conversation. Quilpy started biting another nail. "Fuck it up," Drood continued, spitting the words out like bullets. "They'll all find out, and then you'll be out of here, and I'll get nothing, not even—"

Grewgious stepped over and touched Drood's shoulder and said something to him softly. Drood immediately resumed his earlier posture. Several audience members squirmed in their chairs.

"Sometimes," Grewgious said, "a suggestion results in an unpleasant consequence. We don't need to take this any further." He spoke to Drood again, and Drood's face relaxed into its previous smooth and youthful appearance. Grewgious helped him into his seat and crossed over to Zach.

"I told him not to do it," Quilpy said to Simon.

Simon wanted to think about this, process Drood's reaction, but Grewgious touched Zach's shoulder and then, as with the others, spoke to him quietly. Zach opened his eyes and mumbled a response that Simon couldn't hear. Jennifer Wren slipped back into the banquet hall and took her seat near Lionel.

"I only had a few moments with Zach earlier today, but I believe you mentioned that you earned money for college as a ballroom-dance instructor. Is that correct?"

"Yes," Zach said. Having danced with him at the Fezziwig Ball during the *Christmas Carol* festivities, Simon knew Zach was an excellent dancer, but not this history behind the talent. With Grewgious's help, Zach was now standing.

"Well, everyone here tonight has come to learn how to dance, but we don't have much time. So I'll be changing music quickly; when I call out a type of dance, you'll start doing that one right away. Your partner right now is a lovely young woman. Do I hear a waltz?"

Grewgious stepped back, and Zach started to cross the stage in a waltz promenade, his hands in the leading position, one resting on his invisible partner's back and the other holding her hand. He took a few more steps, turning the imaginary woman, until Grewgious said, "Charleston." Zach immediately dropped his arms to his sides and began doing small forward and backward kicks, crossing his hands in front of his knees, then a few more kicks, when Grewgious shouted out, "Disco!" and Zach started a hustle grapevine, followed by a few *Saturday Night Fever*–worthy moves until Grewgious said, "Polka," and Zach began a quick two-step, bringing one knee in the air, then the other, and twirling his imaginary partner.

"And the music comes to a gradual stop," Grewgious said, and Zach's steps slowed as he finished a turn in the center of the stage and then stopped. "That was very good," Grewgious said. "I'm sure all of your partners learned well from you." He helped Zach back to his chair.

Grewgious faced forward. "I always tell my audiences that hypnosis is simply a process by which the mind overcomes most, if not all, of its resistance to suggestibility. These brave volunteers deserve our thanks for their willingness to let their boundaries down. Let's give them a round of applause."

As the audience clapped, Grewgious spoke briefly to each of the five volunteers. He spent more time with Zach and Drood than with the others.

"As much fun as it is to be relaxed," Grewgious said so that the audience could hear, "it's more enjoyable to be awake and fully aware of your companions' enjoyment of your little escapades. You will feel much more refreshed as you prepare to open your eyes in five, four, three, two, one. And now you're fully awake and alert again."

Bettina, Zach, Drabb, and Neva opened their eyes and looked around. Drood opened his eyes and started to remove his glasses, but then pushed them farther onto the bump of his nose. He turned his head as if his neck were sore. Zach looked at Simon and grinned, his teeth glinting in the lights.

"Again," Grewgious said, "please give our lovely volunteers a hand. They will remember everything they did on stage in five, four, three, two, one."

Drabb looked confused, and then flushed crimson from neck to forehead. Drood frowned. Bettina shook her head and chuckled.

"And with that," Grewgious continued, "our entertainment concludes for the evening. After changing out of my formal wear, I will answer any questions about the performance or about hypnosis in general in the bar. I'm sorry that I won't be able to elucidate on Dickens's use of the technique, but as a result of my presence here, I plan on taking up that issue when I return home. Thank you all, and good evening."

With that, Grewgious stepped down from the stage and, after shaking the hands of the five volunteers, left the banquet room. Audience members stood, and Simon greeted Zach as he and Drood returned to their seats.

"Just a gigolo," said Simon. "What else don't I know about you?"

Zach smiled. "I'll tell you later."

Quilpy was fussing over Drood, who put out his hand so that Quilpy would respect his personal space.

"I'm fine," Drood said. "I'd like a drink, though." The two young men moved toward the door leading into the bar.

"A drink sounds like a great idea," Zach said. "I could use a martini right now—and a big glass of water." He turned to Osma, who was holding her award in one hand and her clutch in the other. "Would you join us?"

"I'd love to," she said. "But I must change first. This dress weighs twenty pounds."

"Would you like help getting to your room?" Simon asked.

At that moment Lionel and Jennifer came up to the group. "We'd be happy to escort the guest of honor," Lionel said. He held out his bent arm for her to take. Osma looked at her clutch and at her plaque.

"I'll help you," Jennifer said, taking the plaque from Osma, who then took Lionel's outstretched arm.

"I'll see you in a few minutes," Osma said, as the three walked away.

Simon and Zach went into the bar. Simon walked toward Quilpy and Drood, but Zach redirected him to a corner booth in an unoccupied section.

"Scotch?" Zach asked.

"A single."

Zach went to the bar and Simon took a seat facing the rest of the lounge. Drabb, Minor, and Cheeryble entered.

"If we had a fourth, we could sing barbershop," Simon

heard Minor say just before he slapped Drabb on the back. The three took a table near Drood and Quilpy. For three men who argued with one another so much, they certainly did spend a lot of time together.

Zach brought back a Glenlivet for Simon, a martini for himself, and a glass of white wine for Osma, all three glasses bunched carefully between his hands. As Zach sat, Grewgious entered the bar from the elevator, now in casual slacks and a variegated pullover sweater. He was carrying a laptop. He nodded at Drood and Quilpy, ordered something in a rocks glass, and sat on a barstool at the corner of the bar. Bettina came in a few minutes later and joined Grewgious at the bar.

"Before Osma comes back," Zach said, "I want to tell you something." He leaned in. "I wasn't hypnotized."

"You gave a convincing performance."

"Grewgious asked me to," Zach said. "That's what he whispered to me. He must have figured it out somehow, or it must not work all of the time. I didn't fight it, but nothing happened. So he asked me to play along, to 'help the show,' as he said, and not to embarrass anyone, especially you." Zach sipped his martini. "So I did."

"You're a good sport," said Simon, kissing the end of Zach's nose. "Were the others playing along?"

"Who knows? Not Drabb, for sure—" Across the way, Minor and Cheeryble were laughing at something, and Drabb looked put out. "And I'm pretty sure Drood and Law weren't faking, either. I don't know about Neva."

"I was fooled," said Simon. "And I know you better than anyone." It felt good to say that.

"And, for the record," Zach said, "I never was a dance instructor. Grewgious made it up as he went along."

"You looked like a pro to me."

"Love has blinded you." Zach kissed him. "My sisters taught me," he added. "They needed someone to practice with when their boyfriends weren't around."

Osma arrived a few minutes later, wearing another of her colorful caftans, this one a daring leopard print. Simon noticed that her ring finger was bare.

"Yes," she said, when he asked about the Heart of Helsinki, "I took it off to moisturize and decided not to put it back on. My fingers swelled from dinner, I think. So much sodium in restaurant food." She took a sip of wine. "I suppose, though, at my age, it doesn't much matter anymore what I eat." She chuckled.

Across the bar, Quilpy got up from his table and walked toward the restroom. As he departed, Grewgious excused himself from Bettina and went over to Drood's table. Bettina took that opportunity to join the Weird Sisters.

This far away, Simon couldn't hear what Grewgious said to Drood. The latter nodded and Grewgious shook Drood's hand and stood, as Quilpy was returning from the restroom. Grewgious then stopped to chat with Drabb and the others. At one point, Simon heard Grewgious give a brief deep laugh, followed by Cheeryble's higher-pitched giggle.

"This has been a great night." Osma's bright lipstick, recently refreshed, was leaving a print on her wineglass. "Thank you so much for all you've done, Simon."

Simon put his hand on hers. Without the Heart of Helsinki to decorate them, Osma's burled knuckles and swollen joints looked painful.

"I did nothing," he said. "You did the work. Grandpa Ebbie would be proud of you."

That reminded Osma of a funny story involving a hatpin that allegedly had belonged to Catherine Dickens, and she started a series of reminiscences about various articles of Dickensiana. Zach fetched a second round of drinks. Grewgious had returned to his perch at the bar with his laptop. His back was to Simon, but Simon could see various windows open to what looked like e-mail correspondence, websites, and search engines. Grewgious ordered another drink. Drabb, Minor, and Cheeryble continued to drink and bicker, also ordering at least one more round. Bettina sat with them but seemed detached from their long-standing disagreements on virtually every topic imaginable. She occasionally checked the screen of her phone.

Sometime later Simon saw Drood leave Quilpy's table, but not before the two men shared an indecorous kiss. Quilpy looked put out and tried to cajole Drood into staying, but Drood shook his head, looked at his watch, and left the bar. Quilpy followed, ambling out of his way to pass Simon, Zach, and Osma.

"Another night alone," Quilpy said with a hangdog sound in his voice.

"You're welcome to join us," Zach said. "We're not so bad."

"Thanks, but this fella is...*frustrated*...by recent events. I think I'll go back to my room. See you dudes and dudette tomorrow."

"How late is it?" Osma asked.

Zach looked at his watch. "Just past midnight."

She finished her wine. "Goodness. I haven't stayed up this late in years. I'll be going immediately to bed when I get back to the room."

"We'll escort you," said Simon. "We should be getting back as well. We've all got a busy day tomorrow."

Zach and Simon each took one of Osma's arms. At the elevator, she stopped them. "I can find my way from here. Good night."

Simon and Zach returned to Gad's Hill Place in their separate cars. When Simon arrived, he found a note from Jude saying that he had fed Miss Tox before leaving but that Simon should check her water bowl.

"I'm exhausted," Simon said as he undressed in his bedroom a few minutes later.

"Me, too," Zach said from the sink in the master bath, where he was brushing his teeth. He was wearing pajama bottoms, his muscular chest with its dusting of groomed black hair looking especially welcoming to Simon. But Simon was tired.

The two men got into bed; Simon turned out the light.

Simon was still sleeping when the landline rang sometime early in the morning, too early.

"Simon," the voice said, "it's Bettina."

"Uh-huh," Simon managed to say in response.

"Something dreadful has happened," Bettina went on. "The Heart of Helsinki has been stolen."

April 17

7:30–9:00 a.m.	Continental Breakfast	Hotel bar
9:15 a.m.–noon	Breakout Sessions:	
	"What was in Mrs. Crisparkle's Cupboard: Food in *Drood*" (seating limited to ten!)	Cassandra Orth Liberty Room, basement
	"New Divots in the Datchery Dilemma"	Dean Minor Columbia River Room
	"Charles Dickens and Wilkie Collins: Friends or Rivals?"	Silas Cheeryble Vernonia Room, basement
12:15–1:45 p.m.	Lunch	Hotel banquet room
2:00–5:00 p.m.	Breakout Sessions:	
	"When 'Heaven's Hard Drunk' Wasn't Enough," or "When Princess Puffer came to Astoria: The Opium Trade in Dickens's London and Nineteenth-Century Astoria"	Osma Dilber; Winifred Duddle, laureate emerita, Clatsop County Historical Society Columbia River Room
	"Miss Twinkleton's Globe: The Geography of *Edwin Drood*"	Louella Pardiggle Vernonia Room
5:30–6:30 p.m.	No-host Bar	Hotel banquet room
7:00–9:00 p.m.	Buffet Dinner: All-you-can-eat No program	Hotel banquet room

DAY THREE

By seven o'clock, Simon was showered, dressed, and in the hotel lobby with Bettina and Bartholomew Cuff. He'd noticed a sheriff's vehicle parked in the loading zone as he'd entered.

"Please tell me what happened," said Simon.

Cuff looked tired; Simon wondered how long he had been awake. "Ms. Dilber went directly to bed after she left you last night," Cuff said. "When she awoke this morning and was preparing to come down to breakfast, she opened her jewelry case where she had stored the ring after dinner, and it was gone. She searched the room before she called hotel security. We also have searched the room without success. The sheriff's deputies are in the room now."

"How is Osma?"

"She's upset," Bettina said. She looked agitated, too, although it had not interfered with her ability to dress professionally in a sleek, black, raw-silk pencil skirt and jacket over a white shell. Her eye makeup was impeccable as well. "But she's doing all right. Jennifer took her downstairs to the meeting rooms to be out of the hubbub."

"I'll go see her soon," said Simon. "May I see her room before I go?"

Cuff looked at his shoes. "I'm not sure the sheriff's office will want you to get involved, Mr. Alastair."

Simon didn't want to be rude; Cuff was only doing his job. "I'll take that risk."

"I need to find Bucky Drabb," Bettina said. She took the stairs to the basement while Simon and Cuff crossed to the elevator.

On the first floor, Cuff walked ahead of Simon as they passed the vintage mahogany doors with etched transom windows above, each room number painted in gold on the window. The hotel library door was ajar, but the room was empty as Cuff and Simon passed. Osma's room was at the end of the hall. The door had been propped open with a wastebasket. A uniformed female deputy stood outside.

"Sorry," said the deputy, "no one can enter until we've conducted our search."

Simon heard a familiar voice call from inside the room. "Excuse me," he said fairly loudly, "is that Detective Boggs?"

The woman who had spoken now stood in the entryway. Clatsop County Detective Sergeant Josephine Boggs,
dressed in a tailored navy skirt, light blue blouse, and
small shoulder bag, looked as fashionable as Simon remembered her from the *Christmas Carol* events. No jewelry except dainty pearl studs, barely visible for the auburn
curly hair worn to her shoulders, today partly pulled
back. Simon imagined that most straight men (the in-
credibly available and handsome Father Blaise Gilmore
of St. Ina's Episcopal Church in Dickens Junction came
to mind) found her attractive. She wore light makeup,
maybe blush and powder, lip gloss, and mascara.

"Simon. I knew I would see you soon enough." She
said it with the hint of a smile.

"I am the conference coordinator," he said, "so I feel
some responsibility toward the guests, particularly toward Osma. I've known her my whole life."

Detective Boggs looked around Osma's room. "We're
pretty much done in here, so I suppose I can at least
show you what we found, which isn't much." She nodded
at the deputy, who stood aside to let Cuff and Simon
into Osma's room.

The room was tastefully furnished, but lacked a river
view. A high four-poster bed with damask duvet cover
dominated the room. A stack of occasional pillows and
bolsters leaned against the wall by the bedside table.
An empty bottle of sparkling water stood on the coffee
table in front of the ecru love seat. Detective Boggs
led Simon and Cuff toward the small bathroom, with
heated floor, cream-tiled double shower, and oversize

sink. Osma's jewelry case and cosmetics bag were on the marble vanity.

"Ms. Dilber told us that she undressed, changed into her nightgown, and then brushed her teeth before going to bed," Detective Boggs said. "Except for her toothpaste, toothbrush, and medication carrier, she touched nothing on the counter, and noticed nothing out of place. It wasn't until she had finished bathing and dressing this morning that she discovered the ring wasn't in her jewelry case where she had put it last night. She did her best to search around before calling Mr. Cuff."

"And of course," Cuff said, "I searched everything before calling the sheriff's office. All we found was an arts brochure fallen behind the love seat. The room was otherwise spotless."

"She must be devastated," said Simon. "The ring is priceless."

"To the world," Detective Boggs agreed. "But to her, it's the sentimental value it has, not its monetary or appraised value. That's what she told me."

Cuff wrung his giant hands together. "Igna, the night clerk, reported that all guests were accounted for."

(*Igna since when?*) Simon wondered.

"No one entered or exited the hotel after midnight. Igna told me this morning that no one had come down to the lobby or entered either the front or back entrance before Ms. Dilber called me around six fifteen."

"So the ring is still somewhere in the hotel," Detective Boggs said. "Is anyone scheduled to check out today?"

"No," Cuff answered. "Every room is occupied by a conferee."

"We need to start taking statements," Detective Boggs said. "I'd like a room set aside for that, please."

"You can use my office," Cuff said, "behind the front desk. Quiet, discreet."

"Thank you." She turned to Simon. "I suppose you want to continue the conference?"

"We only meet every three years, and people have come from many places," he said. "I'm sure we can accommodate your interviews."

Cuff, Simon, and Detective Boggs stepped into the hall near the library when Simon heard the elevator door open. Grewgious emerged. He was wearing a maroon brocaded robe. The pant cuffs of his satin pajamas brushed against the floor, revealing Swedish memory-foam slippers.

"I was told I might find you here. Are you the sheriff?" he asked Detective Boggs.

"I'm with the Clatsop County Sheriff's Office." She showed him her badge. "What can I do for you?"

"This is Morgan Grewgious," said Simon. "He provided the entertainment for us last night. He is a hypnotist."

"I understand there was a disturbance here last night. Something was stolen."

"Word travels fast," Detective Boggs said.

Grewgious turned to Simon. "You remember last night that I borrowed Ms. Wren's scarf."

"Yes," said Simon.

"Well, at the end of the performance, I forgot to return it to her. When I awoke this morning, I remembered I had left it in my tuxedo jacket. So I went to the closet this morning to retrieve it and return it to her, but it was gone."

"Gone?" Detective Boggs took a small notepad from her bag.

"Missing," said Grewgious. "It wasn't in my coat pocket, nor was it anywhere in the room. It must have been stolen from my room last night while some of us were in the bar."

"Was it valuable?"

"It was Hermès," said Grewgious.

Detective Boggs gave an informed nod.

"Two thefts in one night," said Cuff. "That has never happened before at this hotel. I must discuss this with the owners right away." He started toward the elevator, but Detective Boggs stopped him.

"I'd like to meet with you," she said to Cuff and Simon, "and Ms. Law as soon as possible. We need to develop a communication plan that won't alarm the conference attendees." She then turned to Grewgious. "Please touch nothing else in your room. I'll have a deputy there as soon as possible. And I will need to interview Jennifer Wren right away," she said to Simon.

Simon swallowed hard with his latest realization. "It's hard to believe that one of us is a thief."

"There must be a simpler explanation," Cuff said.

Detective Boggs cocked one eyebrow. "Or not."

Simon called Zach to let him know what was going on; they agreed to meet during a break in the morning sessions. That done, Simon called Bettina and told her about the missing scarf. He then arranged to meet Bettina and Detective Boggs within the hour at Cuff's office. While Bettina was giving a statement to Detective Boggs, Simon agreed to make sure that the conference was off to a reasonable start. It was a necessary task, but Simon also knew he was using it as an excuse to put off talking to Bucky Drabb as long as possible.

He went to the basement. All three breakout rooms had been carefully arranged with proper audiovisual equipment, chairs, and tables. The South African *Vin de Constance* wine and glasses for the "Food in *Drood*" discussion and tasting were in place, Minor's laptop was working properly for his discourse on the possible identities of one of *Edwin Drood*'s more mysterious characters, and Cheeryble was double-checking his materials and handouts for his sure-to-be-entertaining discussion of the friendship and rivalry of Dickens and Wilkie Collins.

Simon had just left Cheeryble's breakout room when he ran into Bucky Drabb. "What are you doing to protect us—to protect me—from a madman on the loose?" Drabb demanded.

"Calm down, Bucky," said Simon. "We don't know anything yet. Two items are missing from guest rooms."

"Two now?" Drabb did an exaggerated double take that Simon had to fight not to roll his eyes about. Drabb shook his head. "The one, at least, is not just any item," Drabb corrected Simon, "but a *priceless* ring, so I hear. What if the thief had stolen Number Plan Six?"

"I wanted to ask you about that," said Simon. "What have you done with it?"

"It's as secure as I can make it," Drabb snarled. "And that's all I'm going to say."

"I wish you would deposit it in the hotel safe."

"Where it will be given all of the protection that this hotel possesses? I'd rather not. I will take full responsibility for the number plan's security." And with that, Drabb walked away toward the elevator.

Simon went into the bar where continental breakfast was available. Osma was sitting with the seemingly inseparable Jennifer Wren and Lionel Tartar. Jennifer was holding Osma's hands. Osma had on a simple white caftan with a Greek key neckline. Jennifer was wearing black slacks and a blue silk blouse. She looked interview-ready. Tartar looked stunning, like a male model in pressed black slacks and a gray heather cashmere V-neck sweater hugging his toned physique, a fashion-plate look achieved seemingly effortlessly. Simon felt old.

"I suppose you've heard everything by now," Osma said as he approached. "I'm rattled. I still can't help thinking that I've mislaid the ring and that this will be a major embarrassment." She removed her hands from Jennifer's and rubbed them together. "I should have stopped in the lobby and left the ring in the hotel safe, but at home I take it off at night and put it by my bedside."

"Don't blame yourself," Jennifer said.

Simon nodded and turned to Jennifer. "There's been a second theft." He told the group about the scarf.

"I wondered what had happened to it," Jennifer said. "I didn't give it a second thought until I awoke this morning. I was sure there was an explanation, but not this one. Why would someone take my scarf, and from inside Mr. Grewgious's jacket pocket in his room?"

"Detective Boggs will want to take your statement. And yours, too," Simon added, looking at Lionel a few seconds longer than was decorous—or monogamous.

"I was in my room," Lionel said. "Alone. I saw or heard nothing, maybe room doors opening and closing on my floor after I went to bed, but nothing out of the ordinary."

"And I was also alone," Jennifer said. "I heard nothing."

"We can cancel your afternoon presentation if you wish," said Simon to Osma.

Osma's eyes widened. "Most certainly not," she said. "Winnie Duddle and I have been working on it for months."

Simon smiled. "If you insist."

"Besides," Osma continued, "I know the ring will turn up."

"Is it insured?" Lionel asked. His faced seemed tense, although Simon had the impression he was working hard not to show it.

"Yes," Osma said. "On the advice of my agent."

"May I ask how much?" Lionel asked.

"I'm embarrassed to say," Osma said, "because the policy was for so much more money than I thought it should be. But we insured it for the appraised value—two million dollars."

Lionel put his lips together as if he were going to whistle, but he remained silent, his lips falling into a frown that didn't sully his beauty.

"I have already notified my agent," Osma said. "Under the circumstances, she tells me, the insurance company may send an investigator to look into the disappearance."

The growing sound of chairs scraping the floor caused Simon to check his watch—a few minutes before nine. Conferees were leaving the breakfast area and beginning to disperse to the breakout sessions.

Jennifer released Osma's hands. "Will you be all right if I speak to the detective now?"

"I'll be fine," Osma said. "I want to attend Cassandra Orth's food lecture. I have never had *Vin de Constance.*" She gave Simon a winsome look. "It's only a ring, after all, and life goes on. This may be my last time with my Droodists."

Jennifer touched Osma's shoulder. "I'll see you at lunch, if not before." She left the breakfast table.

"I will escort you to your session," Lionel said.

Simon stood. "And I need to attend to a few administrative matters."

In spite of the excitement surrounding the thefts, conferees filled up all three of the breakout sessions. Simon passed Quilpy and Drood walking toward Cheeryble's session.

"Pretty exciting, isn't it?" Quilpy said. His face was lit from within. "I've already blogged about it. A thief in the night, a fox in the henhouse, a snake in the grass."

"Enough already," Drood said. Simon looked at Drood's hair, the vaguest hint of darker roots beneath the platinum bristled spikes, freshly gelled. *He must have to do that every morning*, Simon thought. *How time-consuming.* Still, it gave the young man a memorable appearance. Along with the clunky glasses and bumpy nose.

Quilpy wrinkled his nose. "I sure wish I had seen something last night," he said. "I was awake for a long time," he said, looking at Drood. "Thinking."

"I was out like a light," Drood said. "I went to bed the minute I got back from the bar. Didn't move until I got my wake-up call."

"I could have run into the thief myself," Quilpy said. "My room is right across from Grewgious's." He frowned. "But I didn't. I heard a couple of doors open and shut before I fell asleep. Probably Grewgious and Drabb coming back from the bar. Drabb's room is near mine."

"The sheriff must have other suspects than us," Drood said.

"I don't know," said Simon, although that wasn't totally true. The hotel was full of Droodists, and no one had exited the hotel. "But try to put it out of your minds, gentlemen, and enjoy the morning events."

At Simon's meeting with Cuff, Bettina, and Detective Boggs, the emphasis was on continuing the conference with minimal disruptions. At Detective Boggs's request, Cuff had drawn up a list of conferees and their room assignments by floor. Using that, the detective created a roster for interviews that, in her estimation, would last through the morning and potentially until early afternoon.

The few people she had been able to talk to so far had all reported nothing out of the ordinary. Grewgious's rooms revealed nothing. Interviews would include fingerprinting.

Cuff was already helping Boggs's team fingerprint and interview the housekeeping staff.

Bettina filled in Detective Boggs about Drabb's document, and his reluctance to put it in the hotel safe.

"It's his personal property," the detective said, "and we have no evidence so far that the thief, or thieves, intend further crimes. We don't know anything."

"Mr. Quill has already blogged about the thefts," said Simon.

Cuff opened his laptop and quickly brought up the relevant pages. "'Thief Strikes at the Heart of Helsinki!!!'" Cuff showed the screen to the others. One of the pictures that accompanied the story was a head shot of Jennifer Wren, clearly for reasons more titillating than journalistic.

"Must he use so many exclamation points?" Bettina asked no one in particular.

"Perhaps," Detective Boggs said, "one of you can influence him to be less sensational in his reporting."

"I'm not going to worry about him now," said Simon. "We've got bigger problems." Simon asked if Detective Boggs knew about the insurance value of the ring.

"Yes," she answered. "Ms. Dilber informed me. I have already received a text message from the investigator. He'll be here late tomorrow. From Geneva."

"Our job," Bettina said, "is to make sure the conference continues with as few disruptions as possible while Detective Boggs goes about her business."

"I agree," said Bartholomew Cuff.

"Of course," said Simon.

But was that *all* of his job? If he had not pursued his own line of inquiry during the *Christmas Carol* events, would the killer have been brought to justice? He wondered.

Simon did his best for the remainder of the morning to be the conference host, but he couldn't concentrate on any of the sessions. If the thefts were not resolved quickly, Astoria and Dickens Junction could be tainted by scandal for a second time in four months. The Junction's reputation as a world-renowned Dickensian haven might be eclipsed or tarnished. Complex negotiations might falter: Simon was working on having the national touring company for the Broadway musical version of *A Tale of Two Cities* make a stop at the Crummles Theatre in the Junction next year, the Jarley traveling waxwork display of Dickens characters was considering the Junction as a venue, and a film company had expressed interest in using Dickens Square as a setting for a celebration of Morris dancing to be broadcast on public television. All of these opportunities might vanish if the public saw the Junction as unsafe.

No one lived and breathed Dickens Junction as Simon did; no one had as much at risk in terms of pride and reputation. So he wouldn't, couldn't, fulfill his pledge to Detective Boggs not to get involved.

After the meeting, Simon let Bettina hurry ahead of him while he waited for Detective Boggs to shut the door of her temporary interview room, and then he approached Bartholomew Cuff. Cuff looked uncomfortably overdressed and overtrussed in a shirt collar that bunched up the extra flesh at his neck. But he was a generous and kind man who, Simon knew, was devoted to his wife and four children. He hoped some of that generosity might shine his way now.

"Bart," said Simon, "may I have a copy of the room-assignment list that you gave the detective? I'd like to understand where the conferees were when the thefts might have occurred."

"Don't you think you should ask her for that?" Cuff hesitated. He had to know, as did most of the locals, what role Simon had played in the *Christmas Carol* events. "I suppose it wouldn't hurt," he added, "as long as you don't interfere."

"Of course not," said Simon. "I have the utmost respect for the law."

During lunch, everyone buzzed about the thefts. Theories ranged from a professional gang of thieves collecting famous jewels for a private collector all the way to Osma having lost the Heart down the bathroom drain. But Simon was sure that the thief walked among them; he was suspicious of everyone but himself and Zach.

After seeing that Osma was fully installed and ready for her afternoon session with her co-presenter, the vivacious and potty-mouthed delight that was Winifred Duddle, Simon caught up with Zach.

"You've had quite the morning," Zach said.

"I hope there isn't more to come," said Simon.

Jennifer Wren and Lionel Tartar made their way toward Osma's session; they were, Simon thought, even more *entre nous* than the night before. Perhaps Mr. Tartar had a unique ability to console Jennifer over the loss of her scarf. Grewgious approached and made a point of apologizing profusely to Jennifer.

"I don't know whether to be upset or thankful," she said. "If I'd had the scarf, the thief might have broken into my room instead of yours." She said this with virtually no inflection; it was merely an observation.

"I hadn't considered it from that angle," Grewgious said. "Fortunately, neither of us was put in physical danger."

"This time," Lionel said. He put his arm at Jennifer's waist and pulled her into the session.

Danger was something Simon had not wanted to contemplate, but Grewgious had put it on the table. Was anyone—Osma, Grewgious, Jennifer—in danger? Was everyone? And, if so, what kind? As if thinking the same thing, Zach placed his hand on Simon's back.

Neva Tupman approached; Simon called out to her. "Ms. Tupman."

"Please," she said. "You can call me Neva."

"Neva, then. I notice"—he tapped the room-assignment list that Cuff had given him—"that you are on the first floor; how is your room situated relative to Ms. Dilber's?"

"She has the room next to mine," Neva said.

Simon calmed his nerves. She could have demanded to know why he was asking, why he knew where her room was, but she hadn't. Yes, he could do this. Again. Too much was at stake not to try. Neva was passive and pliant, another characteristic that distinguished her from virtually all of the other conferees. *Why was she here?*

Cuff's showed that the other rooms on the first floor were not guest suites but storage closets and offices for hotel staff. Even though Simon had attended numerous cocktail events in the hotel library before, he hadn't paid attention to the layout until now.

"Did you hear anything unusual last night?" Simon asked.

"I went to my room right after the performance. I read in bed after taking a long soak in the tub. It's a luxury I don't have at home." She twisted a lock of her hair absentmindedly as she spoke. "I heard a noise sometime after midnight."

"That was probably Ms. Dilber returning to her room."

"Could have been," Neva said. "I must have dozed, because I awoke sometime after that, maybe one thirty or closer to two."

"Did something wake you up?"

Her face moved strangely, a curve of the mouth, as if she were recalling something new. Her glasses were again askew, and she straightened them before answering. "I heard other doors closing."

"Doors?" Zach asked.

"Or one door closing more than once. At least I think that's what I heard." Neva looked confused. "Should I have told this to the detective when she interviewed me?" Suddenly she looked more frightened than confused.

Simon's cell phone vibrated, signaling a text. He looked at the screen. "Excuse me," he said to Neva and then turned to Zach and squeezed his hand. "I need to meet with Detective Boggs. I'll tell her you have remembered something new," Simon told Neva. "Don't be surprised if she has more questions for you later."

Neva seemed disturbed by their discussion. Simon watched her as she walked into Louella Pardiggle's session and took a chair in the back row. Simon suspected she would leave early.

"I probably won't see you until evening at home," Zach said, holding Simon back. "I'm working on some *very* interesting items."

"Hints?"

Zach smiled. "Think *Pirates of the Caribbean*." And he turned around and took the stairs to the lobby.

After seeing that all sessions were underway, Simon returned to the lobby. The desk clerk (Lovisa since 2012) was on the phone, but mouthed "Library" to Simon, so he took the elevator to the first floor.

As the elevator door opened, he turned and saw the layout he had just been discussing with Neva. Nearest him were storage closets and administrative offices. Then came the double doors to the library on the right, beyond those the stairwell door. Osma's room was at the far end of the hall, now showing no signs of the earlier presence of the sheriff's deputies. To the left of Osma's room, across from the library, was another room—this must be Neva's. He checked the number painted on the transom glass—the same as on Cuff's sheet.

He knocked on the library doors and opened them. Detective Boggs, Bettina, and Cuff were already seated at a table that had been returned to the library after the opening night's cocktail party.

"Lock the doors," Cuff said.

Simon turned the deadbolt and pulled to make sure both doors had locked. He took the vacant seat across from Detective Boggs, who had her notepad in front of her.

"It is unconventional," Detective Boggs said, "to share any information with civilians during an investigation, but the sheriff herself has stressed the importance of this conference continuing without disruption, as long as safety concerns are addressed. So I have permission to share details with you as I deem necessary, without compromising my investigation." She looked at Simon. "Provided, of course, that you do nothing that interferes with official law-enforcement responsibilities."

Cuff shot Simon a look.

"Unfortunately," Detective Boggs continued, "we have no real leads yet. Fingerprint results are not in, but we aren't hopeful that they will reveal anything out of the ordinary." She looked at Simon, then at Bettina. "Your group is pretty quiet. Everyone who wasn't in the bar reported being in their rooms alone, either reading or asleep."

Simon repeated his conversation with Neva.

Detective Boggs made a note on her pad and then turned to Bart Cuff. "Is it possible that the sounds she heard were coming from another floor?"

Cuff frowned. "I doubt it. Our floors are thicker than the walls, so we seldom have complaints coming from other levels. But the transom windows are historic repro-ductions, and not double-pane," he said, looking up at the library's own etched faux transoms. "So sometimes guests hear doors open and close on their own floor. The doors are heavy and are designed to close firmly."

"If Ms. Tupman's recollection is correct," said Simon, "then someone came into the library after Osma went to her room."

"But the Heart of Helsinki would already have been taken by then," Cuff said.

"True," said Detective Boggs.

"Perhaps a guest couldn't sleep and decided to look for a book or check e-mail," Bettina said.

"No one offered that as an alibi," Detective Boggs said. "So we have a mystery to uncover that may or may not be related to the thefts."

"And Jennifer Wren's scarf?" Simon asked.

"Ms. Wren claims that the scarf has no special signifi-cance. She says it's not the first time she's lost an article of clothing. Forgotten somewhere, as we all have done or, in her case, accidentally left behind, then taken by a fan. She didn't seem concerned, except for her safety. Like any celebrity, she said, she has to be alert for over-enthusiastic fans."

"Everyone here has treated her like an equal," said Simon, "except Quilpy."

"She isn't worried about him. She thinks he is"—Detective Boggs read from her notepad—"'cute.'" She flipped to another page. "And you said that Mr. Grewgious was still in the bar when you left?"

Bettina looked at Simon. "He was when I came to bed," she said.

"Drood left first," said Simon. "He said he went directly to bed after leaving the bar."

Bettina looked at Simon. "He said that?" she asked. "That's interesting, because I could swear that I saw his light on behind the transom glass when I went to my room almost an hour later. Our rooms are across from one another on the third floor."

Boggs looked at the room list that Cuff had prepared for her. Simon kept his inside his sport coat pocket. "I'll follow up with him," Detective Boggs said as she made a note.

Cuff furrowed his brow. "But with Grewgious being the last out of the bar," he said, "that gave the thief more time to enter his room and steal the scarf."

"Even if we put aside the question of why," said Simon, "how did the thief enter two locked rooms?"

"The thief must have a passkey," Cuff said, "as improbable as that sounds." He turned to Detective Boggs. "We deliberately chose to keep the old-style locks on the rooms when we renovated the hotel."

"Can you have the locks changed?" Bettina asked. "Many people have valuables in their rooms."

"Plus," Simon added, "we have a potentially priceless document in the hotel, and a stubborn owner."

"I have an idea," Cuff said. "What if I tell him that, in the interests of guest safety, he must turn the document over to me or leave the hotel."

Bettina and Simon looked at one another. "He'll be furious," Bettina said.

"What choice do I have?" Cuff said. "He is one person, and the hotel management has the safety of all its guests to consider."

"It might work," Detective Boggs said.

"We won't be able to have the locks changed until tomorrow or the next day," Cuff said, "so it's the least I can offer."

"I'll tell him," said Simon. "I feel responsible."

"I'll do it," Bettina said. "I'm the chair of the conference."

"Why don't I try it," suggested Detective Boggs.

Each of the other three visibly relaxed. Simon hadn't realized how tense he had become.

"You're crazy," Drabb said when, a few minutes later, he arrived at the library to see Simon, Bettina, Detective Boggs, and Bart Cuff waiting for him. "I don't have to do it," he said the minute Detective Boggs had finished her request.

"The hotel reserves the right to dismiss any guest for violating its rules," Cuff said. "You are jeopardizing the safety of other guests."

"Preposterous. So a ring and scarf have gone missing. What of it?"

"The ring is worth two million dollars," Bettina said.

"So it's true?" Drabb paused. "Even so, it's nothing compared with the value of Number Plan Six."

"No harm will come to your document," Bettina said. "Mr. Cuff will release it to you for your presentation."

"You'll throw me out if I don't?" Drabb was looking at Simon.

"We'll have no choice," said Simon.

Drabb pushed himself away from the table. "I'll get it."

Simon stood to accompany him, but Drabb leaned forward. "I can do this myself," he snapped. He turned on them and left the library, slamming the doors behind him.

"That went well," Bettina said.

Detective Boggs turned to Cuff. "Please let me know as soon as you've made contact with the locksmith," she said.

Bettina and Simon discussed options for notifying the conferees about the locks; they were still talking when Drabb returned with a manila envelope. He handed it to Cuff.

"The envelope is sealed. I will be the only person to open it the morning of my presentation. If I find that it has been tampered with, I'll sue all of you." He said this through clenched teeth that Simon thought were on the small and sharp side.

"That is a priceless document?" Detective Boggs asked. Cuff held it at arm's length.

"The Dickens world will change because of it," Drabb said. "The most important piece of Dickensiana since—well, since ever." Bettina reached out as if to comfort Drabb, but he pulled his hands away. "I shall write to the international society to notify them of my displeasure. This has put a blight on my presentation." He was, Simon thought, having a hard time sustaining his anger. "You have managed to make it less special."

In spite of everything, Simon had compassion for this dusty scholar, the months and years spent in libraries, sorting mouldering stacks of fading letters in fusty cardboard boxes, digging for more and more arcane pieces of the Dickens puzzle. Such workhorses (and that's how he thought of Drabb, despite Drabb's dandified exterior) enriched the world of literature, each in his or her way. And, at the end of the day, Simon was a beneficiary of that learning.

"I'm sorry, Buck—Buckminster," he said. "We will do our best to make sure your presentation loses none of its luster."

How he would do that, Simon didn't know.

Although Simon would have preferred a romantic dinner with Zach (send Jude home early and cook for Zach himself: baby arugula with Meyer lemon vinaigrette, sautéed skate wings on garlic chard, and dessert of a more imaginative nature), he knew he needed to be at the conferees' dinner to assure that everything was staying as smooth and as calm as circumstances would allow.

The buffet had been an inspiration of the hotel: all-you-can-eat fresh fish and shellfish—tureens of crab bisque and clam chowder; oysters on the half-shell with champagne mignonette and mussels sautéed to order; baked, poached, or grilled salmon with tarragon/dill butter; cracked Dungeness crab legs and a rich crab macaroni and cheese, crab Louis for those eating light; and desserts. Tables of desserts.

"I eat like this once a year, if even that," Osma said to Simon as she accepted made-to-order Dungeness crab legs sautéed in tarragon brown butter. To make up for the crab legs, she added a generous helping of gathered greens and mâche lightly dressed with aged balsamic vinegar. "I suppose," she continued, "that I should have lost my appetite completely because of the thefts, but I'm peckish."

"Well," said Simon, deciding not to sound another note about the theft, "I've learned a few things about scholars over the years: They love to eat good food—and *good* means *lots*."

Simon kept things simple for himself with a small fillet of poached halibut, steamed haricots verts, and herbed new potatoes. In front of him, Silas Cheeryble had piled his tray with mounds of oysters, both raw and Rockefeller, plus bowls of chowder and bisque. Crab cakes topped with habañero rouille were stacked precariously at the edge of the overfull plate.

Simon saw Quilpy and Drood at a table for four. He hadn't visited much with either and hoped to find out more about Drood who, name notwithstanding, continued to seem a fish out of water.

"May I join you?" Simon asked.

"Sure, dude," Quilpy said.

Drood, chewing on a cocktail sauce-drenched prawn, nodded. His glasses jiggled but stayed in place, held by the bump on his nose. The gelled platinum spikes of his hair glowed like holiday lights.

"What a spread," Quilpy said.

"I'm glad you like it," said Simon. "Do you get much fresh seafood in Minot?" Simon had noted Quilpy's residence when he was reviewing the registrations with Bettina.

"Not on a blogger's pay, even one as famous as I am," Quilpy said. He made short work of a half-dozen oysters, shooting them down his throat and slurping up the mignonette. "Although advertising cash flow has improved since the Dickens bicentennial."

Simon looked across the room. Osma was dining with Lionel and Jennifer. From his vantage, Simon had an unobstructed view of Jennifer, radiant tonight in a low-cut maroon cocktail dress with spaghetti straps and ruched bodice. A teardrop diamond lavaliere sparkled. Simon noticed Drood watching her, too; when she looked their way, however, Drood averted his gaze. Simon nodded and smiled; she returned the gesture.

"Quite the Betty, isn't she," Quilpy said. "If I was straight, I'd hit that." He then pointed the end of a scampi at Lionel. "But I'd hit *that* anyday."

"Down, boy," Drood said affectionately. He took another furtive look at Jennifer Wren, then looked at his plate of food and began eating more earnestly.

"Only for you," Quilpy said.

Simon wasn't sure if this banter qualified as courting among young gay men; their breezy brazen talk made him uneasy. He had never been that way—but maybe that had been part of his problem?

As he considered what topic he might bring up next, he saw Cecily Tartar enter the dining room alone. According to Detective Boggs, Cecily said she had gone to her room directly after dinner the previous night. She had retired early and reported nothing unusual.

But something unusual was happening now. She held a small plate, mostly salad, in one hand. She looked even more glamorous than Jennifer Wren, her silken dark hair framing her oval face. She wore a smoky eye shadow and showed off her curvaceous figure in a short, off-the-shoulder blue ombré bandage dress and taupe four-inch pumps.

Cecily took a few steps toward the table where her brother sat, but as she did, Lionel caught her glance. The side-eye Lionel gave his sister (while Osma and Jennifer talked to each other) would have frozen Simon to the spot if he had been the one receiving it. Cecily, however, pivoted on one foot and, with a toss of her head as if she had changed her mind, sat with Bettina and Louella Pardiggle in a corner of the room.

"So," said Simon, turning his face back to Drood after a moment of silent eating except for Quilpy's cooing at the flavor of the crab bisque, "how did it feel to be hypnotized? Your reaction was different from the rest."

Drood's face darkened. "It was okay," he said. "I have been hypnotized before, so I knew what to expect—at least how it would feel, not necessarily what I would say. I had no idea what Mr. Grewgious would say to me."

"When had you been hypnotized before?"

Drood touched the bridge of his nose. "I had some counseling when I was a teenager," he said in a quiet voice. "Hypnosis was part of the treatment."

"I'm sorry," said Simon. "I didn't mean to pry into private matters. It seemed odd for such a young man—"

"No worries," Drood answered, his face lightening again. That might have been because Quilpy's hand was inching up Drood's left thigh. "In the past. I don't mind talking about it—"

"I don't like the Great Grewgious," Quilpy said abruptly. His hands were again occupied with his food as he slathered butter on a Parker House roll. "He's a phony. And dangerous. Taking what people tell him and trying to make it into entertainment when they're helpless—if they're helpless. It's lame."

"But not unlike Dickens's own occasional use of mesmerism," said Simon. He hoped it hadn't sounded too patronizing.

"Dickens was whacked about some things," Quilpy said. "Like his treatment of Catherine, his beliefs about race, his thoughts on sex—and definitely about hypnosis." Simon had been wrong. Maybe Quilpy wasn't a dilettante when it came to the Inimitable Boz. His list was on the nose.

"My apologies," said Simon, striving this time for sincerity. He was liking Quilpy more by the minute. "Dickens was, as you say, whacked about a number of issues. Sometimes we neglect, or overlook, these aspects of him."

Grewgious entered the dining area with a full plate. He searched about for a spot, but glided past the empty chair next to Simon, opting instead to make a fourth at the table with the Weird Sisters.

Simon turned back to Drood. "Are you enjoying the conference?"

"You'd better say yes," Quilpy said. Out of the corner of his eye, Simon watched Quilpy's hand slide higher up Drood's leg. Drood shifted away.

"Most of it," Drood said. "It was kind of expensive for me to get here and take time off work, since I don't get paid vacation yet."

"What do you do?" Simon asked.

Across the room, Jennifer, Osma, and Lionel rose from their table, Osma taking Lionel's arm. Simon watched Drood watch them leave the banquet room.

"I'm sorry?" Drood asked. He looked confused.

Simon repeated the question.

"I have a soulless existence in a chain bookstore," Drood said.

Simon cocked his head, as if Drood would say more, something with a dollop of irony. But none came. Drood was providing a description, not an analysis.

"I see," said Simon.

Quilpy's hand was still rising up Drood's leg. Drood looked down, but this time let Quilpy's hand continue to move.

This was Simon's clue that it was time to go, so he stood. "I need to mingle." He looked at Quilpy. "You should channel some of your frustration at Dickens into research. You could produce some provocative scholarship."

"I'd rather shock people by reporting the theft of a world-famous jewel, or saying that Jennifer Wren is sleeping with a hot Spanish stud, or wherever exotic place that dude is from," he said.

"The Seychelles," said Simon.

"So he says," Quilpy said. "I'd be suspicious of him, that's for sure. He has shifty eyes. So does his sister. Just like thieves."

"Mr. Tartar has impeccable credentials."

"Just because he's a dreamboat and a scholar doesn't mean he isn't a shit. Look at that one over there." Quilpy pointed with his fork this time at Drabb, who appeared, once again, to be arguing with Minor and Cheeryble. Though this time the argument sounded particularly heated. "For example. Think how many Eye-talian suits he could buy after pawning that Heart of Helsinki."

"I should see what's causing the commotion," said Simon.

He nodded at Drood, then Quilpy, whose hand had scaled Drood's thigh to a new level of intimacy, a level that young Edwin had decided not to rebuff. Drood showed a goofy, crooked, yet contented smile on his face, as he watched Quilpy's other hand dive for one last oyster shooter.

Simon arrived as Drabb pushed his chair away from the table. "You'll rue the day you said that." He spat the words at Minor.

"People don't talk like that anymore, Bucky," Cheeryble said. "Really."

"What's the matter?" Simon asked.

Grewgious rested his hands on his large belly. "They are arguing—again, apparently—about the virtues of Mr. Obadiah Twinn." He showed Simon a smooth brow that, for a man of his age, had probably been assisted by injection. "Such interesting theories," he continued. "I came across this Twinn in my Internet dabblings into Dickens and mesmerism. He's quite controversial."

Drabb squinted at him. "He won't be in two days. His name—and mine—will be known throughout the Dickens world."

"They already are," Minor said. He pushed away his plate of half-eaten shrimp cocktail. "Crackpots in a pod."

Simon didn't think Minor really meant this—at least not about Drabb. Twinn was a different matter.

"Twinn has been dead since 2006," Cheeryble said. "Let his theories rest in peace."

"I believe 2008," Grewgious said.

"You're right," Minor said, giving Grewgious a quizzical look. "You have a good memory for trivia."

"A blessing," Grewgious said. He wiped his brow with his napkin.

"Dead or not," Drabb said, his voice thick, "he'll be vindicated next week." Simon noticed a nearly empty bottle of white wine next to Drabb's plate and only one other glass besides his at the table. Drabb rose unsteadily from his chair; Simon caught his arm so he didn't stumble. "You're all just jealous," Drabb said. As if he had just realized who was holding him, he pulled away from Simon. "I certainly don't need more help from you." Drabb loped out of the banquet room toward the bar.

"I guess," said Simon, "I should be glad that things over here are relatively normal, and that you're not letting the thefts interfere with your enjoyment of the conference."

"What can we do about it?" Minor asked. "It's poor Osma I'm worried about."

"She's handling everything pretty well."

"Any news on Ms. Wren's scarf?" Grewgious asked Simon.

"None."

"The sheriff's office was most respectful of my belongings," Grewgious said. "Please thank them for me."

"Well, gentlemen," said Simon, "if there's nothing more I can do for you, I'll say goodnight. We have another big day ahead of us tomorrow."

—♦—

Zach was sitting in the kitchen, laptop open, and drinking Darjeeling from a Dickens World coffee mug when Simon returned from dinner. Several stacks of papers, books, and folders were strewn around the kitchen and nook. Miss Tox was curled up on the bench seat under the window.

Simon first got a glass of water from the sink, then gave Zach a kiss and sat beside him. Zach's shirt was open at the neck, giving him a rakish and sexy look, a welcome sight to Simon after his tussling with Droodists for the last few hours. "You look tired," Zach said. "Did you learn anything interesting?"

"Only that Drood and Quilpy have become an item. I'm trying to remember the last time I saw people hook up at a Droodist conference. It's not usually done."

"At least not by you," Zach said with a crooked grin. "Or not that you've said."

"That Quilpy," Simon continued, "has more on the ball than I thought. He could be a presence in the

Dickens world, if he would focus more on scholarship instead of glitz and 'goss.'" Such slang felt like copper in Simon's mouth.

"The world is changing, Simon. You, not so much." Zach paused. "That's not a criticism. It's one of the things I love about you. You're predictable."

The last time Simon had been the life of the party was...*File that under "Never."* Quilpy and Drood were so casual about their needs and desires for each other at the dinner table. *What would that freedom be like?*

"Boring, you mean," said Simon.

"Not boring. Stable." Zach shuffled pages of Internet printouts.

Simon pulled a few pages toward him. "So, you've spent the day hunched over a keyboard. You promised pirates, I believe?"

"In a manner of speaking." Zach pulled one of the sheets back toward him. "Out of curiosity," he continued, "how many times in the last few days have you heard about cruises?"

Simon thought. Something in Quilpy's column, a contest; and Grewgious; and Bettina...He said aloud the ones he remembered.

"Good memory," Zach said. "Look at this."

He showed Simon a lengthy news article called "Lost—and Found—at Sea." The subject was the disappearance of a famous gem—the Caracas Carbuncle, a renowned star sapphire that had been worn by a guest, one Musetta de le Reina Compostela of Tegucigalpa, on the SS *Excess of the Seas*, a cruise ship that made stops at St. Kitts, Turks and Caicos, and Caracas. Between ports, the dowager de la Reina Compostela noticed that, after dancing the merengue with shirtless crew members on deck thirteen and enjoying the midnight chocolate madness buffet, her magnificent sapphire pendant was missing. She was sure it had spent the evening nestled in her capacious bosom. The captain docked at Caracas but, in an unprecedented move, decided not to let passengers off the ship without an extensive search of rooms and luggage. Later that day, before the search had gone much beyond the countess's own sun deck, the jewel was found in the deck thirteen lounge, despite two prior unsuccessful sweeps of that room by cruise ship staff, improbably wrapped in a lipstick-stained cocktail napkin and shoved between the tufts of a banquette. Dowager de la Compostela was relieved to have the priceless gem returned to her.

Simon read the article closely. When he was done, he looked at Zach. "A similar loss. What makes this significant?"

Zach pointed to three different photographs that accompanied the article below the caption, "Suspects? Or Innocent Bystanders?"

Simon took a closer look. In the first, a young woman stood with her back and head partially obscuring a young bandy-legged man in cargo shorts and a striped tank top, holding an impossibly large tropical drink with umbrella decoration. "Is that Quilpy?"

"Looks like him to me," Zach said.

The second photograph showed five people milling around; two were uniformed crew members looking closely at adjoining café tables. Next to one stood a leggy beauty wearing a swim toga and sandals. Her long hair was pulled back in a simple bun. Her beauty was unmistakable.

"Cecily Tartar," said Simon.

Zach moved his finger; under it was a large man wearing an open white shirt, striped shorts, and a Panama hat that partially obscured his brow. But the goateed chin was a dead giveaway.

"That's Grewgious," said Simon. "Inches away from Cecily."

The third photograph was a wider shot. Quilpy was again partially obscured by the longhaired woman, but it was clear that Quilpy, Grewgious, and Cecily Tartar, at some time before last night, had been within a few feet of one another.

"Fascinating," said Simon.

"A follow-up article," Zach said, "states that police were suspicious of theft but, given that the dowager de la Reina Compostela wanted no publicity—she was apparently recuperating from an extensive 'vacation' at a Rio plastic surgery center—no further investigation was done after the carbuncle was found."

"We must give this to Detective Boggs in the morning," said Simon. "I'm sure it will change her lines of inquiry, at least with these three."

"There's more," Zach said. He pulled another Internet article from his stack. "Another gemstone scandal, this time in Antwerp, where a small sachet of diamonds went missing at an international exhibition. The diamonds were never found, and the members of the committee involved in the exhibition were all asked to relinquish their positions in their association for, at minimum, a failure to follow gem-handling protocols. Look at the list." He pushed it toward Simon.

"Hermann Onderdonk," Simon read, "Monique Van Eerrpflug, Klaus Kostt, Cecily Tartar…" Simon pushed the article away.

"I find no evidence online that she's ever been accused of a crime, but—"

"—no smoke without fire," Simon finished for him.

"You really know how to turn a phrase, sweetie."

"Did this lead you elsewhere? Something about her brother, perhaps? Or about their connection to the Seychelles?"

"Next on my list."

"You've uncovered a lot in one day." Simon ran his hand through Zach's hair. Clues made him amorous. Maybe Simon could learn a thing or two from young Quilpy.

Miss Tox rose from her place on the floor and ambled through the kitchen toward the hall leading upstairs to the main bedrooms.

"I've been doing further work on young Drood, too," he said, "but still no real information. Have you learned anything?"

"Just that he isn't a stranger to hypnosis," said Simon. "He started to tell me about some counseling he had as a younger man that included hypnotherapy, but Quilpy cut him off before he got very far."

"You think it's suspicious?"

"I think everything unexplained is suspicious," said Simon. He began to run his finger underneath Zach's open shirt collar. "Especially when a two-million-dollar ring is missing."

Zach stood, taking Simon with him. "Looks like I'll be staying the night again," he said. "Good that I packed spare clothes and a toothbrush."

Simon felt Zach's hand in a more familiar place. "When you move in," he said, "I might give you your own drawer."

The next morning Simon had just gotten out of bed when his cell phone rang.

"It's Bettina," she said, out of breath. "I've got terrible news. This is getting to be a habit."

Zach turned over in bed, exposing a broad expanse of chest and abdomen. The tossed sheets draped provocatively over his lower body.

"What is it?"

"Drabb's number plan has been stolen."

"How can that be?" Simon was already walking to the shower.

"I don't know yet. But there's something worse."

"What can be worse than that?" Simon asked.

"Mr. Edwin Drood," Bettina said, taking a breath, "is missing."

April 18

7:30–9:00 a.m.	Continental Breakfast	Hotel bar
9:00 a.m.–4:00 p.m.	Bus Trip to Dickens Junction: dedication of the Sapsea Head, Dickens Junction; shopping; Dickens Family mausoleum	Meet in hotel lobby
6:00–7:00 p.m.	No-host Bar	Hotel rooftop lounge (staircase near room 501)
7:00–9:00 p.m.	Dinner on your own	
9:00p.m.–late	Entertainment (optional)	The Dueling Duoos Brothers, accordionists extraordinaire Suomi Hall (transportation available, see staff)

DAY FOUR

Simon arrived at the hotel at seven thirty and went directly to the basement. Conferees buzzed in clusters with sensational spins on the merest nuggets of truth. In a corner, Cecily and Lionel Tartar stood close together, their discussion heated and terse.

Simon returned to the lobby in time to catch Bettina, Drabb, and Cuff coming from Cuff's office. Even this early in the morning, Cuff had loosened his tie, removed his suit jacket, and displayed signs of flop sweat. He was holding Drabb's envelope. What had gone wrong?

Drabb was flailing his arms and screaming. "Of

course it's your fault! If security in this hotel were well maintained, this wouldn't have happened."

"Thank goodness you're here," Bettina said as Simon approached.

"Calm down," Cuff said. "I have your document right here."

Drabb clenched his teeth and then grabbed the envelope from Cuff. He ripped off one end of the sealed envelope and shook it. Shreds of paper rained onto the hotel desk. Bettina gasped.

"I didn't *actually* give it to you, you idiot!" Drabb screamed.

Simon stepped forward. Drabb's face was red. His eyes, too. He was wearing the same clothes he had worn last night at dinner.

"Slow down, Bucky," said Simon firmly. Someone needed to establish order. "Explain what happened."

Drabb took a deep breath and pulled at his disheveled shirt. "I didn't trust you with the number plan, so I gave you this instead." He stirred a dirty fingernail into the heap of confetti. "I kept the real number plan hidden in my room. I made sure it was safe before I went to dinner." He stopped and put his hand to his head. "I have a headache."

Bettina stepped away and returned with coffee and aspirin.

Drabb took them and gave a perfunctory nod of thanks. "I had more to drink at dinner than I should, and even more than that in the bar." He swallowed. "I may have said a few inappropriate remarks to some women—perhaps even Ms. Wren." His face clouded over. "Then I went, by myself, to a waterfront bar—it isn't far away—and had a few more drinks. I don't quite know how I got back here—maybe someone walked me. The night clerk unlocked my door, and I fell into bed sometime in the early morning—don't know exactly when. Sometime after two, I suppose. I didn't move until the wake-up call this morning. When I went to where I had hidden the number plan, it was gone."

"Where had you hidden it?" Simon asked.

"I shouldn't have trusted that wretched Poe." Drabb's shoulders drooped and something, possibly regret, passed across his face. "'The Purloined Letter.'"

Cuff looked confused.

"An Edgar Allan Poe short story," Simon explained. "Bucky means he hid it in plain sight." Simon paused. "With the hotel stationery in the desk, perhaps?"

Drabb nodded, his eyes revealing self-awareness of his foolishness now exposed.

Cuff's face was puffy and red. "Mr. Drabb, why would you do that? We told you that our room locks were not secure until replaced, probably later today. Why didn't you listen?"

By this time Drabb had exhausted himself with his tirade, or perhaps his head hurt more than he would admit to. In any case, he was now subdued. "I don't know," he said, defeat in his voice.

"No one has checked out of the hotel," Cuff said.

"But Drood is not in his room," said Bettina.

Simon checked his watch. Almost eight o'clock. The tour bus had pulled up in front of the hotel, ready to escort the conferees to Dickens Junction at nine for a day of touring, dedicating the new bronze head for Dickens Square, and shopping.

"Tell me about Drood," said Simon.

"We don't know much," Cuff said. "I received a call this morning from Mr. Quill, informing me that Drood didn't answer his room or cell phone, and would I check on him. We checked his room with the passkey. It doesn't appear that his bed was slept in. His suitcase is there, along with all of his conference materials. His cell phone was on the dressing table near the bed."

"Have you notified Detective Boggs?"

"Yes," Cuff said. "She will be here any time now."

Bettina bit her carefully glossed lower lip. Even this early in the morning, and under such stress, her makeup was impeccable: deep frosted shadow perfectly applied to her tawny eyelids, a dark blush used with restraint, a lustrous mascara. "Should we cancel the trip to Dickens Junction?"

"Let's discuss that when Detective Boggs arrives." Simon turned to Drabb. "You're going to have to repeat your story to the detective, and I don't think she's going to be very happy about it." Then he turned to Cuff. "In the meantime, may I see Drood's room?"

"I don't know, Mr. Alastair—"

"I won't touch anything, I promise."

Bettina put her hand on Cuff's arm. "We must do something."

"All right," Cuff said.

Bettina looked around the lobby. "I'll tell the conferees that we have everything under control," she said.

She turned to Simon. "We *do* have everything under control, don't we?"

Drabb seemed more rational, as if he had just recognized how bad he looked. "I had better go to my room and clean up. And I need to call Lloyd's of London."

"You had the document insured?"

"For five million dollars."

Cuff whistled.

"It's priceless," Drabb said.

"Apparently not," said Simon.

With that, the group broke up. Drabb, Simon, and Cuff took the elevator. Drabb got off on the second floor; Cuff and Simon continued to the third floor. When the door opened, Jennifer Wren was in the hallway. She appeared startled.

"Good morning," said Cuff and Simon simultaneously.

She relaxed her face but stood stiffly, her hands clasped. "I was looking for Lionel," she said. "But he isn't answering my knock."

"I saw him at breakfast," said Simon, "with his sister."

"I will not be attending today's visit to Dickens Junction," Jennifer said to Simon.

"I'm sorry to hear that. Are you concerned about—"

"—my safety," she interrupted, without any dramatic inflection. "I would prefer to discuss it first with Detective Boggs. I understand that she is on her way to investigate last night's events."

"She is," Cuff said.

Jennifer looked at Cuff, her eyes wide, the pupils small. "I wish to see her right away. Meanwhile, I will stay in my room. I ask not to be disturbed except by the detective."

"Of course," Cuff said.

"Mr. Edwin Drood," she said, "he is, in fact, missing?"

"It appears so, Ms. Wren," Cuff said.

Jennifer's face again appeared taut. "I would prefer not to say more at this time," she added, turning to Simon. "You've been so kind, Mr. Alastair. As soon as I've spoken to the detective, I hope to help you understand my behavior." With that, she entered the elevator, and the door closed behind her.

Now on the third floor, Cuff searched for the passkey on his key ring while Simon checked the room-assignment list Cuff had given him yesterday. Drood shared the third floor with, among other conferees, Lionel and Bettina. Drood's room was at the end of the hall, two floors directly above Osma's. Cuff finally retrieved the key and opened Drood's door.

"You said you wouldn't touch anything," Cuff reminded Simon.

Except for a few items on the bedside table (cell phone, a pair of earplugs, a travel alarm clock), Simon would have guessed that the room had been unoccupied. The bed was made, and certainly hadn't been slept in. In the bathroom, Drood's shaving kit was open. Simon peered inside but could find nothing beyond the expected items: razor, shaving cream, toothbrush, toothpaste, three different hair gels, a tube of concealer. A small rectangular container, probably a pill box. But no prescription bottles—perhaps not unusual for a young man.

"Look, Cuff," said Simon.

Next to the shaving kit were Drood's glasses, standing open as though ready to leap onto Drood's face. The lenses pointed toward the mirror.

Simon leaned down and looked through them.

"Don't touch anything," Cuff said.

"I won't," said Simon. "Look." He stood aside.

Cuff lowered his substantial frame into a crouch and peered through the lenses at his own reflection in the bathroom mirror. "So?" he asked. "I don't see anything."

"Exactly," said Simon. "Those lenses have no correction in them. They're clear glass."

"Maybe he wanted to look like an egghead," Cuff said. "After all, this is a pretty egghead-y group."

Simon frowned. "Maybe..." Simon would wait and discuss his thoughts with Detective Boggs.

The rest of the room, that Simon could readily see, revealed nothing. Cuff wouldn't let Simon open the closet door, for fear of leaving fingerprints.

"Thank you for allowing me to satisfy my curiosity," said Simon.

They left the room and returned to the lobby.

Bettina, Detective Boggs, and a uniformed deputy (a very young, muscular, sandy-haired man Boggs introduced as Deputy Abel Gjovik) were waiting for them at the front desk.

"Another theft?" Boggs was asking. "And a missing person? How is this possible?"

Bettina told what they knew.

"Where is Mr. Drabb right now?" Detective Boggs asked.

"Upstairs, taking a shower and notifying his insurance company."

"That means another investigator, I suppose," said the detective. She looked outside. The front and back doors of the bus were open, waiting for the conferees to embark.

Simon looked out, too. At least a few seats were already occupied by anxious, or at least eager, Droodists. Simon showed Detective Boggs the daily conference agenda. "All will be attending except Ms. Wren," he said. "She wishes to see you right away on an urgent matter."

Detective Boggs cocked an eyebrow. "Regarding the theft?"

"She preferred not to discuss it with us."

"Is she in her room?"

"Yes," Cuff answered, "Presidential suite. Top floor."

"Should we postpone our field trip?" Bettina asked.

Detective Boggs considered the question. "What time do you leave?"

"Nine o'clock," said Simon. It was eight thirty now. "The mayor and other Junxonians are expecting us for the dedication of the new head at ten."

"Go ahead and go," the detective said. "I'll have Deputy Gjovik accompany you. I'll interview Mr. Drabb and Ms. Wren, and then join you at the Junction. The deputy can begin taking statements as your visit allows."

It was a short distance from downtown Astoria to Dickens Junction, but Simon had hoped for, and received, a scenic drive. Rather than the usual blustery cold rain, the day was mostly sunny.

Simon's grandfather had commissioned a larger-than-life bronze of Dickens as the centerpiece of Dickens Square, but when Grandpa Ebbie learned that Dickens's will expressly forbade any statuary in his honor, the already-cast figure was altered so that the body of the statue could be fitted with any of a series of interchangeable bronze heads, as the seasons and Junxonian celebrations determined. In honor of the Droodists' visit, the town had commissioned an Oregon bronzesmith to produce a head of Thomas Sapsea, the pompous mayor of *The Mystery of Edwin Drood.*

Mayor Sapsea's bronze head had been screwed on to the statue base the day before and now sat draped with a ceremonial tarpaulin. That was the vision the Droodists saw as the bus arrived and disgorged its passengers. Simon, however, saw Zach, who had planned to meet Simon for the ceremony even before they'd learned of the previous night's mysteries.

Simon and Dean Minor helped Osma down from the bus to the flagstones of Dickens Square; she held a cane. Simon saw the white band below her knuckle where the Heart of Helsinki belonged. Her hand looked so distorted with the ring missing.

"I'm worried about that young man," she said to Simon about Drood. "I can't believe he's a thief."

Grewgious moved his bulk off the bus and stood next to Osma. "I'm sure there's an explanation for everything."

Quilpy had practically bounced off the bus windows during the brief trip to the Junction, and now he clung to Simon and, when he arrived, Zach.

"Something is cocked up," he said, at least seven times in thirty seconds. "Seriously cocked up." He started biting his knuckles.

"Calm down, dude," Zach said. He put his arm around Quilpy's shoulder.

"Droody's the best thing that's happened to me since those frat boys on the cruise two years ago," Quilpy said.

Zach raised an eyebrow. Simon decided it wasn't time to ask Quilpy about the cruise, or the Caracas Carbuncle.

Mayor Solomon Dick, Simon's distant cousin, a large, gregarious man, emerged from his sandwich shop. He shook everyone's hand as Simon introduced him to the Droodists. Simon had called the previous evening to tell him what had happened, and he was thankful that the mayor was helping to keep the visit light and celebratory.

"The viewing stands are ready," Mayor Dick said and escorted the group over to the statue. Simon checked his watch: almost ten.

A number of Junxonians were present for the dedication: Viola Mintun, whose Crystal Palace Tearoom would be supplying the luncheon for the Droodists; Bradford Sturgess of *Household Words*; Mavis Spurlock, Brock's mother and innkeeper at Bleak House Bed & Breakfast; and Mimsie Tricket, new proprietress of Bark: Us Is Willin' Pet Supply and Day Care. Mimsie's assistant, Apassionata Midge, was also the newly installed Head Custodian (Junxonians spoke the description with capital letters) of the

Dickens Square statue, and she, all eighty-eight pounds of her, would be assisting the mayor by removing the tarpaulin from the statue at the dramatic reveal.

Zach escorted Osma to the bank of portable bleachers that had been erected in front of the statue. Neva Tupman, looking ill at ease in a Carnaby Street–inspired lime-green trench coat and a fluttering white marabou boa, sat next to Silas Cheeryble, who was bundled up in a parka with a faux-fur hood. Cecily Tartar had moved toward where her brother sat but, before she got there, Lionel welcomed Quilpy to sit beside him. The young journalist was befuddled by the attention of the much more physically imposing man, and sat without question. Grewgious ended up sitting next to Zach in the front row. Next to him, Zach looked a bit crowded.

Simon and the mayor stood behind a dais next to the statue while the diminutive Ms. Midge, in her late forties and with a tight perm that might last have been popular two or three generations ago, stood nearby, basking in the honor of her new office and holding the golden cord attached to the tarpaulin.

"Welcome Droodists and fellow Junxonians," Mayor Dick began. "We are here today to dedicate the newest citizen of Dickens Junction, Mayor Thomas Sapsea of Cloisterham, who will watch over Dickens Square this year from April 1 to May 1. Naturally, I bear some affinity toward this august personage, and I am glad to welcome him here. But he was more than just mayor: His departed wife's tomb was almost certain to have played an important role in the solution to *The Mystery of Edwin Drood.*"

Minor coughed. "Better not be solved," he said, "particularly by Bucky Drabb."

"I feel particularly honored," Dick continued, "for the role that I played in selecting Mr. Sapsea as our next revolving head, as it were. I want to thank the other members of the committee, Mr. Simon Alastair and Ms. Apassionata Midge, and also the sculptor, Mr. Digger Stuggins"—the mayor gestured toward a bearded angular man who sat previously unnoticed at the far end of the first row of bleachers—"for his faithful rendition of the mayor as Dickens might have imagined him. In honor of Stuggins's vision, let us consider the words that Mr. Sapsea himself said to someone contemplating the hand of the artist: 'STRANGER PAUSE And ask thyself the Question, CANST THOU DO LIKEWISE? If Not, WITH A BLUSH RETIRE.'"

At the recitation of Mayor Sapsea's bloated proposed inscription on the monument to his late wife, Ethelinda, Ms. Midge pulled at the golden cord and revealed the new head from under its canvas mantilla.

Stuggins had done an excellent job of matching the new head to the patina of the existing bronzed torso. And, Simon had to admit, Mayor Dick had been right: Sapsea's jowly head looked good on the statue's body, better, perhaps, than other suggestions, including one to make the new head that of a woman—Miss Pross from *A Tale of Two Cities.*

"Thank you all for coming," Mayor Dick concluded, following a polite round of applause.

"If I may have the Droodists' attention," said Simon, "you are free to visit the shops until noon. Identify yourself as a Droodist, and Dickens Square merchants, including my assistant at Pip's Pages, will give you a ten percent discount on your purchases. Lunch will be served at the Crystal Palace, following which we shall stop by the Astoria/Dickens Junction Cemetery where you can view Oregon's Dickens family mausoleum."

After helping Ms. Midge fold up the tarpaulin for its next official use and conferring with Zach, Simon decided he would roam the square while Zach kept a close eye on the agitated Quilpy.

Simon popped in to the Crystal Palace to speak with Viola Mintun about the lunch.

"You're having a run of bad luck over there, aren't you?" Viola asked. A no-nonsense woman of fifty-five, Viola shook her short red hair. "But I'll take good care of the Droodists. Miss Havisham's Day Old Wedding Cake will cheer them up."

"I'm sure it will," said Simon. He decided to skip lunch himself, opting for a protein bar and a latte. He hadn't been to the bookstore in two days and wanted to spend lunchtime getting caught up on paperwork.

"Hey, boss," Brock said when Simon entered Pip's Pages. "I didn't expect you today." His T-shirt stretched tight across his well-defined chest. Probably had done a two-hour workout before opening the store.

A few Droodists followed Simon into the store and, after introducing Brock, Simon went to his office in a separate room at the back of the store. He could hear Brock ringing up some sales; a few minutes after that, Brock joined him in the back.

"No more Droodists," Brock said.

Simon looked up from his paperwork. Brock was trying to grow a goatee. Simon was sure that it would be gone before the wedding, at Bethany's insistence. Whatever Brock's many charms might be, and they were legion, facial-hair expertise was not among them. He looked like a young Hollywood type trying to show "maturity"—and failing. He would still have a boyishly handsome face at fifty.

"Simon," he said, bowing his head, "I want to ask you a favor."

"What is it?"

"So...the wedding is coming up in June..." Brock said.

"That's no time at all," said Simon. "I know Bethany has her dress, Ladasha's doing the cake, Finching's doing the flowers."

Brock took a breath. "I want you to be my best man," he said, all in a rush.

Simon pushed aside the paperwork in front of him. "This is a surprise." And it truly was.

"I've thought about it a long time," Brock said.

"What about Art Clenham?" Simon asked. Art was Brock's BFF—co-captain with Brock when they were on the high school cross-country team and still twice-weekly running partner. "I thought for sure you would ask him."

"Art's a great guy," Brock said, "but I talked this over with Bethany, and she agrees with me. You have known me since I was a kid—"

"Since you were born," said Simon, trying not to sound *too* old.

"And Mom tells me often what a help you and your grandparents were to her when she was alone and raising a kid—me—on her own." He shuffled his feet. "You helped me with my education—my fitness trainer's certification—and gave me this job. You're the best man I know."

Simon thought he might cry. Instead, he shuffled the papers until he had his emotions in tow, and then stood. He gave Brock a hug. "I would be honored to be your best man."

After an awkward silence, Brock shifted on his feet and resumed his more normal attitude. "Thanks, boss," he said.

"I'll need to get measured for a tux," said Simon, "since I suspect the one I have is more subdued than what you've chosen."

"We're registered, or whatever, at Mulberry Hawk Formal Wear."

"I'll visit them as soon as the conference is over," said Simon. He paused. Another awkward moment. "My duties as best man, I believe, usually include—"

Brock gave a crooked smile. "The bachelor party," he said. "Art can handle that. He probably knows a little more about what would make my posse happy than you."

Simon was relieved.

"But you and Zach have got to come," Brock continued. "For the food, if not for the entertainment."

"It's a deal."

"Great," Brock said. "I can't wait to tell Bethany." And he didn't wait. As Brock turned and went to the front of the store, he was already texting away.

Simon was inclined to do the same and let Zach know about Brock's request, but he would see Zach soon enough. He paid bills, answered e-mails, and reviewed inventory reports until it was time for the Droodists to make the short trip to the cemetery where he was scheduled to discuss his grandfather's mausoleum, a task he always did with mixed feelings.

The Dickensian in him was happy to talk about Ebenezer Dickens's fascination with the architecture of the tomb and the inspiration that Grandpa Ebbie had received from *The Mystery of Edwin Drood*, but another part of Simon thought: *This is where my grandparents and parents are buried and where, someday, I will be, too.* It was a sacred place.

At one thirty, Simon found the bus parked in back of the Six Jolly Fellowship Porters. Lionel had Osma by one arm; as they approached the bus, Cecily came up and took Osma's other arm.

"We can manage," her brother said to Cecily.

"I'd like to help," Cecily said to Osma.

Osma looked at one, then at the other twin. "I think you have been quarreling," she said kindly. "I hope not about me?"

Deputy Gjovik strolled discreetly behind them.

Cecily brushed her silky hair away from her face. "Sibling rivalry," she said with a light tone. "We know each other so well."

"Too well," Lionel said. He almost bared his teeth but smiled instead. He helped Osma complete the first step onto the bus; the bus driver then took over.

Cecily and Lionel followed Osma, with Simon behind them. Cecily sat on the aisle seat next to Osma, leaving Lionel to fend for himself. Simon took a window seat.

Through the streaked bus window, Simon saw Minor sprinting toward the bus, Cheeryble trying to keep up with him. Cheeryble had a large shopping bag decorated with the Bark: Us Is Willin' logo, a Chihuahua wearing a rakishly tilted porkpie hat.

"Thank goodness we're not late," Cheeryble said, huffing as he stumbled to his seat. "There's so much to see and do here. And there's never enough time for shopping."

Bettina now stepped on the bus, with Grewgious behind her. A moment later, Neva walked quickly toward the bus; Zach and Quilpy brought up the rear, and took the seats behind Simon, leaving Simon free to easily get up from his seat as needed, to attend to the group.

Simon did his head count. Allowing for the fact that Drabb and Jennifer had stayed behind and Drood was missing, all of the Droodists and Deputy Gjovik were on the bus, and Simon instructed the driver to leave for the cemetery, just over the hill from Dickens Junction and past the transfer station and waterworks.

"I've left text messages all morning," Quilpy said. "But no answer."

Simon decided not to reveal that Drood, wherever he was, did not have his cell phone with him. Simon checked his cell to see whether he had missed a text or call from Detective Boggs, but saw nothing.

"I'm sure everything is going to turn out all right," Zach said, giving Simon a look as he patted Quilpy's shoulders.

The Astoria/Dickens Junction Cemetery occupied a city block not far from the road leading to the Astoria Column at the top of Coxcomb Hill, about halfway between downtown Astoria and Dickens Junction. The cemetery was on uneven ground dotted with ancient birches and oaks beginning to put out their spring greenery. Simon cautioned the others to watch their footing as they disembarked. Hillocks and other little rises converged at the off-center highest point of the block, where Ebenezer Dickens had built his family mausoleum, by far the largest structure in the cemetery, long since closed to new gravesites. The narrow footpath wound past sturdy gravestones and smaller, more humble markers now mostly illegible. A few stones had collapsed or fallen; others leaned precariously from the vertical, like crooked teeth emerging from the moss and high grass unmowed since fall.

Simon took the lead, watching for puddles in the gravel pathway, and made his way to the top of the rise and the Dickens mausoleum, a squat sandstone edifice, two heavy Ionic columns framing the iron door with its overwrought and rusted fittings. The door was partially open, but no shaft of sun illuminated the inside of the tomb. Simon had called the sexton the day before to make sure the mausoleum door would be open in time for the visit. No one really worried about vandals in this part of town, and the cemetery was infrequently visited these days, except on Memorial Day weekend; relatives of those interred there barely remembered their forebears.

The earthy smell of dirt and humus struck Simon's nostrils as he stopped near the front of the mausoleum, positioning himself directly below the word *Dickens*, now green with lichen, carved into the lintel. The Droodists gathered in a loose semicircle around Simon, careful not to step on a fallen headstone or a patch of mud.

"Welcome to the resting place of my ancestors," said Simon. "My grandfather, the founder of Dickens Junction, was a lifelong devotee of Dickens's works, and celebrated them in more ways than I can count. Although *The Mystery of Edwin Drood* was not among his favorite Dickens novels, he never failed to laugh at Mayor Sapsea, whose bombastic and self-congratulatory eulogy for his wife our own Mayor Dick quoted earlier. My grandfather, however, did believe in allowing Dickens and Victoriana to inspire every aspect of his life—and his afterlife as well."

This made several Droodists chuckle. Out of the corner of his eye, Simon saw Neva, boa fluttering behind her, edge around the crowd so that she was standing close to the mausoleum door.

"Grandpa Ebbie," Simon continued, "worked with architects and stone masons to construct a family tomb inspired by mid-Victorian designs."

Simon scanned the faces in the crowd. Silas Cheeryble was looking at Lionel Tartar, who was glowering at his sister now peering through the door of the tomb.

"Before we go inside—"

Simon was interrupted by a piercing scream coming from inside the mausoleum.

Droodists rushed toward the mausoleum door. In the melee, Simon found himself near the back of the crowd. He could see Zach push wide the iron door before Droodists started to crowd the entrance. Several other people now gasped or screamed and began backing away. Osma leaned on her cane at the back of the crowd, looking frightened. Someone was crying.

Simon and Deputy Gjovik pushed themselves to the front and entered the mausoleum, where a smaller group—including Cecily and Lionel, along with Neva—stood. Zach was pointing a portable flashlight toward the ground with one hand. His other arm cradled Quilpy to his chest, Quilpy's sobs muted in the crook of Zach's arm. Neva's face was buried in marabou fringe and Cecily's shoulder.

Simon looked from Cecily's unreadable face to the mausoleum floor.

Below the concrete bier containing the remains of Simon's parents lay the body of Edwin Drood, arms and legs unnaturally bent, one arm outstretched. The body was nearly covered in a white powder that didn't fully obscure Jennifer's Hermès scarf, which had been knotted around Drood's purplish neck and covered part of his chin. Something was wrong with Drood's nose; the prominent bump that had held his glasses in place was missing. Even though the no-longer-handsome face was distorted, Simon could see clearly: The bridge of Drood's nose was smooth and aquiline.

"Don't touch anything," said Deputy Gjovik, as Lionel began to lean down toward Drood's extended hand.

"But look," Lionel said, pointing to something inches away from Drood's twisted fingers.

Even the white dust didn't dull the flecks of light that glistened from the object just out of Drood's grasp: the Heart of Helsinki.

Detective Boggs arrived within ten minutes of Deputy Gjovik's call, bringing with her the scene-of-crime team, who immediately cordoned off the mausoleum and surrounding area. Zach and Lionel returned to the hotel with the Droodists; Simon remained behind, on the phone with Bartholomew Cuff, who was getting the library ready for Detective Boggs to use as an interview room for the witnesses.

"Drabb wants to know whether the deceased had his document," Cuff said.

"I don't know anything yet," said Simon, watching as the coroner began doing her work, while other officers photographed the body, the door of the mausoleum, the biers, the bits of white dust.

"When did the Droodists know that you would be stopping at the cemetery?" Detective Boggs asked, after Simon ended his call to Cuff.

"It was on the final version of the conference announcement. Most have known for weeks."

"The lock doesn't appear to have been forced."

"No." Simon explained about his call to the sexton.

"Did anyone know about that call?"

"Several people were nearby when I made it, and I might have mentioned it to several more. I'll have to think about that." He paused. "Do you know much about *The Mystery of Edwin Drood?*"

The detective shook her head. "I'm more a Jodi Picoult type."

Simon pursed his lips. So that's why he hadn't seen her browsing at Pip's Pages.

"Well," he said, "in the novel the young Edwin Drood disappears, but where he has gone, and whether he is alive or dead, forms the true mystery that Droodists have been debating since Dickens died with the book only half-finished."

While Simon spoke, Boggs watched the officers performing their work. Simon wished he had worn his winter coat; he hadn't expected to be outside so long and, while it wasn't raining, the wind was stronger here near the top of the hill.

"Many scholars believe that Dickens's solution to the mystery would have Drood's body hidden in a tomb and covered in quicklime to hasten its decomposition."

"Lime doesn't work that way," Detective Boggs said.

"Yes," Simon admitted, "but Droodists think Dickens didn't know that. In any case, even though the body was to have been decomposed beyond recognition, most scholars who theorize that Edwin Drood was murdered believe that he would have been identified by a rose-shaped ruby-and-diamond ring that he carried on his person, a fact that was unknown to the murderer."

Detective Boggs cocked an eyebrow. "That's interesting. Both the quicklime and the ring. I don't think that's quicklime in there, though," she said.

"Neither do I," said Simon. "I'm not a forensics officer, obviously, but it looks like flour."

"We'll know soon," said Detective Boggs.

"It's too eerie a connection not to be deliberate," said Simon. He pulled his coat more tightly around him to fend off the wind. "The young man—he's not who he said he was, is he?"

If Detective Boggs had been surprised at Simon's question, she did a good job of dissembling. "I can't discuss that with you," she said. "I'm waiting for instructions from the sheriff."

"I take it that Jennifer Wren had an interesting tale to tell."

"Given what has happened," said Detective Boggs, "I would call that an understatement."

The coroner's staff was now emerging from the mausoleum, carrying the body of Edwin Drood—or whoever he might turn out to be—in a black body bag. Simon lowered his head.

"You don't have to watch this," said Detective Boggs. "I can take you back to the hotel now."

Simon looked away. He had been such a nice young man.

"He was wearing a disguise," said Simon. He decided to tell her about his trip to Drood's room and the eyeglasses, and what he had noticed about Drood's nose.

"That will come out soon enough," said Detective Boggs, as she and Simon walked toward her unmarked car.

Back at the hotel, Simon and Detective Boggs separated. "I'll draw up my interview list from what you told me in the car," she said. "Those preliminary interviews will probably take about two hours or so. Why don't we meet in the library around five thirty? I'll call you."

Simon checked his watch. Three fifteen. "All right."

He found Bettina and Zach in the bar.

"I've canceled tonight's dance with the Dueling Duooses," Bettina said. "No one's in the mood for a polka after what happened today." She noticed Simon looking at the cocktail in her hand—bourbon rocks. "I decided it was five o'clock somewhere," she added, not at all defensively. Zach sipped a mineral water.

"I'll pass," Simon told the bartender (Bruuno since 2006). "I need to think clearly." He looked around. "Where's Quilpy?"

"In his room," Zach said. "He decided he didn't want to go to the emergency room."

"I gave him a Xanax," Bettina said. "He should sleep for a little while."

"And Osma? How is she holding up?"

"She's also in her room," Bettina said. "She's taken this quite hard. She really liked the young man and can't believe that he stole the Heart of Helsinki."

"Maybe he didn't," said Simon.

"Who was he—really?" Zach asked.

Simon shrugged his shoulders.

Bettina sipped her bourbon. "I'm going to check my conference records as soon as I finish this," she said. "But whoever he is, why would somebody kill him?"

Zach looked at Simon. "I think we're going to try to find that out," he said.

It was almost six o'clock before Simon received his call from Detective Boggs saying that she was ready to see him in Cuff's office, not the library. Cuff and Bettina were already there when Simon arrived. Cuff shut the door behind Simon, then locked it.

"I thought we were meeting in the library," said Simon.

Cuff looked at Detective Boggs. "We were," he said. "I went to prepare it and found the door locked. None of the guests mentioned it earlier; apparently no one has been trying to use the business center."

"Most people have their own laptops these days," Bettina offered. "And after the earlier event, I can imagine people wanting to stay holed up in their rooms."

"So I unlocked the door, and—"

"We believe that the library is where the man you know as Edwin Drood was killed," said the detective. "The crime scene officers are there right now, taking pictures and gathering evidence."

"There were signs of a struggle—" said Cuff.

"We don't know that for sure," Detective Boggs said, giving him a sideways glance, "but items were disturbed: a few books on the floor, chairs moved, etcetera."

"The window was open, too, and—"

Detective Boggs interrupted Cuff again. "We'll tell you what we can when we know," she said, looking at Simon.

She took a breath and then turned to Bettina. "Tell me about Edwin Drood. At least everything you know about his coming to this conference."

Bettina had made some notes and held a few faxes she had received from the International Society. "He registered for the conference online the day before it started, under the name Edwin Drood. That's why he wasn't on our preliminary rosters. He listed a Portland post office box as his mailing address."

Detective Boggs made a note. "Can you tell me when Jennifer Wren registered?"

Bettina looked confused but shuffled her papers. "I have all of the registrations with me. Ms. Wren registered two weeks before Mr. Drood," she said.

"It was covered in Quilpy's blog," said Simon.

"I have a copy of that blog post here." Detective Boggs pushed forward Quilpy's April 2 entry. It was dated one day after Jennifer had registered.

"What is the connection between Edwin Drood and Jennifer Wren?" Simon asked.

Detective Boggs took her cell from the desk and placed a call. "Are you prepared to see us now?" she asked, after exchanging greetings. "Yes. All right. We'll be right there." The detective ended the call and looked at Simon, then at Bettina and Cuff. "Ms. Wren wishes to tell you this herself. Against my advice, I might add."

They took the elevator to the fifth floor; the presidential suite was at the northeast corner of the hotel. Detective Boggs knocked lightly; Jennifer answered. She was wearing skinny indigo jeans, a winter-white boatneck sweater, and black flats. Her long hair was pulled back in a simple ponytail, a very youthful look.

"Please come in," Jennifer said.

The suite had a kitchen with small dining area on one end and, at the other, a full living room dominated by a baby grand piano and large brushed-steel fireplace. A maple spiral staircase led to a loft above, presumably the sleeping area, since no bed was visible on the main floor. The appointments were exquisite, maple accented with a lighter bird's-eye maple veneer on the cabinets in the kitchen and surrounding the granite kitchen.

Jennifer had arranged the room for her guests, and now gestured for them to sit. Large picture windows gave a commanding view of the Columbia River above the tops of the buildings on the other side of Commercial Street. As usual, several barges and container ships were lined up either waiting for a port berth farther upriver or to be piloted across the treacherous bar into the Pacific Ocean beyond. Tugboats moved between them like insects.

"May I offer you anything to drink?" Jennifer asked. "I don't often consume alcohol, myself, but I have a selection here if you'd like."

Although Bettina looked inclined to accept, all of them politely turned down her offer. Jennifer had already set glasses and a large pitcher of ice water on the low table within the circle of matching shell chairs and couch on which the four guests sat. Jennifer sat slightly apart, in a damask-striped accent chair. She tucked her legs underneath her.

"Thank you all for coming," she said. "I know this is unusual, but when I heard about the death of...the young man you called Edwin Drood, I was devastated. I told Detective Boggs this morning about an episode that happened last night that in itself was upsetting enough, but now that the young man is dead—" She ran her hands along her thighs and sat upright, gathering her emotions. "Last night, Lionel and I were having a conversation with Osma in the bar. She was sharing fascinating tales of her parents' childhood in Finland and their immigration here, and the stories behind the Heart of Helsinki. I'm sure we talked until well after midnight.

"Lionel accompanied us as far as the first floor and then continued to his own room. Osma and I began walking down the hall toward her room at the end. Mr. Drood, as I'll refer to him for now, was coming from the stairwell as we approached. I gave him a casual glance as we passed. I noticed that he wasn't wearing his glasses, and he seemed not to notice us at all—he was looking straight ahead. At that moment, Neva emerged from her room holding her room-service tray. Apparently she tripped on the carpet, lost her footing somehow—I don't know what—but suddenly her tray and its contents hit the floor. It made a horrible sound that stopped all four of us. Neva looked at Osma and me, then at Mr. Drood. I saw a look on his face that I can't describe. And I recognized him. For who he truly is. Was. He gasped, looked away from me, and then disappeared into the library. I heard the door lock behind him.

"I was agitated and scared, but I didn't want Osma to know. She had gone to ask Neva whether she needed help. Neva was mortified and apologetic, and the three of us cleaned up the tray and left it in the hall. I then saw Osma to her room. I went inside with her; I didn't want to see that man again, in case he emerged from the library right away, so I gave the pretense that I wanted to be sure Osma was completely safe. I stayed in her room a few minutes, and then left.

"I looked at the transom above the library, and the lights were still on. I almost tried the door, but I didn't want a confrontation, so I returned to my room and, despite the late hour, called my lawyers in Los Angeles."

Jennifer paused and took a drink of ice water. She looked at Detective Boggs over the glass.

"Let me tell this part," said the detective. "We believe that the deceased's real name is Newman Crump, and in 2008, Judge Winslow Fang of the county of Los Angeles issued an injunction barring Mr. Crump from appearing within fifty feet of Ms. Wren."

"He was a stalker?" Simon had not expected to be more shocked this day.

"Everything started innocently," Jennifer explained. "I remember seeing him for the first time—he didn't look the way he did here, no spiked hair, no glasses, no broken nose—a shy young man who came up to me at a restaurant, not long after the network airing of *Oliver Twist*, and asked for my autograph." She paused. "I'm a working actress, and I try to be nice to my fans when they are polite to me. I signed something for him. And then he started showing up near where I lived: at the grocery store, the dry cleaner's, various public events I attended. Then the private security firm that patrols my neighborhood found him searching the garbage cans. My lawyer sent a firm but polite letter asking him to stop stalking me."

Jennifer took a breath. "If anything," she said, after a pause, "the letter made things worse. The dry cleaner found him trying to break in the back of the shop to take a piece of my clothing. Mr. Crump found my cell phone number and started calling it multiple times daily, leaving messages about wanting to meet me, wanting to own something that belonged to me." Jennifer's eyes were tearing up, but no drops fell. "Eventually, Mr. Crump was arrested and was required to undergo a psychiatric evaluation. In early 2008, Judge Fang granted our request for a restraining order. It was the last time I heard from or about Mr. Crump."

"That's a long time ago," said Simon.

"I had almost forgotten him until the other night. It was the combination of him not wearing glasses, and the look of surprise on his face—that's when I realized who he was, and he must have realized that I had discovered his secret."

"If only some clue had come sooner," said Simon. "His Dickens knowledge was thin, but that is true of several people here." He paused and then looked back at Jennifer. "So you didn't see him again after he went into the library?"

Jennifer shook her head. "He had a troubled childhood, we learned from the psychological evaluation."

Jennifer looked at Detective Boggs. "Perhaps I shouldn't say more about that."

"No," said Detective Boggs. She looked at Simon and Bettina. "Mr. Crump's mother has been notified. She lives in Portland, where Mr. Crump also lived. She will be here tonight to identify the body."

"That's so tragic," Bettina said. "I would like to know how to extend my sympathies to her."

"I will let her know that when I see her," Detective Boggs said. She stood to leave.

"One more thing, Detective," Jennifer said, standing along with Bettina, Cuff, and Simon. "My agent called today and asked if I could go to Portland tomorrow for several television interviews related to an upcoming project and to have dinner and a meeting with a director considering me for a major movie role. I could be back here the following morning for any additional questions you might have of me." She looked genuinely pained by her request. "I'm not trying to be difficult, but it could be very important to my career."

Detective Boggs considered her request. "I have one condition. Because of the theft of Mr. Drabb's valuable document, and since we weren't able to conduct a thorough search before the discovery of Mr. Crump's body, would you consent to a search of your bag and any personal belongings?"

Jennifer didn't hesitate. "Of course," she said. She looked at Simon and Bettina. "I feel as if my attendance at this conference has caused such difficulty. I'm so sorry."

"It's not your fault," Bettina said. "Mr. Drood—I mean, Mr. Crump—was a troubled young man."

Simon turned to Detective Boggs. "Can we assume from your request of Ms. Wren, then, that the number plan was not found on the body?"

"You can assume nothing, Simon," Detective Boggs said. "I do not yet have preliminary reports from the coroner's office or the deputies who were in the library. The only thing I can tell you is that the insurance company for the Heart of Helsinki has called off its investigator. I hope to return the ring to Ms. Dilber as soon as it is no longer needed as evidence."

After agreeing that they would see Jennifer when she returned, all left the suite and moved toward the elevator.

Bart Cuff pushed the button to summon the elevator. "May I see whether your deputies have finished with the library?" he asked. "I'd like to open it to our guests again as soon as possible."

"You can," Detective Boggs answered, "but I can't guarantee that they'll be finished. It might not be ready before morning."

"Then we shall have to set up a temporary business center, perhaps in the lobby," he said. "We might have guests who need those services."

"Of course," said the detective. "I'm sure that wouldn't be a problem."

All four stepped into the elevator when it opened.

"I must call the society," Bettina said. "They've been texting me all day to find out what's going on. They may want me to cancel the rest of the conference."

"And not have Drabb give his presentation?" Simon asked. "That will be controversial... Of course, so is murder."

"I'll follow what they want me to do," Bettina said, "but I'll try to persuade them that the conference can continue."

"You can tell the society that my recommendation," said Detective Boggs, "is to proceed as normally as possible. We'll continue our interviews and investigation with the fewest possible disruptions."

They reached the first floor, and Cuff and Detective Boggs got off the elevator.

"I'm going to check on Neva Tupman and Osma Dilber," the detective said before the doors closed. "I need to double-check their versions of what Ms. Wren saw. Perhaps we can meet again before the evening is through. I have a feeling I'll be here at the hotel awhile."

Zach had texted Simon to meet him in the bar. When he got there, Zach was sitting with Quilpy; while Zach appeared to be nursing his first martini, Quilpy sat behind an empty glass with a half-full one in his hand.

"How are you?" Simon asked. Quilpy clearly had been crying: His eyes and cheeks were red.

"I'm a little better now," he said. "Zach has been überchill."

Simon looked at Zach, who shrugged his shoulders.

"I can't believe Droody's dead," Quilpy continued. "I

had started to believe that I might actually be boyfriend material after all."

"I need to make a stop," Zach said. "When I get back, why don't we take this man to dinner?" he suggested to Simon.

"Would you do that?" Simon asked Quilpy. "Let us treat you to dinner?"

"Sure," he said, sliding over to let Zach get out. Zach left the booth and crossed the bar toward the restrooms.

Simon, feeling unexpectedly avuncular, sat and put his arm around Quilpy. "So you and Droody were already getting serious? That soon?" Of course, the same had been true of him and Zach...

"You saw us together," Quilpy said. He took a swig from his martini. "We hit it off right away, you know, pinch-and-tickle things, some flirting, then a little more. I was pissed that he left me high and dry at the bar near midnight—*frustrated*, you know what I mean—and then everything yesterday was back to normal, getting more serious again as evening came along, and then, bam, he did it again."

"Did what?"

"Practically ran out my room, his shirt half off, saying he had something he had to do. I had my hand full, you know." He sniffled. "That was the last time I saw him." He started to cry quietly. Simon put his other arm around him and held Quilpy while he cried.

Zach returned and sat on the opposite side of the booth in silence until Quilpy pulled away from Simon's shoulder. "I think I'll be okay now," he said. "Thanks, dude." He pulled a nasty handkerchief from his jeans pocket and blew his nose.

"Let's get you fed," Zach said. "We can walk down the street to Jinx's for pizza and beer." He picked up his messenger bag from the table.

"Comfort food," Quilpy said, smiling and sniffling.

After ordering a double pepperoni and sausage pizza and pitcher of Black Butte Porter, Zach, Simon, and Quilpy sat at one of the rough-carved trestle tables, on backless short benches, in a corner away from Jinx's pool table and dartboard. The country music coming from the speakers in front didn't drift to the back, so they had this section of the restaurant all to themselves. Simon waved at locals that he knew. A few of the Droodists had wandered there as well.

"It's funny," Quilpy said, as if there hadn't been a break in their discussion, "that we hit it off so well, especially after we got into the argument about the Great Bloody Grewgious."

Simon poured beers for the three of them. "Go on," he said.

"Well," Quilpy started, after sipping the beer and wiping the foam from his lip, "I told him when it was over that it was a big fake."

Zach pulled out his messenger bag and shuffled around inside. "Say more about that," he said.

"Yeah," Quilpy said. "I saw the dude's show on my first Caribbean cruise two years ago, and I knew the minute I saw that chick do her crazy stuff that I'd seen it all before."

"Neva Tupman?" Simon asked.

"Yeah, her," Quilpy said. "She was in his show on the ship, acting like a chicken, everything she did the other night."

Zach pulled out the photos he had downloaded from the Internet and placed them on the table.

"See?" Quilpy said. "That's her." He pointed at the long-haired woman whose head had partially blocked Grewgious. "She was on the ship, so was Grewgious, and so was the hottie's sister." He meant Cecily, clearly, and pointed her out. "How'd you dudes find this?"

"I'm a reporter," Zach said. Simon was sure Zach was trying not to be unkind to Quilpy, another ostensible member of the "press."

"Talk about a zoo," Quilpy continued. "When that Carmichael was stolen—"

"Carbuncle," said Simon. "The Caracas Carbuncle."

The pizza arrived. Quilpy shoved a quarter of a slice into his mouth. "What. Ever," he mumbled. He chewed and swallowed. "When that rock was stolen, you'd have thought someone had stolen the frickin' Sistine Chapel."

Simon considered this interesting visual.

"Anyway," Quilpy continued, "there was a lot of suspicion on Hottie's sister, since she had been the dinner companion for the wrinkly old señora who owned the gem. Sister denied everything, and then the jewel showed up next day shoved behind a cushion or something like that."

"Something like that," Zach repeated.

"But tell us about Neva Tupman," said Simon. "You think—"

"She's a stooge," Quilpy said. "I know that word at least. Chunky, but nice legs, if you're into straight chicks." He looked at Zach. "Maybe you," he said and then nodded at Simon. "Not you."

"I wasn't hypnotized, either," Zach said. He recounted to Quilpy his on-stage whispering with Grewgious.

"See?" Quilpy pointed at Simon with the tip of his next slice of pizza. "I told Droody it was lame-o, but he insisted he had been hypnotized, because he'd had it done before, he said, lots of times."

Simon weighed whether he should discuss Jennifer Wren's revelations. He decided he should; this would be a safe place for Quilpy to express his feelings about what Simon was about to tell him. Otherwise, who knew how Quilpy would react? Plus, he really wanted Zach to know.

"Does the name Crump mean anything to you, Quilpy?" Simon asked. "Newman Crump?"

"No," Quilpy said. "Do I know the dude?"

Simon took a sip of beer. "That was the real name of the man we knew as Edwin Drood."

Quilpy started chewing. He had a smudge of pizza sauce on the tip of his turned-up nose; he looked fourteen years old. "He wouldn't tell me his real name," Quilpy said. "He told me lots of things—probably some of it TMI—but not his real name. I knew that Drood couldn't be right. After all, he's not even on itsmyface.com. And he wasn't a Dickens junkie. At least he didn't know much about any novels except *The Mystery of Edwin Drood* and *Oliver Twist,* and the only topic he seemed focused on with *Drood* was about that Obadiah Twinn dude." Quilpy looked at Simon. "Wasn't Twinn a doofus?"

"Many think so," Simon answered. "But he has his fans,

of course, Bucky Drabb and, apparently, Lionel Tartar—Hottie, to you—among them."

"Anyway, the rest of Droody's Dickens education was lame. After I kissed him for the first time, I said something like, 'We could be just like Eugene and Mortimer,' and he clearly didn't know what I was talking about."

"What kinds of things did he tell you?" Zach asked while Simon chewed on the pizza. Nice clean flavors, zesty sauce, real mozzarella. Quilpy had loaded his with red pepper flakes and extra parmesan from a dubious shaker at the table.

"He'd been through a lot of stuff as a child," Quilpy said. "Whatever it was, it landed him in therapy, and then he started shoplifting. He said he was a different person when he shoplifted, like the Artful Dodger. Except he wasn't so good at dodging. But that all stopped when he discovered Jennifer Wren."

"You knew about his…interest…in Jennifer?" Simon asked.

"Obsession would be more like it. He talked about her so much that I could barely get a word in to show him my own charms, you know? If I had ever gotten him into bed, I wonder whose name he would have shouted at the big *O*." Quilpy chewed his pizza; he appeared to be thinking. "He said that he was nearly over her, though, and this was the last time he would have to—no, he said *need* to—see her."

"Interesting choice of words." Simon then briefly explained to both of them what he had learned about Newman Crump's legal entanglements.

"So he had issues," Quilpy said defensively when Simon finished. "Doesn't everybody?"

Such cynicism so young, Simon thought. On second thought, the way Quilpy had said it didn't make him sound as much cynical as realistic.

"You said he was a different person when he shoplifted," said Simon. "Were those the words he used?"

"He used a bigger word. He said he 'dissociated.' I assume that means he checked out."

"I think it's more serious than that," said Simon.

"You mean he went Sybil on people?"

Simon decoded this. If he were going to be around Quilpy, he'd have to spend more time online at urbandictionary.com. "More or less," said Simon. "Did you tell any of this to Detective Boggs?"

Quilpy shook his head. "I answered the questions she asked. Nothing besides that. Did I know where he was, blah, blah, blah."

"You need to tell her these things when we get back to the hotel." Simon looked at Zach. "His mother will be arriving later tonight."

Quilpy started to tear up again; he wiped his eyes and nose with his hoodie. The pizza sauce smudge was now on his sleeve. "Man," he said, "he could have been a good boyfriend. I usually meet such flakes. I guess I did it again."

Zach put his arm around Quilpy's shoulders and pulled the smaller man toward him. "You'll find the man of your dreams some day. When you're not looking." He smiled his beautiful smile at Simon.

Zach picked up the bill for dinner, and the three men stood to leave. Simon ran through the things he wanted to discuss with Detective Boggs. Neva Tupman's relationship to Grewgious. The Caracas Carbuncle. Cecily Tartar. Newman Crump's *need* to see Jennifer Wren one last time.

Across the restaurant, Silas Cheeryble and Dean Minor were talking earnestly; they looked up and waved at Simon.

"Why don't you go back to the hotel," said Simon to Zach and Quilpy. "I want to talk to these two about a few things."

"You're going to play detective the way you did at Christmas, aren't you?" Quilpy asked. He was smiling.

"I'm not playing," said Simon. "But I want to help out however I can."

Zach gave him a peck on the cheek as he and Quilpy left the restaurant. Simon went over to the table with Cheeryble and Minor.

"May I join you?" he asked.

"Sure," said Cheeryble. "We've been talking about what all of us most likely are discussing at dinner tonight."

Simon sat facing Minor. He had on the same limp corduroy jacket he had worn to these conferences for years—not threadbare, but it had seen better days. His shirt collar had a blood spot on it from shaving that morning (or at some time in the past), and at least one of the lenses of his glasses was smudged with something that would have driven Simon crazy (if he still wore glasses). Cheeryble had changed into a colorful crazy-knit sweater so out of style that he actually looked eccentrically stylish.

"Of course the murder of that young man is terrible," Minor said. "Do you think he was the thief?" He was eating a spinach salad, probably the only one served at Jinx's that evening.

"Things look bad." Cheeryble had ordered deep-fried mozzarella sticks that he dipped into a tiny cast-iron cauldron of ranch dressing. The remnants of a small pizza were on the plate beside him. "But if he stole Drabb's document, where is it?"

"That's the mystery," Minor said.

"Not really," said Simon, finding this irritating. "Who killed Edwin Drood is the mystery."

"I hope there's a solution," Minor said. "Dickens never gave us one the first time around."

Simon decided not to divulge Newman Crump's identity; these two could find out along with everyone else.

"How did you gentlemen spend last evening after dinner?" Simon asked.

"I was in my room," Cheeryble said. Cheeryble and Minor, Simon knew from the chart Cuff had given him, had fourth-floor rooms on opposite sides of the main hall. Cecily occupied the room at the end of the hall. "I had a nightcap and did some pleasure reading. I'm working my way through the oeuvre of Sheridan Le Fanu for the third time."

"A remarkable, if questionable, achievement," said Simon.

Cheeryble giggled. "I didn't hear a thing," he continued. "I use earplugs. So many hotels make noises in the night, or the guests do."

"I had work to do," Minor said. "I didn't return to my room until after midnight. I was having trouble with my Internet connection, so I went down to the library to use the computer."

"Really?" Simon asked. "How late?"

"At least until midnight." Minor paused. "Oh, I see. That's where Drood was murdered, wasn't he?"

"Detective Boggs hasn't confirmed that, but it appears likely."

"Well," Minor continued, "Nothing happened while I was there. And when I returned to my room, I'm pretty sure both Silas's and Ms. Tartar's transoms were dark."

"Of course, that doesn't mean we were in our rooms," Cheeryble said. "I suppose I'm a suspect, although I had not met Mr. Drood before this conference, and I'm not sure I exchanged twenty words with him while he was here."

"I had never seen him before, either," Minor said. "Had anyone?"

Simon had been contemplating this exact question. Only Jennifer Wren claimed a prior knowledge of Newman Crump; could she have been the murderer, covering her guilt by outing Edwin Drood after the fact? Anything was possible. No one else at the conference claimed to know Drood, yet someone had reason enough to kill the young man and desecrate not only his body but Simon's family's mausoleum. Simon pushed away his feelings.

Minor continued talking. "I had a pleasant brief conversation with him at the opening get-together. His Dickens knowledge was spotty, but I find that to be the case in almost all young people these days," he added. "They think they can substitute Masterpiece Theatre DVDs for a close reading of the texts."

That comment made Cheeryble laugh; even Simon chuckled. As Brock had told him several times in the store, "It's all good." The world would keep turning.

Simon turned back to Dean Minor. Keeping in mind what Boggs had told him about the room, he asked, "What were the condition of the books in the library when you were there?"

"The books? I didn't touch them. I had my own materials with me. The only thing I did was open and close the laptop that's on the desk."

"Did you open a window?"

Minor frowned. "At this time of year?"

"What will happen with Bucky's presentation?" Silas asked. "People want to know."

Simon wondered that himself. "I'm going to try to find Bettina when I get back to the hotel," he said. "We may need to have an executive committee emergency meeting. But the real power rests with the international committee. They could cancel us if they think the publicity is harmful to the society."

"When will we find out whether Mr. Drood stole the number plan?"

"Soon," said Simon. "At least, I hope it will be soon."

When Simon checked his cell again, he found a text from Bettina asking him to meet with her and Bucky Drabb in the bar. Bettina was having a martini. As Simon sat beside Bucky, he smelled the bourbon. The drink in Bucky's hand clearly wasn't his first, or second, of the evening.

"I'm so glad you're back," Bettina said. "I'm almost at my wits' end." She didn't look it, of course; her makeup and dress were as strikingly perfect as ever. She was a fashion machine.

"Have you heard from the international society?"

"Several times," she said, with exasperation. "The time difference between here and London makes things difficult. It's dawn there, so the international secretary has been up most of the night discussing our little event here in Oregon. I'm surprised some of them could even find us on the map."

"What have they said?" Simon asked.

"At first," she said, sipping her drink, "they wanted everything canceled."

"Damn fools," Drabb said. He swirled his bourbon, clinking the ice cubes.

"I told them I thought that was both unnecessary and inconvenient," Bettina continued. "Detective Boggs told me that she will have questions for many of us and hopes that the conferees will stay put."

"Except for Jennifer Wren," said Simon.

"Yes," Bettina admitted. "So the committee asked me to compromise—delay the conference by one day, to show sympathy for the death, and then continue the day after that with Buckminster's presentation."

"I can do it without the original, of course," he said. "But I wanted a show." At least, Simon thought, he was being honest about that.

"What is happening with the insurance?" Simon asked.

Normally, Drabb would have found questions, particularly from Simon, annoying. But his own culpability in the loss of the number plan had subdued him. Either that or the bourbon had shaved away the surface hostility.

"Paperwork," Drabb said. "I've filled out online forms and have talked with people both in London and in New York. They're very anxious about having to pay a claim. They want to send an investigator; I think someone will be here before everyone leaves the conference."

"How is Osma, by the way?" Simon asked.

"She went to her room early," Bettina said, "on the advice of Detective Boggs. The more she thought about Cr— Drood," she corrected herself, "the more agitated she got. So she ordered room service and said she would see us in the morning. I made sure she was snug before I came down here."

"Then I won't call her," said Simon. "I want her to rest."

"This is hard on all of us," said Drabb, taking the final sip of his drink. He shook his glass in the air until the bartender saw him and nodded.

"So," Bettina said, "what do you think about a delay? I've talked with the hotel staff, and they believe they can shuffle the few guests scheduled to come in so we can have the hotel another day. The next conference isn't due to begin until after the weekend, and we'll be long gone before that."

"It sounds reasonable to me," said Simon, "if you're agreeable, Bucky."

"When have I ever been agreeable?" he asked.

A brief silence ensued.

"Then that's that," Bettina said. "I'll have a notice delivered to all of the conferees in their rooms within an hour." She turned to Drabb. "Your scholarship will receive the attention it deserves. People came to hear about the number plan. With an extra day, we stand a better chance that the detective will find it. Perhaps she has it already."

"They should search every guest's room—starting with Dean Minor's."

"You don't think he stole it, or killed that young man, do you?" Bettina asked.

"Why not?" Drabb asked. "Somebody here did. Who would you like it to be? The pushy little blogger? The jet-setting brother or sister? Maybe even Simon?" He gave Simon a leer.

"This is monstrous," Bettina said.

Simon frowned. "I hate to say it, but I think Bucky is right. It almost certainly has to be one of us. So who would you like to believe murdered that young man?"

When Simon returned to the hotel lobby, Detective Boggs was standing near the lobby desk, talking to Neva Tupman. When Neva saw Simon, she thanked Detective Boggs and moved to the elevator. She took one more look at Simon as she entered the elevator before the door closed behind her.

"I have some news about her," said Simon, "news that Daniel Quill didn't mention to you earlier. And several other bits about Newman Crump."

"And I have news about both of them as well," said Detective Boggs. "Why don't you come into Mr. Cuff's office and we'll talk."

She led him behind the desk into the warren of staff offices and cubbyholes, including an overflow storage pantry for the commercial kitchen in the basement. As Simon and Bettina approached Cuff's door, a catering employee lifted a sack of sugar from a low metal shelf in the open pantry and placed it on a cart, pulled the door closed behind him, then wheeled the cart toward the service elevator.

Inside Cuff's closed office, Detective Boggs took the chair behind Cuff's desk, while Simon sat in an old-fashioned polished-oak guest chair.

Simon repeated most of what Quilpy had told him and Zach, leaving out a few of Quilpy's more leading suggestions about where his relationship with Crump might have been going, since Simon didn't think they had any bearing on Crump's murder.

"So Quilpy, Neva Tupman, Grewgious, and Cecily Tartar were all on the same cruise ship when this famous jewel, the Caracas Carbuncle, went missing," said Simon. "And more interesting, Quilpy remembered seeing Neva Tupman perform exactly as she did here."

"You've said several interesting things," said Detective Boggs. "But let's start with Neva Tupman's identity. She just confessed to me, although she most curiously did not mention the missing...carbuncle." She had to look at her notes for the word. "As she tells her story, she has been employed from time to time as a performer in the Great

Grewgious's stage shows. She's a graduate student in psychology, and her minor as an undergrad was theater, so she thought she was a natural to feign hypnosis. She has been employed by Grewgious and at least two other stage hypnotists to, as she says, 'augment' their performances."

"Augment?"

"She has two assignments. Her first is to scout the crowd, looking for the best candidates for hypnosis. She looks for an outgoing personality, someone with a playful nature, and someone who presents as imaginative, highly suggestible, or dramatic."

Simon thought of the people chosen: Drabb, dramatic; Drood, suggestible; Law, theatrical, to a keen eye. Only Zach didn't seem to fit the bill—he was outgoing but not suggestible or dramatic—and maybe that was why the hypnosis wasn't successful for him, if it were successful for anyone.

"She swears Grewgious is the real deal, and she's there to make sure that the very worst doesn't happen, that Grewgious misses his mark for all of the participants."

Simon told Detective Boggs that Zach had not been hypnotized but that Drood had sworn to Quilpy that he had been under Grewgious's influence.

"From Neva Tupman's perspective," Detective Boggs said, "the performance here was typical, except for Mr. Crump's less than funny behavior on stage."

"I have a comment about that," said Simon, "but we'll come back to it when we're done talking about Neva."

"I followed up with Ms. Tupman about meeting Jennifer Wren and Mr. Crump in the hall. Unfortunately, she had no insight about that. She was embarrassed by the noise she had caused at that late hour, and she was concerned that she had upset Osma Dilber. She remembered that Mr. Crump had been in the hallway, she said, and didn't remember anything other than that he went into the library and shut the door behind him."

"And she didn't hear anything later? When Drood was being murdered practically next door to her?"

Detective Boggs pursed her lips. "She claims to be a sound sleeper. I haven't yet told you what the scene-of-crime officers found. It appears most likely that Newman Crump was strangled in the library sometime after midnight. We believe his body was tossed out the library window to the alley below, and then transported to the mausoleum. The flour was tossed around to give the impression of quicklime, as you have described." She checked her notes. "One of the deputies is an amateur Droodist herself. She's the one who agreed with your assessment."

"How grisly," said Simon. "How unfeeling."

"Murder tends to be that way," said Detective Boggs. "Either no feelings or too many feelings leads to the disrespect for life."

"The number plan," said Simon. "Was it found on the body?"

"It is still missing." Detective Boggs flipped a few pages back in her notes. "But to finish up with Neva Tupman. She wanted me to be sure that she could have no reason to be involved in any of these crimes—the thefts nor the murder—and she thought the best thing to do was to tell everything she knows."

"Not everything," said Simon, "if she didn't tell you about the Carbuncle."

"Perhaps," said Detective Boggs. "She wants to leave in the morning. She has another job in Seattle this weekend, and the stage hypnotist that she'll be working with wants to go over his expectations for her performance."

"Are you going to let her go?"

"I see no reason to keep her here. I have all of her information, and she was quite cooperative. But before she leaves, I will make sure I ask her about the theft and do a thorough search of her luggage for the number plan. Now, tell me what else you know of this cruise."

Simon told Detective Boggs what Zach had uncovered on the Internet and confirmed by Quilpy. "Apparently," said Simon, "most of the suspicion about the disappearance of the carbuncle swirled around Cecily Tartar, but when the jewel was found, the investigation was stopped at the owner's request."

"Ms. Tartar said that she went for a late-night walk the night Crump was killed," Detective Boggs said. "And the desk clerk could confirm that she was out during that time."

"What a strange time to be taking a walk."

"She claimed that she walked to the river and watched the ships. She said it was peaceful, and helped calm her from some issues between her and her brother. They argued earlier in the evening."

"Issues?"

"She declined to elaborate," said the detective. "She said they were family matters not connected to any of the crimes."

"Do you believe her? Maybe she's trying to cover up something, trying to protect her brother."

Detective Boggs had the faintest smile at the corners of her mouth. "At least as far as Newman Crump's murder, Lionel Tartar doesn't need any further protection."

"What does that mean?" Simon asked.

"Well," said the detective, "unless there's a conspiracy that I'm too dense to see, Mr. Tartar has an alibi for the entire time Mr. Crump could have been murdered."

"What is that?"

"After Ms. Wren returned to her room, she called Mr. Tartar. And, she says, from then until just after dawn, he never left her company in the presidential suite."

With that, Detective Boggs looked at her watch.

"Now," she continued, after taking what Simon considered a dramatic pause, "what I have told you will come out eventually, but you don't need to tell anyone else, even Zach. I need to be ready to receive Myrtle Crump, Newman's mother. She is scheduled to arrive here around ten o'clock tonight. She said she couldn't afford to miss her shift at work, poor woman. We've arranged for her to stay here after she identifies the body."

"I would like to express my condolences to her," said Simon, "as would Bettina and, I'm sure, a few of the others."

"I'll tell her, but I suggest you wait until morning."

Simon stood, as did Detective Boggs.

"Now," she added, "I'm going to be tied up for the rest of the night with Ms. Crump. And I'm guessing that you and Zach will be descending like Holmes and Watson on the Great Grewgious, won't you?"

That was already uppermost in Simon's mind.

"I wish you wouldn't," she said. She came around Cuff's desk and opened the door for Simon. "But I know you will. Remember: Last time you could have been seriously hurt because of your 'assistance.'"

Simon was going to protest that he had done more than 'assist' the detective but decided against it.

"I will take your advice to heart," he said. "But I might have to visit the bar for a nightcap before I go home. And you never know who I might find there."

During his discussion with Detective Boggs, Simon had received a voice mail from Zach; after watching Quilpy down three lemon drops at the bar while Simon had been with Detective Boggs, Zach had decided that Quilpy would be in better hands sleeping things off at Gad's Hill Place, so he had taken him there and put him in the Growlery, one of Simon's guest rooms (and the same place Zach had spent the night that Simon met him). Zach would see Simon when he returned home.

That was good news. Simon felt sorry for Quilpy. Simon wanted to believe that Newman Crump, whatever problems he must have had (and Simon was convinced they were considerable), was fundamentally a good young man. So what had happened? Why had he stolen Osma's ring—if he did steal it? And why did he steal Drabb's number plan—if he did steal it? Where was the number plan? And why was Crump murdered, and by whom? The only sure thing right now was that Newman Crump was dead and his poor mother, in the next hour or so, would have to identify his body. Simon could think of nothing more heartbreaking than that.

Lionel Tartar and Grewgious were sitting together in the bar when Simon poked his head in. "There's a pair to draw to," Simon's grandfather would have said. What could the two of them possibly have in common, besides Grewgious's tenuous—but interesting—connection to Cecily? Simon was about to find out.

"May I join you?" he asked.

Grewgious's arm flourish was fit for the stage; Lionel was polite but reserved. Grewgious was drinking a martini, while Lionel sipped white wine.

"I hope the conference is not totally ruined," Grewgious said. "We see that Bettina has issued a postponement."

"Yes," said Simon. "I saw the bulletin board as I came in." He turned to Lionel. "Will that be an inconvenience for you?"

"It will," Lionel answered, "but I can't leave here without hearing Drabb give his talk. I have a feeling he will fulfill his promise and blow the lid off the Droodist world."

Lionel was the Dickens future—cockier, more self-assured, than the generations that preceded him.

"Do I understand that you are of the Twinn tradition?" Simon asked.

"I am," Lionel said.

Simon turned to Grewgious. "I should apologize. I don't usually talk shop in the presence of non-Dickensians."

"Go right ahead," Grewgious said. "I'm beginning to find these topics fascinating. Tell me about the various theories that you Droodists espouse."

"Well," said Simon, "there are two basic schools—the Jasper tradition and the Twinn tradition. Jasperites, and I am one, believe that Dickens's mystery is not so much *who* killed Edwin—since Jasperites are almost unanimous in our belief that Drood was murdered by his uncle, John Jasper—as *how* the crime was committed. And the answer is, possibly under the influence of opium, or in a dissociative state. Some believe that, if Dickens had finished the novel, Robert Louis Stevenson would never have needed to write *The Strange Case of Doctor Jekyll and Mr. Hyde,* since Dickens would have introduced the concept of split personality, with all of its symbolic connection to the dual nature of Victorian morality."

"Well summarized," Lionel said. "The Twinn tradition is the product of the prodigious mind of Obadiah Twinn, who wrote extensively on the potential endings of *Edwin Drood,* the novel, that is. Using both textual and police-procedural methodologies, Twinn espoused several possible endings to the book, none of which had John Jasper as the murderer, at least not directly."

"Fascinating," Grewgious said.

"One of Twinn's theories," Lionel continued, "the one that Bucky Drabb is most likely to claim as the true theory when he gives his presentation—is that the exotic female twin Helena Landless murdered Drood while under the mesmeric influence of Jasper."

"That would show a primitive understanding of how hypnosis actually works," Grewgious said.

Simon leaned forward. "Really?"

"Hypnosis plays upon the suggestibility of the subject," Grewgious said. "But modern hypnosis therapy posits that a subject will only perform acts that he or she believes are reasonable. A subject will not, under most if not all circumstances, perform an act that he or she thinks morally repugnant. There are limits to suggestibility."

"Professor Twinn had an answer for that," Lionel said. "At least, he had a speculation. He believed that Dickens knew the truth of what you are saying but, at the end of his creative life, thought that cheating in the interests of a dramatic story would be worth the sensation that such an idea would cause."

"I will have to defer to you on that," Grewgious said. "Authors often manipulate truths to serve their fictional ends."

"Twinn had other theories, too," Simon added. "He was not alone in believing that one of the possible endings would have Edwin Drood returning alive with some sensational explanation for his disappearance."

"How unfortunate that such won't happen with *our* Edwin Drood," Grewgious said, his voice low and somber.

Simon paused. For a glimmer of a second, that possibility passed through him with a thrill, a hope that made his stomach flutter. Then the impossibility of it returned with an image of the mottled face on the floor of the family mausoleum. "Yes," he said, his voice catching.

"But to finish up with Twinn," Lionel said, "since you're so fascinated with him. His theories about Helena

Landless murdering Edwin Drood are what have caused his posthumous reputation to be so uneven and unstable right now."

"The murder of a young man by a woman, a twin," Grewgious said. "Something I'm sure, Lionel, that you hope is not true in this case."

Simon almost gasped at this. Lionel certainly didn't like it, and stood immediately.

Grewgious realized his faux pas and held out his hand. "I apologize for my insensitivity. I meant to imply nothing."

"Yes," Lionel said, his neck tight, the cords standing out from the sides. "Excuse me, gentlemen, but I need to return to my room. I need to catch up on e-mails and some work for my dissertation. Good night." He left the bar with a determined stride.

"I meant no harm," Grewgious said.

"Of course not," said Simon, not so sure he meant his words. "Everyone is on tenterhooks right now." He took a sip of his drink. "I'm surprised you're staying on at the conference," Simon continued.

"I had contemplated leaving," Grewgious said, "but my room and rental car are paid for. I have a house sitter in Phoenix, and my next engagement isn't until next week, so I decided to stay, perhaps see the local sights tomorrow, and enjoy the relatively slow pace of this pleasant town—slow, I imagine, outside of the hotel and the events of the last few days." His voice continued its dangerously soothing quality.

"Your assistant, Neva Tupman, has decided to leave tomorrow."

Grewgious raised an eyebrow, opened his mouth as if to speak, and then instead took a sip of his cocktail. "I'm not surprised," he said after a long pause. "She called earlier today, and I knew from her voice that she was under strain. Apparently she had spent a very pleasant half-hour with Edwin."

"You aren't embarrassed that I know you used a stooge?"

Grewgious spread his palms across his belly. "I have had a long and interesting career. I have not always been a performer. And I have learned not to be 'embarrassed,' as you say, by the realities of the form of show business I perform. Neva, and your friend Zach, feigned hypnosis for entertainment purposes. Were people not entertained?"

"Is that the question?"

"It is for me," Grewgious replied. "My contract specifies that I am an entertainer, not a clinical psychologist performing therapy for patients. I must be sure that I will always have entertainment on the stage, in the unlikely event that the volunteers do not submit to the hypnosis or to my occasional requests to simulate it. I assure you that I have legitimate credentials."

"I don't doubt that," said Simon. "You must have been surprised," he continued, "to see Cecily Tartar here at the conference when you arrived."

Grewgious again raised his eyebrow. "Because?"

"Because you and she were on the SS *Excess of the Seas* when the Caracas Carbuncle disappeared."

"You know about that."

"Quilpy—Daniel Quill—was also on that cruise and remembered you."

"I don't remember seeing him on the cruise, but Ms. Tartar—she is unforgettable, don't you think?"

"She is a beautiful woman," said Simon.

"And mysterious, and exotic, and very, *very* dangerous," Grewgious said. "If you know about the cruise, you know then that much of the suspicion about the jewel's disappearance centered on her."

"So I've gathered from Internet news accounts."

"I had the pleasure of meeting her at the captain's reception," Grewgious said, "and then didn't see her again until in the dining room on the day the jewel disappeared. Along with the dowager Whozit from Wherezit, Cecily and I were seated at the captain's table. I thought it amusing, actually, because Cecily had told me at the reception that she didn't believe in what I did and wouldn't attend my performances as a result. She dismissed me in the most charming way, as you can imagine."

"Of course," said Simon.

"I hold no ill will toward her for her misconceptions about hypnosis." Grewgious scrutinized his empty glass. "What else have the sheriff's deputies learned? Do they know how and when young Edwin died?"

"I only know a few details," said Simon. "But I believe he was murdered here at the hotel after midnight, and then his body was taken to the mausoleum and staged, presumably for us to discover the next day."

"Such a pity. He was an amiable young man. I was in bed early last night. I thought I heard a noise coming from across the hall well after midnight, but I could have been mistaken. Whatever it was, I did not rise to investigate."

"It might have been Bucky Drabb," said Simon, knowing from Cuff's chart that Grewgious and Drabb both had rooms on the second floor. "He apparently had a few too many drinks and was late returning to his room."

Grewgious put his empty glass on the table. "That should serve as a signal to me that I have had enough myself for the night. I must maintain a clear head for my day tomorrow." He stood and extended his meaty paw. "I hope I will see you sometime tomorrow, Simon. You have a keen mind I would like to know better."

Zach was drinking chamomile tea in the nook with a stack of papers and his laptop open in front of him when Simon arrived. Zach was shirtless with pajama bottoms, so apparently (to Simon's delight) he had decided to stay the night at Gad's Hill. Simon kissed him, poured himself a Glenfarclas on the rocks, and sat across from Zach.

"How is Quilpy?" Simon asked.

"Out like the proverbial light. I practically had to carry him into bed once he got here. Fortunately, I haven't heard any noises coming from the guest bath, so I'm hoping he'll sleep it off and not get sick."

"I feel sorry for him," said Simon. "He's a good young man, even if he is high maintenance."

Zach smiled. "I hope you don't think that about me."

Instead of answering aloud, Simon admired Zach's well-defined chest, the hair trailing down and disappearing beneath the drawstring waistband of the pajamas. First things first, however...

"Neva Tupman spilled the beans to Detective Boggs," said Simon. "And she's leaving the conference in the morning. The interesting thing is that Grewgious didn't seem to mind."

"It's probably not the first time he's been caught," Zach said.

Simon looked through the stack of papers and found the information about the Carbuncle of Caracas. He read it through again quickly. "Grewgious pretty much confirmed what this says," he told Zach. "He called Cecily a dangerous woman. I didn't ask him why."

"She stands next to disappearing jewels too often if you ask me."

"But if she's a thief, she hasn't been caught," said Simon.

"Yet," Zach said. "The Tartars are still phonies, though, both of them."

"How?" Simon asked. "I've seen Lionel's credentials and have read at least two of his papers in *The Dickensian*."

"I mean about being from the Seychelles. I brought it up again today, asked him when he was last in Port Moresby, the capital. He said they left the islands when he was young, about eight, and hadn't been back since."

"And the problem with that is?"

"Port Moresby is the capital of Papua New Guinea, not the Seychelles. The capital city of the Seychelles is Victoria. An old trick, I admit, but it worked here."

"Why would someone make up something like that?" Simon held his drink in one hand; with the other he traced his finger along the line of Zach's sternum.

"Beats me," Zach said. "Hey, that tickles."

"Good," said Simon. A different thought crossed his mind; he checked his watch. "It's after ten. I suppose by now that Mrs. Crump has identified her son's body." Simon told Zach about the time of the murder and how Crump's body was pushed out of the library window.

"That's gruesome," said Zach.

"And risky," said Simon. "It makes me think that the murder was possibly an accident, or at least unplanned."

"How did the murderer leave and return to the hotel unnoticed?" Zach asked. He reached out and started to unbutton Simon's shirt.

"There's a back entrance," said Simon. "So there might be a back stairs also." He felt Zach's warm finger now matching his own, running down his chest, around his left nipple. "I'll have to check them out tomorrow."

Zach pulled Simon's shirttails out from his chinos. "Yes, more investigating to do."

"By the way," said Simon, trying to pull his day together in his mind, despite the current distractions, "Brock asked me if I would be his best man."

"Awesome," Zach said. His finger now circled Simon's right nipple. "You'll be great at that. We already know that you look hot in a tuxedo."

"Why thank you," said Simon. He let his mind wander, as Zach's hand did the same. "Nothing makes sense. We don't know why the jewel was stolen, why Drood was killed, or where Drabb's number plan is. And how did Jennifer's scarf end up around Drood's neck? My head can't handle all of the questions." He pulled at the drawstring on Zach's pajamas, loosening the knot.

"Then give it a rest," said Zach. He stood, pulling Simon up with him, and then kissed him. "You have other investigating to do right now."

April 19

7:30–9:00 a.m.	Continental Breakfast	Hotel bar
9:15 a.m.–noon	Plenary Session: "At Last! The Truth of Number Plan Six"	Buckminster Drabb, Columbia River Room
Noon–12:15 p.m.	Closing Remarks/ Droodist cheer	Bettina Law; Simon Alastair, conference coordinator Columbia River Room
12:15–2:00 p.m.	Conference ends/Check out	Hotel lobby

The events scheduled for today have been postponed until the same time tomorrow. Please see Bettina Law or Simon Alastair if you have any questions.

DAY FIVE

Simon and Zach were at breakfast when Quilpy staggered into the kitchen. The pajamas Zach had found for him, light blue with big white clouds, were much too big—the legs dragged on the ground and the pajama top fell almost to his knees.

"Dude," Jude Hexam said, handing him a full mug of fine Sumatran, "you need this bad."

Quilpy took the coffee from him, mumbled an introduction, and plopped down in the empty chair between Simon and Zach.

"Christ, was I drunk last night," he said. "Did I do anything—anyone—that I would regret?"

Zach chuckled. "Everyone's virtue has remained intact."

Jude placed a plate of scrambled eggs with pommes Anna and a buttered English muffin with gooseberry jelly in front of Quilpy. "Here, mate," he said, "eat up."

After giving Jude an up-and-down look of pleasant surprise—at Jude's cooking or his physique, Simon wondered—Quilpy attacked the food as if he hadn't eaten for days.

"Since the conference events are postponed," Zach said to Simon, "what are your plans for the day?"

Simon finished his poached egg and the last bit of his pumpernickel toast. "I would like to check in with Brock at the store, then go to the hotel and look at the back entrance."

"Why do you want to do that?" Quilpy asked.

Simon almost reached over to dab a smudge of jam away from Quilpy's cheek. "Trying to understand what happened when Newman Crump was murdered." He didn't need to get too detailed with Quilpy right now.

Simon's cell vibrated with an incoming text message from Detective Boggs.

"But my first event of the day will be to meet Newman Crump's mother," he said. He watched as Quilpy devoured half of the English muffin in two bites. "She would like to see you, too."

Myrtle Crump was a small, slender woman, not more than five feet tall. Her brown hair had started to gray and was pulled into a simple knot behind. She had soft blue eyes, dainty hands rough from some kind of work and, Simon guessed, was anywhere from forty-five to fifty-five, although she looked older. She had on a simple wool coat over a flower-print dress.

"I'm so sorry for your loss," said Simon.

Detective Boggs sat behind Cuff's desk, and Myrtle Crump sat in front. Simon and Quilpy took the two chairs beside the desk.

Quilpy started to tear up; he took Ms. Crump's hand but wasn't able to say much more than his name.

"You're the young man Newman mentioned," she said. "In his last call to me." Her voice sounded tired; Simon assumed she had been crying, but her eyes were dry now.

"He talked about me?" Quilpy sniffled. Simon handed him a tissue.

"He talked a lot about being here," she said. "At first he felt guilty for having come, but after he talked with Ms. Tupman and with you, he started enjoying himself more. I had hoped to meet her also, but Detective Boggs told me she left early this morning. But he talked most about you," Ms. Crump said, her tired blue eyes searching Quilpy's face. "He thought you were a special young man."

Quilpy tried to say something but blew his nose instead.

Detective Boggs, dressed in navy pants and a pastel lime blouse, leaned forward. "I know you had a difficult time last night," she said. "I hoped this morning you would be able to tell us about your son. Perhaps you know something of significance."

Myrtle Crump rested her hands in her lap, but they didn't stay rested—she constantly moved them as she talked, rubbing them together. "I won't lie," she said, "Newman had a difficult childhood, and much of it was my fault, because I was working all of the time. I divorced his father, Colum, when Newman was young, and his father and I didn't see one another after that, although he dutifully paid his child support. So I often left Newman in the company of my brother, Hiram."

She took a tissue from her small black purse and rubbed her eyes. "He...abused...Newman for almost two years," she continued, "from the time Newman was ten until his twelfth birthday, when Newman told me everything. Hiram went to prison, but Newman started having problems after that."

"What sort of problems, Ms. Crump?" Detective Boggs asked.

"Stealing. Shoplifting. He got caught several times. I was able to keep him out of a detention center, although it cost me everything I had. And sometimes he changed. The psychologist called it dissociation—you know, multiple personalities. Newman sometimes became a different person, with a different name—Jack Dawkins—and a different past. I didn't see Jack Dawkins often. Most of the time he came out during therapy, or just before Newman stole something. But when I saw him, somehow I was Jack Dawkins's mother, too."

Quilpy was crying quietly.

"Then, when Newman was fifteen," Ms. Crump continued, "two things happened that changed everything, part for better, part for worse. First, his father died. Without telling me, Colum had taken out a life-insurance policy with Newman as beneficiary, and the benefit paid at his death was more than one hundred thousand dollars, enough for Newman to go to college and have a better life than I could give him."

Myrtle Crump stopped talking; Simon watched her face. He assumed she was reliving some memory.

After a pause, Detective Boggs spoke. "What else happened?"

"Newman saw Jennifer Wren. On television, playing that prostitute in *Oliver Twist*. After that, he became obsessed with her—not in a sexual way, but obsessed. He stopped dissociating at about the same time, as if his fascination with her gave him a focus that required his full time as Newman. I never saw the Jack Dawkins personality after that television show." She looked around the office. "May I have some water, please?"

Quilpy jumped up, flew out of the office, and returned with a bottle of water and a glass with ice. He put them on the desk in front of Ms. Crump. She reached out and put her hand on his. "Thank you so much."

Quilpy quickly sat and sniffled again.

Ms. Crump sipped at her water and smoothed her dress before talking again. "Newman attended the University of Oregon and graduated with a bachelor's degree in English. He came out during his freshman year, and even brought boyfriends home to meet me. But his relationships didn't last long."

"Why was that?" Detective Boggs asked.

"He never fully understood," she said, "but I think it was because he was so tentative about everything, afraid that letting his emotions go might somehow cause Jack Dawkins to reappear. He was so afraid of that, even as he became more obsessed with Jennifer Wren, and as she became a real movie star. When he graduated, he moved to Los Angeles; that's when he started trying to meet Jennifer—when he began stalking her."

She paused and took another drink of water. "I love my son," she said, first looking at Detective Boggs, then at Simon and Quilpy, "but he has done some things that were wrong, shameful. The last straw was when he was caught rummaging in her garbage. That's when the restraining order was issued. I begged him to return to Portland, to live with me until he could get over his feelings about her. He went back into therapy and started improving." At this comment, Ms. Crump smiled. The smile wavered and disappeared.

"Everything was better, until a few months ago. He had moved out into his own place, had gotten the job at the bookstore, and was talking about his future, starting to hope he would meet a life partner and build something lasting, he said." She paused again for another sip of water. "Then he saw something on the Internet a few weeks ago about Jennifer Wren appearing here, in Oregon, at this conference. And he decided he had to go, see her one more time, get her out of his system, he told me. I tried to stop him, but he promised me this would be the very last time." She reached into her purse and took out a small photograph. She handed it to Quilpy. "Here is my son, the real Newman. Without the spiked hair, without the false nose and eyeglasses that he bought so that Jennifer Wren wouldn't recognize him."

Simon peeked over Quilpy's shaking shoulder. The real Newman Crump had been a handsome young man; in this picture, he had a crooked smile but also confidence in his eyes, and the slight tousle to his soft, shorter brown hair gave him a carefree appearance the young man probably had never felt.

"You may keep that," she said to Quilpy, closing his hand in hers. Quilpy nodded, and kept crying.

"Did your son say anything else in his e-mails or phone calls to you that might have some bearing on this case?" Detective Boggs asked.

Ms. Crump now removed a book from her purse. She placed it on the table. Detective Boggs picked it up and looked at it, shrugged her shoulders, and put it back on the table, pushing it toward Simon. He knew it instantly.

"*The Organ and the Spire*," he read from the spine, "*The Alternate World of Edwin Drood*, by Obadiah Twinn." He put the book on the desk. "I know this book, Ms. Crump. Did this belong to Newman?"

"Yes," she said. "It was with his things here at the conference. He studied this book intensely, along with the book that Jennifer Wren wrote, which he must have left at his apartment. He believed that, if he studied hard enough, he could pass as a scholar here, just long enough to accomplish his goal."

"Which was?" Detective Boggs asked.

"To have something that belonged to Jennifer Wren. An earring, a magazine she had read—"

"A scarf," Quilpy said, his voice scratchy. The three other people in the room looked at him. Quilpy wiped his nose with his sleeve.

"He wanted that scarf. The one by Hermees," he added, mispronouncing the name. "He told me it was as beautiful as she was."

Detective Boggs made a note in the pad she kept in front of her.

"May I borrow this?" Simon asked Ms. Crump, picking up the Obadiah Twinn book again. "I don't own this book, and I would like to reread it. Mr. Twinn's name has been mentioned too many times in the last few days."

"Certainly, Mr. Alastair."

Simon put the Twinn book in his shoulder bag.

"Newman mentioned you also," Ms. Crump continued. "He thought you were a kind man, and he wished he worked for someone like you, instead of the people at the chain store where, he said, people didn't even seem to like books most of the time, let alone love them, as he said you did."

"Thank you so much for telling me that." Simon lowered his head. "I so regret that I didn't get to spend more time with your son. He was charming."

Myrtle Crump turned to Quilpy. "Did you love Newman?" she asked.

Quilpy's eyes widened. "I—I—was ready to," he said finally. "He was Droody to me." He spoke to the photo. "I was on my way." And then Quilpy broke down.

Ms. Crump stood, crossed to where Quilpy sat, and put her arms around him. His head was cradled in her neck as he sobbed. "I needed to know," she said, looking now at Detective Boggs, and then at Simon. Softly, she patted Quilpy's back. "I need to believe that my son experienced joy before he died. I couldn't bear it if he had died without hope."

When the interview ended, Ms. Crump explained that she had to return to Portland to arrange Newman's funeral. She and Simon exchanged e-mails and phone numbers; Simon promised to pass them on to Quilpy, who had returned to his room immediately after Detective Boggs said she was finished with her questions.

Simon and Detective Boggs said good-bye to Myrtle Crump, who had already checked out of her room. Bart Cuff helped put her luggage in the car, which he had parked out front for her. As she got into her car, she waved limply to Simon and Detective Boggs and then drove away.

"Were you surprised by any of her story?" Detective Boggs asked Simon.

"Yes and no," he answered. "I liked the young man. I wish I had spent more time talking to him. It makes me more determined than ever that we find out who murdered him."

"That *I* find out who murdered him," the detective said, although she had a slight smile on her face. "You are not a member of the sheriff's office, last time I checked."

"Of course," said Simon. "But you can't stop my curiosity, can you?"

"Not unless you interfere in official business."

"Thank you," said Simon, "for letting me meet and speak with Ms. Crump. It meant a lot to me to hear her story directly."

"It was her wish, not mine," she said. "Do you think that Mr. Quill will be all right?"

"Eventually. The young are resilient, I suppose. But he was more affected than I had understood."

Bart Cuff came over to where Simon and the detective stood.

"Did Jennifer Wren leave already?" Detective Boggs asked Cuff.

"She did. The limousine was here before seven this morning." Cuff turned to Simon. "I just received a call from Osma Dilber in her room. She is hoping you will stop by to visit her when you have some time. She's resting today, she says, so that she can be alert for tomorrow's presentation by Mr. Drabb."

"I'll go see her right now," said Simon.

Osma took a while to answer Simon's knock. When she opened the door, her flowing purple caftan rippled in the breeze caused by the moving door.

"Please come in, Simon," she said. She gestured to him to join her in the small sitting area. Two chairs faced one another. On a small table between the chairs rested a tray with coffee and tea. Osma had plugged in the electric teakettle; it was steaming now and clicked off.

"Will you join me?" she asked. "I brought some tea from

home—Finnish Breakfast, not common here at all, and it reminds me of my childhood."

"I'd love to," said Simon.

Simon saw a breakfast tray on the bed, and the remains of a poached egg and toast. Osma saw him look that way and smiled. "The hotel staff has been so kind. They're treating me like royalty, even offered to move me to the presidential suite now that Jennifer has left, at least for the day. I couldn't possibly. But I *will* indulge in room service."

She prepared the loose tea and dropped the tea ball into a small ceramic teapot. Her craggy hands were slow and stiff.

"I always think myself invincible," she said, "at least when I'm puttering around at home. But these terrible events have upset me and have made me not quite myself. I feel so badly for that lovely young man—and his poor mother!" She put her hands to her face.

Simon described his meeting with Ms. Crump. He left out the more unsavory details of Newman's life; he didn't want to upset Osma even further, but he did tell her about Newman's obsession with Jennifer. He also told Osma about Neva Tupman, her connection to Grewgious, and her departure from the hotel.

"Thank you so much for telling me this," Osma said when Simon finished. "I also feel sorry for that young man, Mr. Quill. It sounds as if he was just about to discover the love of his life."

"Yes, I expect that he will hurt for a while."

Osma poured tea from the pot. Simon took his black; Osma added cream and sugar to hers. The tea was fragrant, like Earl Grey, but more delicately scented with tart herbs and licorice.

"This is delicious," said Simon.

"A touch of *Artemisia absinthia* makes it special," she said. "A blend of native Finnish herbs, good for what ails you." She looked out the window beside her; her eyes, however, Simon imagined, were looking far beyond the hills above downtown Astoria, far back from today. She turned back to him. "I've been in my room for hours and, as nice as it is, I'm beginning to get cabin fever." Her hand around her coffee cup looked like dried vines clinging to the porcelain. "And I've had too much time to think about poor Mr. Drood, or Mr. Crump. And to realize that Jennifer and I may have been the last to see him."

"Except for his murderer," said Simon.

Osma lowered her glance to her teacup; Simon regretted what he had said.

"I was present," he continued, "when Jennifer told her story to Detective Boggs. How Newman walked past and then, after Neva dropped the tray, how he reacted in horror when he realized that Jennifer had recognized him as her stalker."

Osma's cup rattled against its saucer. "Is that how she described what she saw?" she asked. "She didn't tell me—probably to spare me her pain. Detective Boggs didn't tell me, either. She asked me what I saw in the hallway." She rested her hands in her lap, looking directly at Simon. "But how interesting—and strange. Something about what happened in the hallway is bothering me. I will think about it some more and talk with you and Detective Boggs later, when I've figured out what it is." Osma tapped her fingers on the edge of her teacup. "Will you be staying in town today, given that the festivities have been postponed?"

"I don't think so," said Simon. "I have chores, personal business and such that I can't hand off to Jude."

"I suspect that will be the next thing for me, too," she said, "finding someone to help around the house. I'm not as spry as I used to be." She looked around the room and pointed to the fanned-out magazines on the small table beside the tea tray. "I've read practically everything here."

"Would you like me to bring you something? I have a store full of books, and since I've read every one, I know just what you might like. Revisiting *Daniel Deronda*, perhaps, or an early Mrs. Gaskell? Maybe something truly obscure, like a late Wilkie Collins?"

"Thank you," she said. "I will most likely take a walk around the hotel later today. I think I can make it across the hall to the library if I run out of things here." Osma put her hand to her mouth to hide a small yawn. "Oh, my goodness. That was rude of me."

Simon finished his tea and stood. "I don't want to tire you out. Can I help you with anything before I go?"

Osma stood also, and took Simon's hands in hers. "You've been such a good friend all of these years," she said, "everyone in your family. I owe all I am to your grandfather, but you are his worthy successor in every way."

"That means a great deal to me. But let's think positive thoughts: that this wonderful tea will make you strong and ready to do battle tomorrow with whatever Bucky

Drabb has up his sleeve. Because I'm pretty sure it will be controversial, whatever he's got to say."

Osma chuckled, her small lips wrinkling more. "Nothing like dueling scholars for a good show."

Simon thought Osma's tea had made him sleepy also, so before heading back to the bookstore and Gad's Hill Place, he walked two blocks from the hotel toward the river to Krook's Koffee An' Kiosk for a latte. The Koffee An' wasn't really a kiosk anymore; the business had moved into a vacant storefront near the river, but the owner had kept the full original name for nostalgic reasons. Simon ordered his usual twelve-ounce double nonfat extra hot latte. The barista, a willowy attractive young man with a pierced nostril and a crimson streak in his blond hair, took his order.

While Simon waited, he noticed that Cecily and Lionel were seated at a back-corner table. They were hunched forward, talking above a whisper, and both were clearly tense, the cords in their necks showing above the collars of their raincoats. Simon looked away; a moment after he did, he heard the scrape of wood against wood, then a thud as, in his haste to leave the table, Lionel knocked over his chair. He brushed by Simon as he left, seemingly not noticing him.

As tempted as Simon was to look at Cecily, he kept his back to her, took his drink when it was called, and left the café. He paused outside the door, but Cecily stayed inside. He could see Lionel a block ahead, walking with a powerful stride until he turned the corner.

The hotel parking lot was in the block beyond the hotel, so Simon passed by the lobby windows on his way to his car; as he did, he saw Bettina motioning to him to come inside. Dean Minor and Silas Cheeryble were getting off the elevator, Minor's arm around Cheeryble. They both greeted Simon as they left the hotel and Simon entered it.

"They seem happy," said Simon to Bettina.

"Must be something in the water. Either that, or they can't contain their secret delight at Drabb's temporary misfortune."

Simon chuckled. At the same time, he realized that either one might have a motive for stealing Drabb's document. Also the Heart of Helsinki? And killing someone? As Simon had learned at Christmas, anything is possible when murder is involved.

"What can I do for you?" he asked Bettina. "I'm about to leave for Dickens Junction, the bookstore, and home. Would you like to join Zach and me for a home-cooked meal tonight?"

"I'd love to, Simon, and thank you for the gracious offer. But I've got so many things to do: writing reports to the international society and e-mails to society members all over the world wanting to know what's going on, reviewing the hotel bills with Bart Cuff—no, I had better pass and order in tonight. I should also stay around in case one of the conferees needs something."

"Like Drabb."

"Something like that. And I can check on Osma, maybe after dinner. I haven't seen her yet today."

"All right," said Simon, "but you'll be missing out on some fine cooking. Jude is doing pot au feu."

"Tempting, tempting," she said.

"And charlotte russe for dessert."

Bettina stomped her Jimmy Choo in mock anger. "All right, you've twisted my arm. I can review the bills with Cuff tomorrow afternoon after the conference ends and before the executive committee meeting begins."

"Let's say seven," said Simon. "You remember how to find the house?"

"Absolutely," Bettina answered. Her cell phone started to buzz. She took it from her suit-jacket pocket and flipped it open. "Society business," she said. "Excuse me, Simon. Looking forward to tonight."

As Simon walked toward his car, he remembered that he wanted to check the alley and the hotel's back entrance. The service alley between the hotel and the building next to it, a small women's clothing consignment shop, was narrow, and shut out most of the sun, such as it was. Simon tried to imagine it at night. It would be dark; the closest street lamps were at the corner. The alley ran the entire block, with three back doors opening onto it. The Hotel Elliott's door was the one in the middle, marked with a small sign. It had a solid aluminum handle and was locked with a key. Next to the handle was a button with a small sign, *Deliveries press hard.* Simon pulled on the locked door; it didn't budge.

He walked around the block and back into the lobby,

and asked the desk clerk if he could see the back entrance from inside the hotel. As the clerk led Simon past Cuff's office and the other cubicles, Cuff's door opened and the head of security emerged with a man dressed in coveralls and carrying a small toolkit.

"The locksmith." Cuff introduced the man to Simon. "He should be done changing all of the locks before the end of the dinner hour. "I'll let Bettina know so she can post a notice." Cuff paused. "Did you want to see me, Simon?"

"No, I'm investigating the back entrance to the hotel, if you don't mind."

"Go right ahead." Cuff and the locksmith passed into the lobby.

As Simon went farther toward the back of the hotel, he realized that the desk clerk wouldn't be able to hear the back door opening or closing at night if it was done carefully. The back entrance was off a small narrow hallway that led up a set of service stairs that Simon had not previously seen.

He opened the back door. It scraped against a handful of pebbles and some wind-blown leaves, now decaying, from last autumn. He picked up a small rock and stuck it between the door and the sill and let the door close almost all of the way; it barely stuck out from the line of the wall. Simon reached down, removed the rock, and let the door shut behind him.

He could see Cuff's office door and the door to the pantry nearby. He walked toward the pantry and looked inside. There was a small freezer for the overflow of cold items, and shelves of staples lined the walls: plastic tubs of dried beans, giant boxes of pasta, industrial cans of tomato sauce, sacks of sugar and flour, boxes of kosher salt. On the floor near the flour sacks, Simon saw a small mound of whitish powder. He touched it, and looked up. The stitching on one of the flour sacks was partially torn away, leaving a small hole in the bag. *So,* Simon thought, *here is where the murderer got the "quicklime" for the staging at the mausoleum.* From this location, Simon could not see past the dogleg corridor that led to the lobby desk, and was sure he couldn't be seen, either. He brushed his hands clear of flour and left the pantry, closing the door behind him.

He climbed the service stairs one floor, where the stairs ended with a kitchen-style swinging door. He pushed that open and found himself staring at the door to Osma's room.

The transom above Osma's door showed that her lights were out; she was napping. Neva Tupman's room was also dark. The library transom glowed with light from within. Simon opened the double doors and found Bucky Drabb working at his own laptop. The hotel laptop was also on and signed in to a bibliographic website maintained by the Droodist Society.

"I'm sorry," said Simon, "I didn't mean to interrupt."

Drabb had strewn papers and several of his own reference books around him. "I'm trying to put last-minute touches on my presentation," he said, his voice clipped. "So I'd like to be alone unless you absolutely have to be here."

"I'll be a minute," said Simon. He walked across the room to the brocaded floor-length drapes that covered the library windows. He pulled one aside; the brickwork of the consignment store filled the view. The hotel window-sill was scratched in several places, varnish removed and exposing bare wood. Although no expert, Simon thought the scratches appeared recent. No doubt the police had photographed them.

He examined the window; it had been opened recently: The rotating latch wasn't fully shut. Simon turned the latch, lifted the window, and looked below. This was how poor Newman Crump's body was dumped after being strangled with Jennifer Wren's scarf. How awful. He looked both ways down the narrow back alley. Very unlikely that at such a late hour as the murder occurred anyone would have been passing by to hear the body hit the concrete below.

"Close the bloody window!" Bucky Drabb said, his voice almost a shriek.

Simon closed and locked the window and returned the drapes to their previous position.

"That's all you wanted to do?" Bucky asked.

"That's all."

When Simon arrived at Pip's Pages, Brock was alone and reading a travel brochure behind the counter. He and Bethany still hadn't made a final honeymoon decision, even though the wedding was only a few months away.

"What do you think, Simon?" Brock asked. "Where will you go on your honeymoon when you and Zach get married?" Brock had no difficulty talking with Simon about their relationships, even with the difference in ages and objects of desire. To Brock, "a dude was a dude." All men wanted the same thing, he said, whether it was from another man or a woman. And Simon had to acknowledge the fundamental truth of that.

Simon sat on the stool behind the counter, a few feet from Brock. Today Brock had on a navy muscle tee that showed a flash of the bicep tattoo he had gotten on his birthday right after the New Year. Simon still hadn't gotten used to it and had to take Brock's word for it that it was hot.

"I don't know," said Simon. "First, Zach and I would have to decide to get married, wouldn't we? We're not quite that far along; I can't even get him to move in with me."

"So you've asked him?" Brock asked. "Major."

"I made my latest effort a few days ago. He's promised his answer by the end of the conference, if that ever comes."

"I struggled when Bethany asked me to move in with her. A dude's freedom—" Brock stopped, catching himself on the no-dude rule. "A guy's freedom is everything, and Zach's been on his own way longer than me."

Simon overlooked Brock's ungrammatical construction. "But if we get married," said Simon, returning to Brock's original question, "I'd probably let Zach choose the honeymoon site. After all, he's been everywhere from the Seychelles to Secaucus. I've been relatively few places by comparison." He thought about it. "But where would I like to go? Patagonia, Bhutan, maybe the Galapagos.

Someplace that's totally unlike here in geography or history."

"Bethany wants to go sea kayaking in New Zealand, but the timing isn't the best."

"Sea kayaking wouldn't be on my list, that's for sure," said Simon.

It felt good to be out from under the conference, the murder, the narrow focus of the Droodists. Life as a scholar never would have suited Simon; he needed the larger world, even if the world of Dickens Junction might not qualify as nature red in tooth and claw.

Simon's cell vibrated in his pocket. He looked at the screen. "A text from Zach."

"Give him time, Simon," Brock said. "You're a good man. He'll say yes."

Brock's new status as a groom-to-be certainly had put a serious streak in him, maybe a good sign, Simon thought. He opened the text.

+ *Quilpy 4 chow*, it said. *Luv.*

Simon didn't quite understand how a journalist could stand to purposefully misspell words; how much time did it really save? Nevertheless, he shifted his focus to the message, not the medium. He had better notify Jude. He called the house. A familiar voice, though not Jude's, picked up.

"Alastair Detective Agency." The Georgia drawl could only belong to Simon's oldest friend, George Bascomb, a collage artist who lived in Portland but made frequent visits to Dickens Junction.

"George! When did you arrive?"

"Not soon enough," George said, "to keep you from getting your fingers mixed up in murder again." George had played a supportive role during the ordeal at Christmas.

"How long are you staying?" Simon asked.

"If your newest acquisition keeps on dazzling me with the aroma coming from his pot au feu, I might never leave. I have already unpacked my trunks in Boffin's Bower." George's favorite guest suite at Gad's Hill Place. No stairs and a fireplace.

"Well," said Simon, "we'll be a lively group for dinner. Please tell Jude to expect two additional guests besides yourself."

"How festive," George said. "I'll buy flowers straightaway, unless you want to be Mrs. Dalloway and buy them yourself."

Simon chuckled. George was working harder on his literary references all of the time now, it seemed. He heard mumbling on George's side of the line and then George resumed talking.

"Jude says 'no worries.' Why is it that the young have no worries, when they have the strength for them?" George had admitted to being in his midfifties for six or seven years now. "May I ask with whom we shall be dining?"

"Since you surprised me," Simon answered, "in a delightful way, of course, let me surprise you the same way by not telling you. I assure you both people have fascinating different ways of viewing the world."

"I look forward to dinner, my dear," George said.

After hanging up, Simon realized he should have filled George in on the situation between Quilpy and Newman

Crump but trusted George's keen observation powers, and his ability to extract information from Jude between now and dinner.

He finished at the store by six thirty. When he arrived at Gad's Hill Place, Simon saw a familiar sight: people gathered at the kitchen island. Zach, Quilpy, and George were taking animatedly about gay cruises, their benefits and drawbacks. A rich cloud of thyme and cloves filled Simon's nostrils. At the center of the island was George's flower contribution: three or four dozen tulips in an explosion of orange, yellow, and white.

"All those poor, young, shirtless men I see gyrating on deck at all hours of the day and night," George said about his cruise experiences. "It's too bad about their condition."

"Condition?" Quilpy asked. Although not built like Brock or Jude, he wasn't exactly scrawny and probably looked good without a shirt. Being twenty-five helped.

"They're all blind," George said. "Well, aren't they? They certainly can't see *me*."

Everyone chuckled at this, even Jude, whose sexual orientation remained a mystery to Simon. He hadn't mentioned a girlfriend or boyfriend, but a young man of his stunning looks certainly had to be pursued by many. It didn't matter anyway—he was an excellent cook and housekeeper.

George crossed to Simon's side of the island and gave him a big hug. Simon always felt lost, and found, in the big man's substantial warm embrace. "You are a sight for sore eyes," George said.

"It's good to see you, old friend," said Simon. Words would never be enough to describe Simon's sense of calm and security around George. They had been through too much together—Simon's breakups with prior partners, the death of George's partner a year earlier, and laughs too outrageous to count or even remember fully.

"A glass of wine?" Zach asked Simon. He and Quilpy were drinking a California Viognier, more as a cocktail than anything. Simon would pull out one of the bigger guns for the pot au feu.

"I'm glad you could join us," Simon said to Quilpy once his wine was poured and he could lift the glass to the young man. "This should give you some time to unwind."

"I had no idea we would be dining with a celebrity," George said, with a touch more than the usual archness in his voice. "I suppose you could call me a fan of Mr. Quill's oeuvre. Your cruise stories tempt me to enter your Cabin Boy contest," he continued. "Although you wouldn't want an old drone like me around."

"You make me laugh, dude," Quilpy said. "You'd be a babe magnet."

George laughed deeply, and Simon decided that tonight he wouldn't impose the no-dude rule.

George, many years in recovery, sipped a mineral water. "Nothing like your stories has ever happened to me on a cruise. Certainly no Westphalia Wart has gone missing on any ship I've sailed on."

"The Caracas Carbuncle," Simon corrected him.

"What. Ever," George said, mimicking Quilpy's phrase.

"The cruise should be fun," Quilpy said. "All of you should come."

"How romantic," George said to Simon and Zach. "All the ABBA you could ever want, any hour of the day or night."

"You dudes are not up on your music."

The doorbell rang. "I'll get it," said Simon, seeing that Jude was more than fully occupied drizzling *aceito balsamico* on salad plates decorated with endive leaves, pink grapefruit suprêmes, julienned radishes, and crumbled Rogue River bleu cheese.

"Welcome," said Simon to Bettina as he ushered her inside. She had dressed in a vermilion cocktail dress. The short circle skirt accented her trim legs, something Simon noticed as soon as he had taken her raincoat and hung it in the entryway. "I came empty-handed," she said.

"No worries," said Simon. When had that entered his vocabulary?

"I've been on the telephone with the society all afternoon," she said. "They can be such *nudges* when they want." She brought a practiced Yiddish sound to her otherwise flat West Coast American with that one word.

"Did you get a chance to see Osma?" he asked, leading her into the kitchen.

"I didn't," she answered. "I stopped by her room before I left to come here. The light was on behind the transom window, but she didn't answer."

"Probably taking a nice hot soak in that deep tub. Or maybe she popped over to the library to get a book—she told me she might."

Simon introduced Bettina to George and Jude, and soon the whole group was laughing and munching on Jude's chevre-and-quince-paste bruschettas. They eventually wandered into the dining room, where Jude was pouring from a bottle of mature Leonetti cabernet, a second at the ready.

Simon raised his wine glass along with the others, including George and his flute of diet ginger ale. "To Newman Crump," said Simon. "A young man I wish I could have known better." He paused. "And to new friends"—he looked at Quilpy, whose eyes were two half-filled pools of tears—"and old"—now to Bettina and George. "And to family."

Zach gave Simon one of those crooked smiles that melted Simon's heart every time.

The pot au feu, delivered in Grandma Melanie's tureen—along with the side dishes of new potatoes, boiled cabbages, and cornichons—was stupendous. Jude, Simon thought, might be an even better chef than Bethany.

Quilpy, sitting on Simon's right side, picked up a cornichon and looked at it quizzically.

"It's a pickle," said Simon.

"Only smaller," Quilpy said.

"When have I heard *that* before," George added.

The group ate in silence for a few minutes, except for laudatory comments about the food and the chef. Jude turned down an offer to join them at the table; Simon could hear the sounds of cleaning up in the kitchen. Jude returned later to clear and then bring in cordial glasses filled with a frozen greenish concoction. Quilpy looked at Simon.

"A palate cleanser," Jude said. "Gooseberry granita."

"That dude is hawt," Quilpy said. He puckered his lips as he tasted the sweet-tart flavors. Simon felt the ice melt on his tongue.

"Indeed," George whispered across the table. "Thank God Simon lets us beg the scraps from his table."

"Enough," said Simon.

After Jude had cleared away the granita glasses, he poured coffee for those who wanted it and served the charlotte russe, after presenting it complete, inverted on a glass-footed cake stand.

"Finally something I know," Quilpy said. "Cake."

"Sort of," Simon told him.

Like everything else Jude had served, this ladyfinger-and-cream delight was exquisite, Simon thought, although where the berries had come from he had no idea. He'd have to talk with Jude about sustainability one of these days.

When dinner ended slightly after ten o'clock, Zach suggested drinks in the living room. He and Simon went to the liquor cabinet to get the cognac and glasses. Zach kissed him as they stood side by side.

"Good idea not to talk about the murder at dinner, I think," Zach said.

"George has been a godsend. Who would have guessed that he and Bettina knew some of the same people in San Francisco?"

"I didn't learn much today," Zach said. "My attempts

to get more information about Cecily Tartar failed. No more missing jewels, at least when she was around. Did you get a chance to look into the Twinn guy?"

Simon thought about the book in his briefcase, sitting on the table in the nook. "Maybe I can get to it after dinner." He held an empty snifter in his hands. "I better pass on this if I want to do any research tonight."

Simon carried cognac to Bettina. Quilpy passed, settled on hot tea instead. "I'm usually a root beer schnapps guy," he said. "I can't take too much of this in one day."

Jude poked his head into the living room through the hallway French doors. "I'm out of here," he said to Simon. "See you at six, or whenever." Simon heard the back door shut.

Bettina took a sip of cognac, and then tilted her head. At first Simon worried something was off about the cognac, but then he heard a tinny sound coming from the kitchen. "It's my phone," she said, standing, looking at her watch. "I better take it. It's daylight in London now, and the society probably has a whole new list of things for me to do." After passing across the Tibetan carpet, her heels clicked on the caramelized bamboo floor and through the dining room into the kitchen.

"Thanks for everything, Simon," Quilpy said. He had slumped into a chair, and looked very tired. Even he showed signs of wear from the events of the last two days.

"You can stay here tonight if you want," said Simon. "I've got guest rooms to spare."

"It's the Ritz of Dickens Junction," George said.

"No crackers for me," Quilpy said. "I'm full."

Simon saw Bettina's shadow precede her, phone pressed to her ear, into the living room just as his own cell began to vibrate.

"Oh my God," he heard Bettina say as he looked at his own phone's illuminated screen.

"Detective," he said.

He looked up as Bettina's cell clattered to the floor. Her mouth was open and her hands were shaking.

"Simon," Detective Boggs answered, her voice low and measured. "Please come to the hotel right away. Osma Dilber is dead. Murdered."

April 20

7:30–9:00 a.m.	Continental Breakfast	Hotel bar
9:15 a.m.–noon	Plenary Session: "At Last! The Truth of Number Plan Six"	Buckminster Drabb, Columbia River Room
Noon–2:00 p.m.	Conference ends/Check out	Hotel lobby

The remainder of the conference is CANCELED. Partial refunds will be available after May 1 by writing to the International Droodist Society at the address given in your conference materials. Please be checked out of your rooms by 1:00 p.m. If you cannot meet this request, please see Bartholomew Cuff at the front desk.

If you have questions, please see Bettina Law, conference chair.

The Droodist Society is so very sorry for this inconvenience.

DAY SIX

Around midnight, Detective Boggs called Cuff, Bettina, and Simon into Cuff's office, which again had been turned into an interview room. Cuff had managed to get two hot pots of coffee from the skeleton kitchen crew; Simon half-filled a cup for himself, considering it medicine. He didn't think he could stomach anything, yet he knew he would need the caffeine to get through the time ahead.

Detective Boggs removed her pantsuit jacket and folded it across a table behind Cuff's desk. She looked harried, and her note pad looked nearly full. George had taken Quilpy back to Gad's Hill Place after Quilpy had given his statement regarding his whereabouts during the last few hours. Simon had left Zach fighting to find space in the lobby among the journalists and television reporters and cameramen that had already descended on the Hotel Elliott. The night clerk (Igna since 2006) sat behind the lobby desk looking like a frightened child but answering the phone sharply each time it rang.

"What can you tell us?" Simon asked. He had seen the body bag containing Osma Dilber's tiny frame only minutes earlier. It had made him start crying again; now, his dry eyes stung and, he was sure, were blood-red.

Detective Boggs thumbed through her notes before she began talking. Bettina sat with her hands in her lap; for once her perfect makeup was smeared. She had been crying also.

"Mr. Drabb spent most of the afternoon in the library," Detective Boggs began, "working on his presentation for tomorrow. He believes that he left the library, returning to his room with his laptop and program materials around six, to then seek out companions for dinner. He hoped to find Mr. Cheeryble or Mr. Minor to accompany him, but neither answered his call or his knock on their respective doors. So he went to Bisque It for a quick dinner and returned sometime around seven thirty."

"Where were Minor and Cheeryble?" Simon asked.

Detective Boggs seemed irritated at the interruption; Simon apologized.

"I'm tired," she said. "I will come to them in a few minutes." She flipped another page. "Drabb returned to the library, but found the door locked. The transom showed light inside. He went to his room and continued to work on his presentation, but couldn't get as comfortable as he had been, so he returned to the library at around ten fifteen, found it still locked, and came down to the lobby to express his frustration to Mr. Cuff."

"That's correct," Cuff said. He had unbuttoned the top button of his dress shirt but remained in his full suit. His brow was glazed with perspiration. "So I went upstairs to the library with him and knocked loudly on the door. When I didn't get an answer, I used my pass-key to open the door. That's when I found Ms. Dilber on the ground."

"She had been struck several times with a heavy object," Detective Boggs said, "probably by the bust of Dickens from the top shelf of the bookcase, which we found on the library floor wrapped in an oversized linen napkin. There was a room-service tray missing its napkin outside her door and not found in her room."

Bettina started sobbing and dabbed at her eyes with a lacy handkerchief.

"I won't know the full details until later," Detective Boggs continued, "but it appears she was struck from the front, and several contusions on her hands suggest that she attempted to defend herself before receiving the blow that killed her."

"Why in the library?" Cuff asked.

"Unknown," replied Detective Boggs. "Perhaps the killer surprised her there, or she surprised the killer."

"Or they had agreed to meet," Simon suggested. "She told me this morning that something had been bothering her about Jennifer's story about seeing Newman Crump in the hall the night he was murdered."

Detective Boggs made a note. "And she figured out what it was—"

"—and told the murderer what she knew," said Simon.

"Why would she be so reckless?" Bettina asked.

"Where is Jennifer now?" Simon asked.

"She's on her way back to Astoria," Detective Boggs answered. "I received a call from her an hour ago."

"And where were Minor and Cheeryble?" Simon asked. "Out to dinner somewhere?"

"Also unknown," said the detective. "I'm meeting with each of them when we finish here."

"What about Lionel and Cecily Tartar?" Simon asked. "And the others?"

"Cecily Tartar is also en route back to Astoria," Detective Boggs answered.

"She checked out of the hotel abruptly at seven this evening," Cuff said. "A taxi picked her up and drove her to the Portland airport."

"A taxi?" Simon asked. "It's a two-hour drive or more to PDX."

"Money was no object," Detective Boggs said. "She wanted to get away quickly. We apprehended her at the airport and she is returning here, under the escort of the Multnomah County Sheriff's Office. She also should be here at any time."

Simon was confused. "What about Lionel?"

"He claims to have been in his room until seven fifteen, after which time he says he walked around town to calm his nerves."

"Did he know why Cecily had checked out?"

"He told us it was her story to tell."

"He's a cool customer," said Simon.

"I'm not sure there's much love lost between those siblings," said Detective Boggs.

"And Grewgious?"

Detective Boggs turned another page in her notepad. "He was resting in his room, he said. He ordered in, and the housekeeping staff picked up his tray outside the door around ten."

Simon shook his head. "I can't believe that Osma risked her life. She almost told me what she was worried about."

"We'll find the killer," Detective Boggs said. She stood, and so did Simon, Cuff, and Bettina. "You probably want to get some sleep. I'll keep you posted as things develop."

Bettina checked herself in her compact. "I look dreadful. I need to go to my room and clean up." She then flipped open her phone. "And I've got texts and voice mails already from the society. With all those reporters out there, I'm sure the news is already on some of the blog pages, too."

"May I see the library?" Simon asked Detective Boggs. She frowned.

"I want to see how the room feels."

The detective sighed, apparently too tired to argue with Simon this time about his involvement in the case. "When the scene-of-crime officers are done, I don't have any objection."

"Did you check the library laptop?" Simon asked.

"We did," she said. "It had been shut off. The scene-of-crime staff determined that it hadn't been used since Drabb left the library, so we didn't impound it."

Simon turned to Cuff. "May I use it, then?" He reached in his messenger bag and pulled out the Obadiah Twinn book. "I want to check some references. It will be something that will occupy my time, and I don't want to go home right now."

Back in the lobby, Simon watched Multnomah County Sheriff's deputies, one male, one female, escort Cecily Tartar into the hotel. The questions from the reporters, including Zach, who was at the far end of the lobby from Simon, came immediately and loudly. Cecily walked ahead of them and was not handcuffed. A Cable News Northwest reporter and cameraman were next to her almost instantly.

Cecily looked around and nodded toward Detective Boggs, who had stepped out of Cuff's office at the commotion. "I will talk only to the detective," she said. "I have no other comment." A small crowd trailed behind her as she met up with Detective Boggs and the two women disappeared behind the lobby desk toward Cuff's office.

Cuff turned to Simon. "Let's see if the library is clear."

Simon motioned to Zach; he joined them. Cuff led them up the back service staircase, the same route Simon had explored the day before. "This is better," Cuff said.

A Clatsop County deputy was removing the crime scene tape from the library door as the three men turned the corner and entered the main hallway.

"May we use the library now?" Cuff asked.

The deputy nodded and moved aside.

When Cuff turned on the library light, Simon was surprised at the brightness of the room; a faint chemical smell that he didn't recognize touched his nostrils, possibly disinfectant, although he had understood from Detective Boggs that Osma had not bled much externally.

"Why are we here?" Zach asked.

"I wanted to use the laptop to check a few things."

The scene-of-crime officers had moved the conference table normally in the center of the room to one side. Simon looked at a conspicuously bare spot on the floor; that must have been where someone brutally killed Osma Dilber. Simon looked up to the row of busts on the top shelf. Between the plaster visage of Shakespeare and the grim asymmetrical face of Wilkie Collins was an empty spot. And the small reshelving cart was filled with the books that had been disturbed during Newman Crumb's murder.

Simon opened the library laptop.

"Do you need anything else from me?" Cuff asked.

"No, Bart," said Simon. "I think I'll be fine."

Cuff looked around. "We're going to have to redecorate. Or we'll have nut jobs trying to take pieces of the carpet or something like that."

Simon shuddered at the thought. But Cuff was probably right.

Cuff closed the door as he left the library.

"What would you like me to do?" Zach asked. "I'd could file a story or two, but helping you is most important to me."

"Not this time. This is arcane work about Drood, and you don't need to be put through that. I just...I just wanted you with me when I first came in here."

Zach kissed Simon and left the library, shutting the door behind him.

Simon felt the door close, a vacuum pulling air out with Zach as he left. The library was quiet, still warm from the too-many bodies that had been here photographing, measuring, dusting, and testing for clues to the murder of his old, old friend.

Osma had been the librarian when Simon had checked out his first book, *A Christmas Carol*, from the Astoria Public Library, long before the Dickens Junction branch had opened off Dickens Square in the 1980s. He remembered how she had looked to his young eyes: how the Heart of Helsinki had dazzled him; how pretty her hands had been then, and how dwarfed by that ring; how kind her eyes were.

He wiped his eyes with the back of his hand and turned on the computer.

Simon opened the Internet browser page connected to the hotel's Wi-Fi connection. He opened the browser's history and started clicking on several of the links. With the exception of one site called *Girls Do...*, which Simon avoided, the sites Drabb had been using were ones Simon often consulted. And here was the one he wanted first, an online bibliography of Droodist essays and books, painstakingly compiled by one of the world's foremost Dickens scholars, a feisty retired professor from South Africa whom Simon had met at an international conference on *Bleak House* several years ago in New York City. He had used the bibliography many times before, but never to look into anything about Twinn.

Simon typed *Obadiah Twinn* into the site's search field; a long list of articles and books emerged. Simon had never realized how prolific Twinn had been. As someone firmly of the Jasper tradition, Simon had read only enough of Twinn's work to know that he almost never agreed with him. Several of Twinn's articles were available online through a subscription service to which Simon subscribed. He picked a Twinn essay, "The Two Headstones," at random, typed in his password, and began reading.

He had been up a long time, and the coffee wasn't helping; he found his eyes getting tired, but he trudged on. Another essay, "Princess Puffer's Children," an outré theory about the opium smoker, was even harder to get through.

He made his way through five essays before returning to the bibliography's home page. He checked his watch. Three fifteen. Maybe he should call Zach to suggest they go home, or go to the lobby himself and get more coffee. No, just a few more essays; maybe the next one would contain whatever it was he was looking for. He only wished he knew...

The door to the library opened. Simon jerked awake.

"Coffee to the rescue," Zach said.

"You startled me," said Simon. "But I'm grateful."

"Any progress?"

"Not really," said Simon, sipping. He turned away while Zach began looking at the books in the stacks nearby.

Simon turned back to the laptop and typed *Twinn* into the search engine to bring up the list again. He noticed a title he hadn't before.

"Twinn, D. M., 'When Shall We Three Meet Again?,'" Simon read. "Unpublished dissertation. Referenced in Obadiah Twinn's book, *Anyone but Jasper.* I haven't been able to locate it." This last sentence, a note from the bibliographer. The text didn't link anywhere.

Simon looked up. Across the room was the shelf containing Dickens's complete works. He rose and went to pull out the copy of *The Mystery of Edwin Drood* that he had reshelved the other day in its proper place. The books were perfectly aligned on the shelf, but *Edwin Drood* had been moved again, placed between *Great Expectations* and *Our Mutual Friend,* one spot away from where Simon had placed it the other day. He pulled the book and began thumbing through it to find the chapter he was looking for. A half-sheet of pale blue paper slipped from the book. Simon caught it before it fell.

Even as he glanced at it, Simon knew what it was and, a second after that, knew everything that had happened during the last few days. Who had stolen the ring, what had happened to the scarf, and why. Knew who had killed Newman Crump and why. Knew what Osma Dilber had seen in the hallway, and why she had been killed because of it. If he had come in here last night instead of going home to dinner, Osma Dilber would be safe and alive, her would-be murderer already in custody. Simon again wiped his eyes with the back of his free hand and let out a huge sigh.

"Is something wrong?" Zach asked.

Simon carefully shut the volume, pressing the loose piece of paper between the leaves. "I have to see Detective Boggs right away."

"You've found something," Zach said.

"I've found everything," said Simon. He dialed Detective Boggs's cell phone.

"Simon," she answered. "Is this important? I'm about to interview Cecily Tartar. She managed to find a lawyer at this time of night."

"Listen," said Simon. He spoke for the next minute.

"Are you sure?" she asked. "It's far-fetched, don't you think?"

"Yes," he said. "I can't prove all of it yet. You will need to check on a few things." He named them. "Then, if we can gather everyone together here in the library, I think we can get resolution to everything."

"I can't believe I'm going to let you do this again," she said. "The sheriff will have my badge if you're wrong."

"You know I'm not wrong," he said. "Can you bring a few things with you?" He named what he wanted.

"I'll need a few hours to check your assumptions," she said. "And enough time to get Neva Tupman back from Seattle."

"Let's say in the library at ten o'clock, then," said Simon. "That will give you six hours to notify her and for her to drive here. Just enough time."

"You'll have been up more than twenty-four hours by that time," Detective Boggs said.

"I'm running on adrenaline now," said Simon.

Simon stood before the semicircle of nine seated people at the front of the library. At Simon's request, George had arranged them in a casual but not arbitrary order. From Simon's left to right: Quilpy, Dean Minor, Neva Tupman, Bucky Drabb, Cecily Tartar, the Great Grewgious, Jennifer Wren, Lionel Tartar, Silas Cheeryble, and Bettina Law. Zach, George, Bart Cuff, and Detective Boggs stood behind the semicircle at the back of the library. Minutes earlier, Simon had returned from Gad's Hill Place freshly showered and shaved and dressed comfortably in jeans, T-shirt, and sport coat.

"A Droodist conference," Simon began, "is a rare event and, for those who thrive on such things, an exciting opportunity to celebrate the unique charms of Dickens's unfinished novel and participate in bracing discussions about its many mysteries. But this conference brought in several people with more oblique and personal interests, including someone with a singular, shocking intention: to steal a rare artifact and secure it for a private collection, without scruples regarding the artifact's provenance or means of acquisition. Such collectors exist; we read stories about irreplaceable art works too recognizable to be on display anywhere in the world outside their proper homes, held in private galleries for the delight of a select few, or even only one select person with limitless means. In our case, to our particular collector or agent, the artifact was worth having at any price—even murder."

The people Simon was addressing watched him carefully, from time to time glancing at one another.

"But not just one rare object, the purported Number Plan Six, appeared at the Droodist Conference," Simon continued, "a second one, the Heart of Helsinki, attracted attention as well, and these two items together gave the agent a special opportunity to create confusion and increase the possibility of a successful crime. But everything went horribly wrong.

"Let's talk about a few who came here because of some reason not connected with a love of the Inimitable Boz." Simon had a water bottle on the laptop table next to him. He took a drink.

Minor pulled at the cuffs of his frayed dress shirt underneath his corduroy sport coat. No one except for Jennifer Wren, in Simon's estimate, looked his or her best. Jennifer looked radiant this morning; unlike her entrance for the cameras last evening, today she wore no makeup at all. It was her underlying beauty that made it possible for the hair and makeup people to transform her from the streetwalker Nancy to the exotic Helena Landless, a character Simon was sure she could play with passion.

"First, the young man we originally knew as Edwin Drood, revealed after his death to be Newman Crump. He came to Astoria to fulfill a life dream that we might not admire but that we must understand: He wanted to see the object of his long-standing inappropriate fixation, Jennifer Wren. Despite having been the recipient of a restraining order several years ago, Crump decided to make one last attempt to see her, to be near her, and to achieve his ultimate goal: owning an object that had belonged to her. But he was murdered—either as a result, or as a consequence, of that desire."

This revelation caused reactions from a few of those gathered in the library. Cheeryble looked at Jennifer, his mouth a perfect *O* of surprise. Quilpy's eyes watered, and he rubbed his nose with his shirt sleeve.

"Who else wasn't expected here?" Simon asked the group. "Although registered as an attendee, Neva Tupman was not a Dickens scholar or enthusiast and, I'm sorry to say, didn't do a great job of representing herself as one. She was under contract to 'enhance' the stage performance of the Great Grewgious, acting like someone under hypnotic influence in case Grewgious's talent didn't reach everyone. We know, because of Quilpy's excellent memory, that Neva Tupman has performed her act with Grewgious before, perhaps many times, on at least one Caribbean cruise that Quilpy, along with Neva and Cecily Tartar, attended two years ago.

"I don't want to cast doubt on Grewgious's talent, however, because Crump admitted to Quill that he had been hypnotized, as were Buckminster and Bettina, who freely admit that they would not have chosen to reveal those particular talents had they been fully in control of their actions."

Drabb's face flushed, no doubt, Simon thought, from the recollection of his display of vulnerability. Simon looked at the back of the room. He needed to maintain concentration.

"We also have to wonder," he continued, "at Cecily's last-minute conference registration. She and her twin brother, Lionel, claim to have spent their childhood in the Seychelle Islands. Detective Boggs has confirmed, however, that the Tartars were raised in Philadelphia and that Lionel didn't obtain a passport until 2008. Cecily, however, has traveled widely and extensively in her career as a gem specialist and has a proclivity for being near famous gemstones just before they are…mislaid. Could her curiosity about the Heart of Helsinki have been the cause of her presence at the conference? She registered at the last minute, after Quilpy's blog post mentioning Osma's famous ring appeared on the Internet. Anyone who saw Cecily interact with her brother would have noticed his annoyance, concern—something—about her presence. Cecily didn't drop in on the Droodists for a fond sibling reunion. But did she steal the Heart of Helsinki, or was she simply unfortunate—again—to be near the eye of a hurricane, as she had been when the Caracas Carbuncle went missing at sea two years ago?"

Cecily looked hard at Simon, but her face was unmoving—she wasn't about to let him see even a scintilla of her emotion. But Minor and Drabb both expressed surprise, Minor's lips rounding in a moue, Drabb's face pinching into a combination of surprise and disgust. Grewgious examined his cuticles; Lionel looked at the floor.

Simon took another drink of water. "There's at least one other person in this room whose full identity is not the one we saw on display here at the conference. But I'll come back to that."

Detective Boggs moved from the back to the side of the library, from which position she could see faces instead of backs of heads. When Simon looked at her, she returned a face as impassive and noncommittal as Cecily's.

"If these crimes—three thefts, including Jennifer Wren's expensive scarf, and two murders—are connected, then we need to start with the theft of the Heart of Helsinki. Did Newman Crump steal it? If so, how? Better yet, why? If not Crump, then who else had the opportunity to steal Osma's ring from her room? At least four people alive today have alibis for the entire time that Osma was away from her room when the Heart of Helsinki was taken. Bettina and I were in the conference center bar with Osma and Zach Benjamin. As I recall, Grewgious was also in the bar the entire time we were there.

"Osma discovered the theft of the ring the following morning. Moments later, Grewgious reported missing the scarf he had borrowed from Jennifer and inadvertently taken back to his room after his performance. Crump reported that he had gone to bed early, but this has been called into question by Bettina, who saw Crump's light through the transom when she went to her room on the same floor around twelve thirty. All of the rest reported that they were alone in their respective rooms, alibis that cannot be either proved or disproved. If Crump stole the ring himself, then the other subjects' whereabouts are moot."

Cheeryble wiped his forehead with his handkerchief, his skin flushed. With so many people in the room, it had become warm. Simon took another drink of water.

"Detective Boggs tells us that the coroner has established the time of Crump's death to be sometime after midnight, and that Crump was killed in the library with the stolen scarf, his body thrown from the library window into the alley below, and then transported away."

Simon paused. He wanted the room to feel the indignity of this particular act, even though Crump had yet more to suffer. Quilpy let out a sob. Minor moved his chair a few inches away from him. With one hand, Jennifer reached over and took Lionel's hand. With the other she dabbed her eyes with a handkerchief. Bettina was crying also, her mascara running down her cheek.

"Dean Minor reported," Simon continued after the pause, "that he had been in the library until just before that time, and that the door had been locked when he returned there at approximately one in the morning. Additionally, Quilpy reported that he had been in Newman Crump's company until shortly before midnight, when Mr. Crump abruptly said good night and went, we presume, to his room. Buckminster Drabb claims that he was in town having drinks, but he made himself so inconspicuous, something not normally associated with his larger-than-life persona, that no bartender in town remembers him. Although Jennifer, the victim of Crump's stalking efforts, has the best discernible motive for wanting him dead, she and Lionel have provided alibis for one another during the time that Crump was killed and his body removed from the hotel. Cecily claims to have gone for a long walk and saw nothing suspicious when she returned to her room around two o'clock. The rest have no alibi for the time of Crump's murder.

"The excitement of Crump's disappearance was almost trumped by Buckminster's sensational news that *Edwin Drood*'s Number Plan Six had been stolen. The ring gone, the scarf gone, the number plan gone, Crump gone. The answer was simple: Newman Crump had stolen all three objects.

"When his battered body was found by the Droodists later that day at the Dickens mausoleum, it had been staged in a way that would have been instantly recognizable to any Droodist as representing an oft-assumed scene from the unwritten half of the Dickens novel. There was the body, there the quicklime (in our case, all-purpose flour), and there, just out of the dead man's reach, the Heart of Helsinki. Although the ring—and the scarf—were found, the missing number plan was not. Why not? Because I discovered it here, in the library, earlier today."

Simon produced from his sport coat pocket Number Plan Six, carefully protected in a plastic shield. Bucky Drabb leaped from his seat, but Detective Boggs was quick and immediately placed her body between Drabb's and Simon's.

"Give it back," he said through clenched teeth.

"It's evidence," Detective Boggs said.

Simon held the clear plastic to the light before returning it to his coat pocket. "How did the number plan end up here in the library? More about that in a few minutes."

Drabb pulled himself together and took his seat. He ran a hand across his shaved pate, his face a mix of anxiety, relief, and confusion. This news was startling enough, and Cheeryble and Bettina whispered to each other. This was news so shocking that even Minor leaned over and said something to Quilpy.

"Poor Osma," said Simon.

He stopped and swallowed, gathering his emotions together. This part was hard; he pushed through it, telling himself he would not cry for her again until her funeral, scheduled in two days at St. Ina's Episcopal Church in Dickens Junction.

"If Newman Crump's death was sad," he continued, "Osma Dilber's death was tragic. She saw something she shouldn't have seen, and didn't understand, until she decided to ask the murderer about it. Her curiosity, and her lack of cynicism or suspicion, caused her death. The thefts of the ring, the scarf, and the number plan were planned, but Crump's murder, and certainly Osma's murder, were decided in haste, the result of more careful plans gone awry.

"What happened in the hallway three nights ago?" Simon asked. "Let's imagine it now. As Osma and Jennifer walk toward Osma's room and pass Edwin Drood walking the other way, Neva Tupman appears in the hallway and accidentally drops her room-service tray outside her door. Everyone turns around. What does Jennifer see? She sees the face of Edwin Drood without his glasses and recognizes him as Newman Crump, her long-ago stalker. She sees Crump's face change in a horrifying response to her discovery and then sees him disappear into the library to avoid her.

"But what if Jennifer is mistaken?"

The faces around him were tense, now, one in particular. But Simon took special care to look at each person equally. He had to admit, there was something thrilling about this pressure, his heart racing, his muscles tense. He remembered it from when he'd gathered people at Pip's Pages to reveal the *Christmas Carol* murderer.

But he would trade it all away, along with his grandfather's fortune, to have the victims returned.

He looked to the back of the room. George and Zach gave approving smiles, a needed boost as he got to the most difficult part of all of his disclosures.

"Jennifer saw in Newman Crump's face what she *believed* he was feeling, based on her knowledge of Crump's past. Osma, on the other hand, had no knowledge of Newman Crump; what she saw on his face in the hall was a look not of guilt or horror but of shame—shame at being discovered on his way to the library to deliver Number Plan Six, which he had stolen, just as he had delivered the Heart of Helsinki, which he had also stolen the night before, both to the person who would murder him minutes later. So when Osma heard Jennifer's view of Crump's reaction, she was confused. She had seen the same expression, but had interpreted it differently, and had drawn a different conclusion.

"But Osma wanted to think about what she had seen, and its significance, before telling anyone. I believe Osma asked a question that caused her to be murdered later that night when she met the murderer, or came upon the murderer, in this room."

Drabb craned his neck to stare at the rug behind him, as if imagining the place where Osma had been beaten to death with the bust of Dickens. He shuddered and returned his gaze to Simon.

Simon took another drink of water. "Who was waiting for Osma in the library? Not Jennifer. She had left the conference that morning for a meeting in Portland, and her continual whereabouts have been confirmed to the satisfaction of both the Clatsop and the Multnomah County Sheriff's Offices. Lionel and Cecily offer piquant alibis: They were having a knock-out, drag-down argument about Cecily's presence at the conference, and the potentially negative chances her presence—and her reputation—might have on her brother's chances to form a relationship with Jennifer."

At this, Jennifer squeezed Lionel's hand. Cecily remained impassive, a cipher.

"Cecily left the conference in a hurry, and her taxi driver can confirm her alibi from seven o'clock. on. She might have left the hotel immediately after killing Osma, but I don't think that's what happened. And Osma wasn't meeting Quilpy or Bettina: Quilpy was at my house in the presence of witnesses most of the day and evening, and Bettina, after finishing documented telephone calls to the International Droodist Society, was also at my house, in the presence of witnesses. And it wasn't either Dean Minor or Silas Cheeryble," said Simon, looking at each in turn. "During the hours in question, Cheeryble and Minor were enjoying one another's company in a spirited discussion of Dickens's views of sex."

Simon took a breath. By now everyone was watching everyone. He stepped closer to the semicircle, and was now standing next to Drabb. "That leaves you, Bucky. You would have had a strong motive to kill Newman Crump, if you discovered that he had stolen Number Plan Six from you, no matter what his reason might have been. You have no alibi for the theft of the Heart of Helsinki, a weak and unconfirmed alibi for Crump's murder, and another unsubstantiated alibi for Osma's murder." Drabb wiped sweat off his brow.

"Only someone with a criminal and unscrupulous mind could plan and execute multiple thefts without regard to the consequences—or the costs. And the costs were terrible. The murder of a confused young man, the desecration of a family burial place, the cold and heartless murder of a defenseless woman. And all because of the accidental dropping of a tray."

Simon turned to someone in the semicircle. "Isn't that right, Morgan, 'the Great,' Grewgious? Or should I call you David Morgan Grewgious Twinn, son of the late Obadiah Twinn?"

Several people gasped, including Bucky Drabb. Grewgious's great bulk gave off heat as he started to stand, but at that moment the library doors opened and three armed sheriff's deputies blocked the opening. Grewgious gave Simon a strange smile and returned to his chair.

"You and Neva Tupman arrived separately," said Simon, "Neva having no knowledge of your ulterior motive. You began your casual interviews with conferees, looking for suitable candidates for your performance, candidates who would be willing and suggestible while under hypnosis. Neva had done this many times before, and knew what to look for. This time, however, you were looking for someone special. Neva found Newman Crump.

"They got along well immediately; we know from Quilpy that Crump, once over his initial shyness, was a chatterbox. Crump, I believe, told either Neva, or you, Mr. Twinn, or both of you, about his shoplifting past, his familiarity with hypnosis in its therapeutic role during recovery from his dissociative personality disorder, and at some time he told you about his desire to possess something belonging to Jennifer Wren.

"You hit the jackpot with Crump," said Simon, now focusing his gaze directly on Grewgious. "He had everything you needed: suggestibility to hypnosis and a secret desire that you could exploit. You told him that you would help him achieve his goal—to acquire Jennifer's scarf—but you wanted to perform a trick first for the crowd, one that would demonstrate the power of hypnosis, the kind of parlor trick that Charles Dickens himself might have imagined. You didn't tell Crump your real goal: Stealing the Heart of Helsinki was merely a rehearsal for Crump, whom you would use to steal Number Plan Six. And casting suspicion on Cecily Tartar? Well, her unexpected appearance provided you with an excellent red herring. You gave Crump a passkey you had acquired by using hypnosis on one of the hotel clerks early in your stay. I realize now that I witnessed you in action on the day of your arrival, coaxing a passkey from the clerk while ostensibly discussing local sights."

Grewgious remained motionless. So did the three deputy sheriffs in the doorway.

"This is conjecture on my part," Simon continued, "but I'm guessing that Crump offered to take the ring while fully conscious, but you declined, saying you believed that being under a posthypnotic suggestive state would give him more confidence and relax him. What you didn't tell him was that there would be a *second* suggestion, given at the same time, to perform another task the next night.

"And everything worked! Crump stole the ring and gave it to you, probably in this room. But you told him you needed to wait one more day before giving him the scarf, which you had already reported to the police as stolen, a ruse you somehow convinced Crump was in his best interests. I don't know where you hid the ring and the scarf, but you successfully kept them from Detective Boggs and her competent assistants. Then, the next night, still under the posthypnotic state, Newman Crump, passkey in hand, walked into Buckminster's room and found Number Plan Six, which Bucky had chosen to hide in his room. I also suspect that Bucky's act of extreme carelessness was the result of further hypnotic suggestion during your time on stage with him. I have known him for years, and his reckless decision to 'hide' the document in plain sight is beneath his intellect."

Neva was crying quietly. Minor gave her his handkerchief. Through tears Quilpy was still able to look daggers at the mound that was Grewgious.

"But as Crump walked down the hall toward the library, past Osma and Jennifer, not acknowledging them because he was told not to as part of the hypnotic suggestion, Neva appeared in the hallway and accidentally dropped her room-service tray. The clatter startled Crump out of his hypnotic state. He turned around, fully conscious and fully aware of what he was doing, what he had done, too late for you to issue another posthypnotic suggestion that would have wiped his actions away from his memory. Yes, Jennifer was able to recognize him without his unnecessary eyeglasses and because of his facial expression. He wasn't horrified because she had seen him, but ashamed because he knew he was carrying Number Plan Six in his pocket.

"Crump understood immediately what deceit you had practiced on him. He might have been a shoplifter when he was young, and he might (as a practical joke) temporarily remove a jewel from its owner, as I believe he imagined he did, to obtain Jennifer's scarf, but he was not the kind of person who would steal a priceless artifact. The shock of discovery sent him reeling into the library. He knew you would be there soon to collect Number Plan Six, just as you had been there the night before to receive the Heart of Helsinki, so the only thing he could think of was to hide the document. Where? In a book. But which one?"

Simon walked over to the shelf and retrieved a volume, holding it in front of him. "Crump chose one he could easily remember—the book containing his own assumed name, *The Mystery of Edwin Drood*. But he returned it to the wrong place on the shelf. After that, he disrupted several books on the other side of the room as a ruse. You arrived later, surprised to find him not in a hypnotic state. You demanded the document and, when he denied having it, you strangled him with Jennifer Wren's scarf, which you had brought to give him as a token of your appreciation.

"Being the son of Obadiah Twinn, and a Dickens scholar in your own right, you decided to dispose of the body in a way that might cast suspicion on Droodists but not yourself, already self-proclaimed as virtually ignorant of anything Dickensian. You removed the passkey from Crump's pocket, then pushed the body out of the library window, came down the back stairs, took a bit of flour from the pantry as part of your staging, and drove the body to the Dickens mausoleum where you knew it would be discovered the next day. You left the ring beside Crump's body—it hadn't been your intention to keep it and, unlike Number Plan Six, you didn't have a buyer waiting for it—and everything had a neat and tidy ending. Detective Boggs fully expects that forensic evidence will demonstrate that Newman Crump's body spent time in the trunk of your rental car, which she impounded late last night."

Still no movement from Grewgious.

"Unlucky Osma," Simon continued. "She saw Newman Crump at the same time as Jennifer did and, I think, she wondered whether he was operating under hypnosis, although she couldn't figure out why. After all, Jennifer's explanation of the look on Crump's face was authoritative, at least within Jennifer's frame of reference. But Osma was still unconvinced, and I think it bothered her enough that she arranged to meet you in the library and ask you whether Crump had been given a posthypnotic suggestion. You were probably surprised enough, and fearful enough, that you killed her, striking her down with the bust of Dickens you found at hand and then wiping away fingerprints by taking the room-service linen from her tray across the hall. After killing her, you locked the library door and returned to your room, where you worked on an alibi."

Simon rested, taking several swallows of water.

The people in the semicircle turned their heads toward Grewgious—David Morgan Grewgious Twinn. He had his hands in his lap, and he was looking straight ahead at Simon. Then he stood.

"Excuse me, Mr. Twinn," Detective Boggs said. She then gave him his full Miranda rights.

"You will prove nothing," Twinn said, with the same sonorous voice, no hint of tension or nervousness. "I am a Twinn; that is true. I have nothing to be ashamed of. My father was a great man; this number plan you speak of, when Buckminster Drabb reveals it to the world, will vindicate his life's work."

"You are amazing," said Simon. "Until last night, I didn't know who you were, but the Internet is a powerful tool when you know where to start. Your mother was an eminent psychologist specializing in the study of dissociative personality, and your father the most controversial and polarizing Dickens scholar of the modern era. With a few suggestions from me, Detective Boggs and her investigative team have uncovered your past. You had a promising career in psychology until you misused your hypnosis talents for sexual conquests.

"After falling from grace as a clinician, you took your training and turned it into a lucrative form of entertainment, becoming a popular fixture on the cruise-ship circuit. You even survived the potentially career-ending scandal of the missing Caracas Carbuncle. Your role in that remains unclear, but no matter now. You have had financial trouble, a personal bankruptcy. I suspect financial difficulties, plus your Dickens background, led you to discover the shadowy world of private collectors who would pay high prices for precious artifacts like Number Plan Six. You have killed two wonderful human beings," said Simon, suddenly tired, his mouth parched. "And for that, you will be brought to justice."

Detective Boggs took another step toward Grewgious. "I am arresting you for the murders of Newman Crump and Osma Dilber," she said. Bettina began to cry again. One of the deputies moved forward with a pair of handcuffs. Detective Boggs motioned for Twinn to turn around. When he did, he was facing Neva Tupman.

"You stupid, clumsy girl," he said, the one break in his otherwise honeyed façade. After the cuffs were on, he turned back to Simon and Detective Boggs. "You have nothing but a few misrepresentations and no facts."

Detective Boggs held up an evidence baggie; it contained a key. "I received a warrant from Judge Henningsgaard two hours ago, and deputies began their search as soon as you were here in the library. This passkey was found among your belongings."

Simon detected a flicker in Twinn's eyes, a twitch of an eyebrow. "I want a lawyer," he said.

"Of course," said Detective Boggs. "As soon as you are in custody." She motioned to the deputies, who flanked Twinn and covered him from behind. They led him from the library.

"Number Plan Six," said Drabb, "what will happen to it?"

Simon removed the document from his coat pocket and handed it to Detective Boggs. "It will remain in the county evidence room," said Detective Boggs, "where it will stay until the judge decides to return it to you."

"This is your fault," Drabb said to Simon.

"Bucky," said Simon, "you're not making any sense. Calm down. You'll get your document back soon enough."

Simon went over to Neva Tupman. Her face was blotchy, her eye makeup a mess, the rhinestone glasses well below the bridge of her nose and again askew.

"I didn't know what I'd done," she said. "That what I told Grewgious about Edwin would get him killed."

"Don't blame yourself."

"We talked a lot that first day at the cocktail party. He didn't tell me about Jennifer Wren, but I saw the way he looked at her." She smiled. "But he looked at Quilpy that same way. I wanted to be his friend. I was going to tell him about my work for Grewgious. I think he would have forgiven me."

"I have his mother's telephone number." Simon took her hand. "I think you might feel better if you call her and tell her about her son. She wants to hear from you."

Neva sniffled. "I'll do it," she said. "Thank you so much. I'm going back to my room now, and calling my next employer. I'm so done with this. There are better ways to make money than being a stooge."

Cecily came up and gave Simon her elegant and exquisitely manicured hand. "You are a clever and resourceful man. And your theories are most interesting, if they prove to be true."

"That will be for a jury to decide," said Simon. He paused. He would only get one chance, so he might as well ask. "What happened on the *Excess of the Seas*? To the Caracas Carbuncle?"

She smiled a careful smile. "A lapse in judgment? A parlor trick? Unlucky timing on my part? A mystery? I do not choose to know. Would you believe me if I said I was totally unaware of what happened?" She paused, her eyes searching Simon's face. "I thought not. But, as you say, I have bad luck around famous gemstones. Perhaps I need to think about using my training in a more—productive—way."

"One more question?" Simon asked. "Why the Seychelles? It only took Detective Boggs a few minutes to discover that you had never been there."

Now she had a real smile on her face, and looked over at her brother talking with Jennifer.

"My brother and I," Cecily said, "were not always like this. As children, we were united in one thing—the hatred of the guardians who took care of us after our parents were killed. We imagined a place we could be together—safe from the intrusions and cruelties of the people who took care of us. So we invented a different life for us. By that time, Lionel had already discovered the Landless twins in *Edwin Drood* and was inspired by their exotic birthplace of Ceylon. So we spun the globe and stopped it with our fingers on the Seychelles, and that became our haven, a place where we could project our dreams and wishes." She paused, as if reliving this pleasant fiction of her past. "But as we got older, our interests diverged—he went into scholarly pursuits, I chose a riskier path with international flavor and, perhaps, danger. As our lives grew further apart, our exotic imagined childhood served, for me at least, as a pleasant reminder of that time when our shared misery brought us close together.

"Perhaps"—she glanced again at her brother—"in time, I can make amends and renew our childhood closeness. But when we are together, we occasionally know what the other is thinking. And maybe that will always be too dangerous for him." She extended her hand again. "Thank you, Simon. You will not see my name in print again in connection with any missing jewelry, I assure you."

Cecily moved away to speak briefly with her brother. Simon watched Lionel, Jennifer, and Cecily. At first, Lionel appeared agitated, but Jennifer put her hand on Lionel's arm while Cecily continued speaking. When Cecily finished, Jennifer put out both hands and took Cecily's in hers. Lionel stood beside the two women, his face a handsome puzzle of conflicting emotions.

Cheeryble and Minor approached Simon. "Thank you," Cheeryble said, "for the colorful way you characterized our mutual alibis."

"How you spend your time together is your business, and your story to tell," said Simon. "But I'm happy that the two of you can combine multiple interests in such a… creative…way."

Dean Minor stuck out an awkward hand for Simon to shake, but Cheeryble gave Simon a bear hug. He smelled of spearmint.

"I'll see you at the executive committee meeting," Minor said, "whenever Bettina decides it's best to meet."

Jennifer separated herself from the Tartars, who remained in tight conversation with one another. "Thank you, Simon, for ending all of this unpleasantness. If I had understood what Mr. Crump really felt, I probably would have behaved differently. I would have given him the scarf. I feel so powerless…"

"I understand," said Simon. "I wish I felt better myself. This was the best I could do." He paused. "Do you return to Los Angeles now?"

"I must," she said, "I have wardrobe camera tests beginning tomorrow, and a script conference, and…" She stopped. "My busy life. Sometimes I wish I could go back to the day before *Oliver Twist* aired. It was much easier then. I could come to something like this, and no one would notice me unless I made a comment, and then I would be judged on my intellect, not on the designer label on my back."

Simon looked over toward the Tartars. "You have done a good thing, I believe."

Jennifer smiled. "I hope so. I have no family of my own; I hate to see people push aside their blood relations."

"That would make an interesting subject for a Dickens monograph," said Simon. "If you ever have the time to write again."

Jennifer thanked Simon again and moved away. Zach came forward as the library began to clear; George was by his side.

"You were fabulous, once again," said George. "Miss Marple of the crab pots."

"Let's go home," Zach said. "To a warm fire and a drink or two. I've convinced Bettina and Quilpy to join us. Bettina will turn off her cell phone, and Quilpy thinks he'd like to spend an extra night or two touring the Junction before heading back to Minot."

"Sounds like a plan," said Simon.

As they were heading toward the library door, Detective Boggs approached. "You impress me, once again."

"Thank you, Detective."

"Of course, Grewgious...Twinn...admits nothing, but I wouldn't worry about that," Detective Boggs said. "With two counts of aggravated murder facing him, he won't be appearing on any stage for some time."

"Unless he plays Prospero in the state penitentiary's all-male production of *The Tempest*," said George.

Quilpy's Quill

May
Last Update for Now

I know I haven't been blogging lately;
I've been too, too busy with my own
personal life, which I shall discuss
right after I get down all of the skinny
that has happened since my last blog.

Well, the unpleasantness at the Droodist
Conference has been covered elsewhere in
way more detail than is necessary, and
I don't want to prod tender feelings,
so I'm not going there again.

But, since the conference, several important
developments have happened that Quilpy's
readers are desperate to know about!

Number Plan Six, the cause of so much
kerfuffle, was a FRAUD! Poor Bucky Drabb!
Just as those suits from Lloyd's were set
to fork over five million bucks, their
crack investigators, using state-of-the-
art handwriting analysis, were able to
determine that the document Drabb believed
would revolutionize Droodist scholarship was

not written by Charles Dickens, not even
written by John Forster or his widow, but
matched the handwriting of a man named Hugo
Mudge, who ran a grocery store near Covent
Garden at 25 Smidgen Mews in the 1860s and
1870s. The half-page, containing only the
words "the girl did it wif her nif" was not
Dickens's cryptic note indicating that the
illiterate sexton Stony Durdles was going to
accuse Helena Landless of murdering Drood
under hypnotic influence from John Jasper.

Instead, the page was discovered to have
been carefully torn from the manuscript of
Mudge's never-published "Confessions of a
Costermonger," and fit perfectly at the end
of the chapter entitled, "Wot Happen'd to
the 'Tatoes," between unnumbered pages 645
and 646. Now fully restored, the fragment
in context shows that Mudge had written a
note to his wife about a scullion error
that resulted in the potatoes for the
Mudge stew ending up in the dog's dinner
bowl instead. (Yeah, I didn't know what
a scullion was, either. Google it.)

Although not at all a Dickens fragment, the
discovery of its rightful place in literature
has led to a publishing bidding war over the
Mudge manuscript, which is part of the London
Preservation Archive. Proceeds from the sale
of the manuscript (movie-deal pending) will be
used to restore the original Mudge property on
Smidgen Mews, with hopes of turning it into
a Museum of Greengrocery. A happy ending all
around—except, perhaps, for Bucky Drabb.

But not so unhappy for Bucky, after all.
In other movie news, Jennifer Wren reports

that she and Drabb are going to make lemonade out of the number-plan lemons, by collaborating on an all-new script for the proposed film adaptation of THE MYSTERY OF EDWIN DROOD. Jennifer apparently rejected the existing script in favor of Drabb's theory extracted from the bogus number plan, because of the potential for an enhanced role for her own character of Helena Landless. We'll all queue, as they say in London, for that movie when it comes out!

But enough about other people—let's talk about me! I'm so excited to announce that the winner of Quilpy's Cabin Boy Contest is a man from Portland, Oregon, named George Bascomb! George will be my cabin mate this July on the fabulous SS EXCESS OF THE SEAS, as we travel to Aruba, Martinique, and Guadeloupe.

As for Quilpy, I'll have a man in one hand and a mai tai in the other! You'll all love George, by the way—he's the funniest man I've ever met. Thanks to the 5,000+ who entered the contest. For those of you on the cruise, buy me a drink when you see me, and ten minutes later you'll be my new BFF!

I've decided to slow down on blogging for the next few months while I concentrate on a new phase in my life. Quilpy's got a job—a real job! I've accepted employment as the assistant to the manager of Pip's Pages, a fabulous bookstore in Dickens Junction, Oregon, where owner and supersleuth Simon Alastair says I'll be "both a supernumerary and a factotum," in addition to my executive duties at the store. (Remind me when I've got a minute to Google those, too!)

In my free time in the Junction (as we locals call it), I'll be settling down to what I believe to be my life's work—the writing of the Great American Novel of the new millennium. With my vast experience behind me, and the promise I hold for the future, I'm seeing a triple-decker opus to rival THE PICKWICK PAPERS!

Watch for more news as I begin the birthing process! It'll be awesome!

I'll be back (even if not soon),

Quilpy

xoxoxo

(Missing you, Droody…)

EPILOGUE: THE DAWN AGAIN

It is morning in Dickens Junction, an early morning in May, and fingers of sun filter through the kitchen curtains at Gad's Hill Place, lighting on Miss Tox, watchful and awake on the floor. The breakfast nook's flagstone floor is warm beneath Simon's bare feet, and through the open jalousie, notes of wisteria and lilac drift his way. The sounds are light and joyful: the call of a bird flying inland from nearby Youngs Bay, even, Simon thinks, the fluttering of its wings.

Jude has set forth breakfast for Simon—oatmeal, toast, and homemade gooseberry jam—but it remains untouched while Simon fingers the edge of the heavy ecru envelope received the day before, eyeing Bethany's calligraphy. Someone (probably Brock) has even sealed the envelope with wax, something Simon hasn't seen since he used it himself at fourteen to send a note to the boy his grandmother called Simon's first "special" friend.

In the three weeks since the Droodist conference, life for Simon has almost returned to its normal pace. These sheets of embossed paper signal the beginning of another wave of activity, with its obligations, celebrations, plans, and gatherings. Simon has ordered his tuxedo and opened a new account at Tellson's Bank for his eventual wedding present to Brock and Bethany.

Miss Tox snakes between his calves, seeking warmth in one place or another. Her total dominion of Gad's Hill Place has been disrupted by the newest member of the household. Mrs. Pipchin, Osma Dilber's Cavalier King Charles Spaniel, rests in her comfortable cloth bed in the corner, now starting to adjust to her new home. She misses her owner, is still shy around visitors, and walks around the edges of the room to be near Simon or Zach.

Simon misses Osma, too. When Osma's grandniece offered the dog to Simon, saying that she didn't have room for another pet at her townhouse in Seattle, Simon was only too happy to take Mrs. Pipchin, not just because of his affection for the dog but as a remembrance of her owner. Miss Tox examines the curled-up spaniel and, as if satisfied that the dog is not going to challenge her supreme reign, jumps into Simon's lap, kneads herself a comfortable place, and goes to sleep.

Zach has left his laptop on the nook; Simon pulls it over and clicks on one of the bookmarks, bringing up the final entry in Quilpy's Quill. He smiles at Quilpy's glib dismissal of poor Bucky Drabb's years of scholarship, tainted and ridiculed in both the scholarly and popular press. At least, Simon thinks, Bucky's belief in the authenticity of the document was real, which means Drabb will always have hope against hope. A recent e-mail from Bettina includes a tidbit that Drabb is hard at work again, and still on the lookout for the missing piece of Dickens's working notes for *Edwin Drood*.

Simon is also pleased with Quilpy's progress at the store. Brock is training his replacement, which gives Quilpy the added benefit, as he says, of some nice eye candy while he trains. Quilpy is already a hit with local customers. He will move in to Zach's duplex as soon as Zach is fully moved out.

In fact, Zach should be back any minute with the last of the boxes from the vacated apartment. Already Zach has carved out a place for himself in the kitchen, placing his cookbooks (at least the ones that weren't duplicates of Simon's) on a small shelf near Simon's and his clothes in the other half of the his-and-his master-bedroom closet. The few sticks of furniture Zach owns have been put into storage, except the zebra hassock, which he and Simon discussed at length before placing prominently amid Simon's more carefully chosen living room ensemble.

"It gives the room some lived-in whimsy," Zach argued, with partial success. The hassock has small turned legs and tufted faux-zebra upholstery, with a small tear at one corner. Nonetheless, it signals a room combining the tastes of two people, not the relentlessly ordered existence of a man living alone. Simon is almost used to it.

"Honey, I'm home," Zach says as he appears at the mudroom entrance off the kitchen. He has two boxes in his hands, obscuring his face.

"Do you need some help?" Simon asks. "I'm afraid of disturbing Miss Tox's beauty rest."

Zach puts the boxes down in the mudroom and comes into the kitchen. "That should be the last of it," he says, kissing Simon as he removes his leather bomber jacket and tosses it on the island. "It's official. This is home." He sits beside Simon and puts his hand on Miss Tox. In his other hand he holds a legal-size envelope.

"I hope this is what you want," says Simon, unable not to worry one last time.

"It is scary," Zach says, "but if I'm not ready for commitment at forty, when will I be?"

And, after all, isn't that the question for Simon, too? Willing to risk his heart again, hoping this time it will last? He looks in Zach's eyes, so blue, so dangerously inviting. He could sit like this—comfortable, secure, safe—forever, maybe. Neither man can know, however, that, only a few months away, a dinner party and its consequences will disrupt their peaceful lives, as they find themselves embroiled in *The Our Mutual Friend Murders*.

Simon returns to the laptop, and toggles from Quilpy's blog to his e-mail account, where he is in the middle of resolving where to store the maypole until next year's

Barnaby Rudge Days, recently completed. Eclipsing that event is the full hubbub of Brock's and Bethany's wedding, the changes at the bookstore, the changes at home. But all of this activity is better than a quiet life alone. He puts his hand on Zach's.

Simon smiles. "No regrets."

"None," Zach agrees.

"I love you."

"I love you, too." Zach puts the envelope in front of Simon. "Open it."

As Simon reaches for the envelope, a jostled Miss Tox jumps from his lap and runs through the French doors toward the living room and a quieter place.

Simon opens the envelope and removes a brochure with a picture of trees in full fall foliage, someone tapping a sugar maple for sap, and a quaint house. "Sugar Mountain Bed and Breakfast," Simon reads, "Bennington, Vermont."

"The magazine wants me to do a story on gay leaf-peeping," Zach says. *Rainbows*, a gay-travel magazine, had been Zach's full-time employer when Zach arrived in Dickens Junction months earlier. "They offered it to me as long as I stay in the top twenty sexiest journalists next year," he says with a grin. "I accepted the assignment. Will you go with me?" Simon starts to toggle from his e-mail to his calendar, but Zach takes his hands. "I want you to go with me. Be with me. Where we can be legal." Zach's eyes are full, blue, loving. "Will you marry me?"

Simon wants to savor this moment for himself in this glorious light of spring. He releases himself from Zach's grasp, pulls his oatmeal closer and raises his spoon, as if he is about to eat. He's smiles teasingly at Zach's frown.

"Of course I will," says Simon, and then falls to with an appetite.

The End

"Authors often manipulate truths to serve their fictional ends."
—*The Great Grewgious*

A Note on the
Hotel Elliott

The Hotel Elliott is a real hotel in downtown Astoria, Oregon. I stay there often when I visit the area to work on ideas for a Dickens Junction mystery. Because of its many charms, the real hotel had to be modified in several ways in order to be the host site for the crimes that occur in *The Edwin Drood Murders*.

Try as you might, you will not find a library or room service. The real hotel has modern key locks that virtually eliminate any chance of theft, and the transom windows are inconveniently opaque. Most inconvenient, the hotel abuts the building that adjoins it, so I had to separate them with an alley that, in the real Astoria, is a full block away.

Furthermore, the hotel's actual basement is not quite large enough to contain the egos of the volatile Droodists, so I have quietly expanded it and added the necessary conference breakout rooms. The ground floor does not have the back rooms that I required for my purpose, nor a back staircase. The presidential suite is lovely, and much as I describe it, but I have moved its location on the fifth floor so that Jennifer Wren and Simon can look out at the view from the real hotel's club suite 501, my room of choice when I visit.

As of this writing, the hotel is undergoing a renovation of its lobby that, when completed, will contain a new breakfast room. The real basement wine bar (unfortunately lacking the hard liquor that Droodists demand) remains open on weekend nights.

ACKNOWLEDGMENTS

Critical Readers: Rebecca Clemons, Candace Haines. Endless gratitude once again to Carol Frischmann. Extra-special thanks to Larry Rogers, who gave of his time and expertise, and gave the manuscript a critical read.

Technical Advice: Two eminent Dickens scholars honored me by actually taking my interest in *Edwin Drood* seriously enough to correspond with me.

Wendy Jacobsen, author of *The Companion to* The Mystery of Edwin Drood, was kind enough to shed light on the number plans, Dickens's "mems," and gave me the germ of the idea for the rival factions: the Jasper tradition and the Twinn tradition. She also compiled a partial bibliography of critical works on *Edwin Drood* that I consulted while planning the novel.

Arthur J. Cox, perhaps the world's leading expert on the *Edwin Drood* number plans, wrote to me, expanding on work he published in the journal *Dickens Quarterly*. When I described my idea for the novel, he was diplomatic enough to refer to the Forster Fraud as "very unlikely," favoring his own highly informed scholarly research and conclusions. Cox's persuasive theory is that, nearing death, Dickens became so obsessed with secrecy that he didn't write notes even for his own private use about *Edwin Drood*'s denouement, fearing that his papers would be studied after his death (how right he was about that he will never know). I applaud Mr. Cox for taking my interest seriously enough to share his thoughts and an unpublished footnote from his scholarly article. I would like to believe that somewhere between Mr. Cox's theory and the absolute truth there is enough room for my whimsical proposal.

Kristin Thiel is an editor *extraordinaire*. She will quietly remove the italics in the previous sentence, and I will quietly restore them. And thanks to Laura Meehan, who occasionally indulges my quixotic opinions about hyphens and capitalization.

Special thanks to Vinnie Kinsella for answering all of my little questions and patiently guiding me through the process.

I love Tina Granzo's illustrations; she understands the feeling and mood of my books, and strikes the perfect note. You make Dickens Junction come alive.

Alan Dubinksy is a typography nerd. And I'm lucky to have him on my team. He is a man of great detail and infinite patience.

Jessica Glenn has sent me hither and yon, mostly yon, to make sure the world knows about Dickens Junction. And because of that I've met the nicest people, some of whom love books even more than I do.

A Note
on the Type

The *Edwin Drood Murders* is primarily set in **ITC New Baskerville Standard**. John Quaranda designed this version of John Baskerville's eponymous typeface for the International Typeface Corporation (ITC) in 1978, 210 years after its first iteration. Baskerville was reknowned as an innovator of technique and style; his influence would carry beyond his Birmingham, England business to other parts of Europe.

Quilpy's Quill displays in `Andale Mono`. Steve Matteson designed the san serif typeface for Monotype in 1995. It was originally intended as a terminal emulation typeface for a joint project involving Apple and IBM, but Microsoft first distributed `Andale Mono` as an Internet Explorer add-on and continued to do so until eventually replacing it with Lucida Console. It is still available as part of Apple's OS X font library.

Photo by Katherine Adams

ABOUT THE AUTHOR

Christopher Lord was born in Astoria, Oregon, near the very heart of Dickens Junction.

His short stories have appeared in *Men on Men 7, His 3, Everything I Have is Blue, Confrontation, Harrington Quarterly, The James White Review, Blithe House Quarterly,* and *Lodestar Quarterly.* He has been a recipient of an Oregon Literary Fellowship from Literary Arts, Inc.

He and Simon have read almost all of the same books.

He lives in Portland, Oregon, with his partner Evan (who is not a writer).

Please visit Christopher's website: dickensjunction.com for more maps and information about Christopher and Dickens Junction.

CPSIA information can be obtained at www.ICGtesting.com
Printed in the USA
BVOW01s0658240913

331956BV00001B/1/P

9 780985 323639